序 言

　　學好英文的關鍵，是要能夠用英文思考周遭的疑惑，紀錄現實的環境，並抒發心中的感覺；完全掌握生活動態與細節的「如何寫好英文日記」就是針對這些需要所精心編寫而成的，幫助您克服學習英文的瓶頸，提昇寫作能力，創造英文敘事與言情的新境界。

　　英文日記的內容俯拾皆是，英文日記的觀點因人而異，英文日記的形式自由多變，但一篇好的英文日記卻也必須言之有物，簡麗生動。本書包羅萬象，特分四季及生活環境二大部分，從依照季節遞嬗而自成風格的「初春手稿」、「夏日記事」、「深秋小札」、「冬天行腳」到主題豐富，篇篇皆範文的「大自然篇」、「青春篇」、「娛樂篇」、「節日篇」、「心情篇」以及「人物篇」等，涵括各類生活情事，詳記季候情緒變化，使您在生活中獲得學習的精華，在學習中享受生活的情趣。

　　值得一提的是，讀完本書，您不但能融會貫通日記英文的寫作技巧與遣詞用句，還能從新穎實用的附錄部分：如「中外節日一覽表」、「節氣時令用語」、「氣象用語」、「戀愛婚姻名詞」、「人生百態」、「學生用語」、「外國文學家及其代表作」以及「各月幸運花卉、寶石、星座」等，充實寫作參考資料，汲取寫作靈感，隨時隨地寫起英文日記來，都能得心應手，輕鬆有趣。

　　本書在編輯與校對的過程中，均力求嚴謹、完善，唯仍恐有疏失之處，尚祈各界先進不吝斧正。

編者　謹識

本書採用米色宏康護眼印書紙，版面清晰自然，
不傷眼睛。

● 目　　錄 ●

HOW TO KEEP A DIARY

如
何
寫
好
英
文
日
記

HOW TO KEEP A DIARY

Ⅲ- 深秋小札 Autumn ⋯⋯⋯⋯⋯⋯⋯⋯⋯ 107

● 八月 August ⋯⋯⋯⋯⋯⋯⋯⋯⋯⋯⋯⋯⋯⋯ 110

● 九月 September ⋯⋯⋯⋯⋯⋯⋯⋯⋯⋯⋯ 127

如何寫好英文日記

如
何
寫
好
英
文
日
記

Chapter 3 生活環境 Life series ⋯⋯ 207

Ⅰ-大自然篇 Nature ⋯⋯⋯⋯⋯⋯⋯⋯ 208

Ⅱ-娛樂篇 Entertainments ⋯⋯⋯⋯ 223

如何寫好英文日記

HOW TO KEEP A DIARY

學習出版公司　港澳地區版權顧問

RM ENTERPRISES

P.O. Box 99053 Tsim Sha Tsui Post Office, Hong Kong

翻印
必究

1

LET'S ENJOY
KEEPING A DIARY

談談英文日記

One who does not know a foreign
language does not know one's own.

—*Goethe*

不懂得一種外國語文的人，就是不懂
得他自己國家的語文。

Life being very short, and quiet
hours of it few, we ought to waste
none of them in reading valueless
books.

— *John Ruskin*

生命苦短，又少寂靜的時刻，因此我
們不應該浪費時間去讀毫無價值的書
籍。

爲什麼要寫英文日記

在台灣，想把英文學得漂亮而道地的人比比皆是，然而，花了十幾二十年研讀的人雖多，英文寫得呱呱叫的人却屈指可數。從國中、高中到大學，甚至研究所的學生，都應該有必要重新檢討自己的學習方式了。

英文是活的，如果缺乏英語的環境，就得創造一個，能夠用英文思想，用英文記錄，用英文表達生活經驗的學習環境——**寫好英文日記**。

寫不好英文日記，就學不好英文

日記是十分自由的文體，不像作文，必須有起承轉合，依主題發揮；也不是史書，一定得逐日記載大小事件。日記是生活，是思想，是感情，也是您自己的人生觀與世界觀。當您坐在書桌前，正準備好好衝刺一番時，突然停電了，您該說 *the electric current failed*. 愚人節時的記載通常是 " *Today is All Fools' Day. People play all kinds of tricks on their friends.*"（今天是愚人節，人們對他們的朋友作各種惡作劇。）老師要您寫書法時，書法這個字是*calligraphy*，補考得用*make up*，而媽媽做了一道北平烤鴨，英文則是*Peiping duck*。

　　英文日記能夠從您的各種生活細節及感受，讓您學到最生活化的英文詞句。因此，會寫出好的英文日記，您的英文就已經成功了一半。

◉ 日記英文流行語 ◉

　　由於日記是一種經年累月的習慣，所以舉凡**節日、氣象、人生百態、學校用語、文學作品**等等，無所不包；而又以**每月的幸運花卉、寶石與星座**等，大受學生歡迎。譬如氣象常用語就有*drizzle*（毛毛雨）、*rainfall*（雨量）、*low-pressure*（低氣壓）等。而近年來在台灣甚爲人們所重視的情人節，在西方是二月十四日，所謂（*St.*）*Valentine's Day*。但在中國，却是指七夕（農曆七月七日），*Seventh Night of the Seventh Lunar Month*。此外，您可知道校花怎麼說？是*school beauty*。方帽子則是*mortarboard*或者*square cap*。抄筆記是*note-taking*，而品學兼優則用*excellent in character and learning*.「**如何寫好英文日記**」將流行與生活融爲一體，奠定您駕馭英文的基礎。

◉ 日記基本常識面面觀 ◉

　　中英文日記事實上都沒有一定的格式與文體，因爲它原本就是個人抒發苦悶與見解的寄託，有其私密性，而非專供大衆閱讀的範本；然而日記體却是所有應用文中，涵括最廣泛、寫實最深入的，故而最能試煉一個人寫作能力的好壞。因此，對於英文實力尚未臻至爐火純青的人來說，英文日記的書寫方式仍必須有例可循，以免不知所云，而竟沾沾自喜。

　　通常**日記的第一行**，都先註明年、月、日與星期，大都還加註氣候狀況，如果是遊記，則加寫地名。此行稱做「**日期欄**」。可依個人習慣變換一些時間及天氣的形容詞，並沒有硬性規定。

　　此外，日記可以任選抒情、敍事、描寫、說明、議論等各種形式表達，但一般都以**抒情**及**敍事**兩種居多。從生活中取材，可長可短，但切忌寫成流水帳。

● 縮寫知多少 ●

　　日期欄的月份與星期，因為經常重覆的關係，常以縮寫代替，如 *January 1st, Sunday* 就可寫成 *Jan. 1，Sun.* 或 *Sun., Jan. 1*。後面再加上氣候狀況，如 *cloudy*（陰），*rainy*（雨），*windy*（風），*cool*（涼爽）等等。有些人甚至還加註氣溫度數，十分寫真。

週名之縮寫

Sunday	Sun.	（星期日）
Monday	Mon.	（星期一）
Tuesday	Tues.	（星期二）
Wednesday	Wed.	（星期三）
Thursday	Thur. 或 Thurs.	（星期四）
Friday	Fri.	（星期五）
Saturday	Sat.	（星期六）

月名之縮寫

January	Jan.	（一月）
February	Feb.	（二月）
March	Mar.	（三月）
April	Apr.	（四月）
May	May	（五月）
June	Jun.	（六月）
July	Jul.	（七月）
August	Aug.	（八月）
September	Sept.	（九月）
October	Oct.	（十月）
November	Nov.	（十一月）
December	Dec.	（十二月）

＊通常May, June, July 都不縮寫

● I 的省略不可不知 ●

英語的命令語氣，通常都將*You*（你）省略，而在日記中，則常將第一人稱的敍述主詞 *I*（我）略而不寫。〔 除非有副詞片語或子句置於 *I*（我）之前，或者是在萬一省略了 *I*（我），後面的動詞就語焉不詳的情況之下，才一定要寫。 〕如：

" *In the evening went with Mr. Ku to church.* "（傍晚我和顧先生一起去教堂。）和 " *Finished reading `The Old Man and* *the Sea' by Ernest Hemingway.* "（我讀完了海明威的「老人與海」。）都將 *I* 省略掉。但在 " *My brother is a skilful skater, but I am a very poor one.* "（我哥是個溜冰高手，我卻對此笨手笨腳的。）中的 *I* 就絕對不能省略，以免語意混淆不清。

● 英文日記的結構圖示 ●

以下列舉幾種最常見的英文日記的架構：

【例 1 】

　　March 1. ||||||||||||||||||||||||||||||||||||||||||||||||||||||||||||||||||||||||||||||||||||||||||||||||||||
||||||||||||||||||||||||||||||||||||||||||||||||||||||||||||||||||||||||||||||||||||||||||||||||||||
|||||||||||||||||||||||||||||||||||||||||||| .

【例 2 】

July 23rd,　Wed.　Fair, cool weather
　　||||||||||||||||||||||||||||||||||||||||||||||||||||||||||||||||||||||||||||||||||||||||||||||||
||||||||||||||||||||||||||||||||||||||||||||||||||||||||||||||||||||||||||||||||||||||||||||||||||||
||||||||||||||||||||||||||||||||||||||||| .

【例 3 】

Thurs.,　　Jul. 31　Hot and close
　　||||||||||||||||||||||||||||||||||||||||||||||||||||||||||||||||||||||||||||||||||||||||||||||||
||||||||||||||||||||||||||||||||||||||||||||||||||||||||||||||||||||||||||||||||||||||||||||||||||||
||||||||||||||||||||||||||||||||||||||||| .

英文日記有接寫及一頁一篇兩種主要形式，如果正式一點的，則會在日期欄與內文之間加上題目。如：

【例 4.】

Fri.,　　May 20　　　Fine

My birthday

‖‖

‖‖

‖‖‖ .

日記通常不寫年分，除非是旅遊札記或是文學家的手記；因爲基本上，日記是一年一本的，故只要在日記的第一頁或最後一頁加以註明便可。

● 一睹名家範例 ●

多參照名家寫法，多磨鍊寫作技巧，您就能在每天寫英文日記的習慣中，將作文能力無形中提高。因爲日記的用字精簡，取材周廣，而且人人皆是提筆就寫，有話直說，不像寫書信、文章，還有可能先打草稿，再謄寫完畢。

July 23rd,　Wed. Fair, cool weather

From morning we had cool breezes. I read as usual in the morning. Kingsley's "Heroes" was very interesting. My brother James is ill, but I hope he will soon get well.

（The Century Readers）

七月二十三日　　星期三　　晴，冷

　　打從早晨開始就吹著冷冷的微風。我在早上就像平常一樣地閱讀。金斯利所著的「群雄」十分有趣。弟弟詹姆斯病了，我希望他快點復原。

　　　　　　　　　　　　　　　　　　（摘自世紀讀者）

July 31st,　　Thurs.　　Hot and close

　　We are at last at uncle's. After the noisy town life this place is strangely quiet. It is a little Paradise. Cows, dogs, and hens are all running freely about. Many birds are singing in the woods behind the house. In the little river, found some red fish. Uncle keeps a few cows. They give fresh milk for his family. Wrote a letter to my parents tonight.

七月三十一日　　星期四　　悶熱

　　我們終於到達叔叔家了。經過城市嘈雜的生活之後，此地顯得出奇的靜。這是個小天堂。牛、狗和母鷄都自由自在地四處奔跑。許多鳥兒在屋後的林中歌唱。我在小河裏發現了一些紅色的魚。叔叔養了一些牛。牠們供給叔叔一家人新鮮的牛奶。今晚給爸媽寫了一封信。

May 20.

　　I put a good deal on paper yesterday, and yet not all. I was, in truth, hoping against hope, against conviction, against too conscious self-judgement. I scarcely dare own the truth now, yet it relieves my aching heart to set it down. Yes, I love him that is the dreadful fact,

and I can no longer parry, evade, or deny it to myself,
though to the rest of the world it can never be owned...

　　　　　　—— Alicia's Diary — Thomas Hardy

五月二十日

　　我昨天寫了很多，但却不是全部。實際上，我總是希望違
背希望，違背信念，違背太自覺的自我批判。我現在幾乎不敢
承認這個事實，然而它却減輕我痛苦的心，使它安撫下來。是
的，我愛他，那是可怕的事實，而且我不能夠再躲開、逃避，
或者對自己否認，雖然對世界上的其他人而言，這項事實是永
遠不會被承認的……

　　　　　　——「愛莉雪的日記」—湯姆斯‧哈代

2

FOUR SEASONS

四季

Spring

by William Shakespeare

When daisies pied and violets blue,
　　And lady-smocks all silver-white,
And cuckoo-buds of yellow hue
　　Do paint the meadows with delight,
The cuckoo then, on every tree,
Mocks married men, for thus sings he：
"Cuckoo！cuckoo！" O word of fear,
Unpleasing to a married ear.

春　天

當雛菊的斑點和紫羅蘭的靛藍
酢漿草純然的銀白以及
杜鵑花苞的鮮黃
　　將草原塗滿喜悅的時候，
每棵樹上的布穀鳥
就嘲笑著已婚的男子，
叫著：「咕咕！咕咕！」噢可怕極了，
已婚的人聽來眞覺逆耳。

　　　　　　　　　　　　　—錄自莎士比亞。

　　　　　　　　　（英國詩人及劇作家，1564-1616）

初春 1.

SPRING

手稿

Pippa's Song

Robert Browning

The year's at the spring;
And day's at the morn;
Morning's at seven;
The hill-side's dew-pearl'd;
The lark's on the wing;
The snail's on the thorn;
God's in His heaven —
All's right with the world!

比潘之歌

這是一年之中的春天，
一天之中的早晨，
早晨七點鐘。
山坡綴滿露珠，
雲雀自在飛舞，
蝸牛在荊棘上，
上帝在天堂 —
世界上一切順遂美好

—錄自勃朗寧。
（英國詩人；1812-1889）

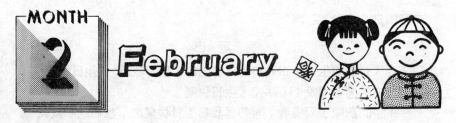

Wed., Feb. 3　　*Clear*

Movies

Today was very clear with no wind.

I practiced basketball in the morning. Then I went to the movies with Sandy. We saw "White Nights". It was a very nice movie ! I liked "Say you, say me" best of all the songs. I'm fond of seeing musicals. The dancing is very beautiful and the music is pretty.

二月三日　星期三　晴

電　影

今天是晴空萬里，沒有風的日子。

早上我練習籃球，然後和珊蒂一起去看電影「飛越蘇聯」，它眞是相當好的一部片子，所有歌曲中我最喜歡「說你，說我」，我喜歡看歌舞片，舞蹈十分美妙，而音樂也好聽得很。

---

be fond of 喜歡　　musical〔'mjuzɪkḷ〕*n.* 以音樂爲主的電影片或舞臺劇

Thurs., Feb. 4　　*Very Fine.*

My birthday

It was my birthday. At the homeroom meeting, Mr. Su said to me, "Happy birthday."

All of my classmates said, "Happy birthday to you, Linda!"

We had a party in the afternoon. They sang the Birthday Song for me. We had cake and ice cream; though it is still cold. We also played cards together. I was very happy.

二月四日　星期 四 晴

長　尾　巴

今天是我的生日，在教室遇見蘇老師，他對我說：「生日快樂!」
所有的同學都說：「琳達！生日快樂。」

下午我們開了同樂會，他們爲我唱生日快樂歌，我們吃了蛋糕
和冰淇淋，雖然天氣仍然變冷的。我們還一起玩牌，我好快樂。

**─────────────────────

homeroom〔'hom,rum〕*n.* 教室

have a party 舉行宴會　　*the Birthday Song* 生日快樂歌

card〔kɑrd〕*n.* 紙牌

Fri., *Feb.* 5　　*Fine*

My cousin got married

Cousin Jenny has finally tied the knot with John. I don't
think she's doing the right thing. I don't like her husband, he
is rich but very immature. I think Jenny is going to be a mother more than a wife to John. At least she'll be rich. So I
felt the marriage party is both boring and uncheerful.

二月五日　星期五　晴

吃　喜　酒

珍妮表姊終於和約翰結婚了。我並不認爲她做對了。我不喜歡
她先生，他有錢，却很不成熟。珍妮不只是做約翰的太太，更將當
他的媽媽。至少，她會很有錢。我認爲珍妮是做約翰的媽媽，遠超
過做他的太太。

**─────────────────────

immature〔,ɪmə'tjur〕*adj.* 未成熟的

uncheerful〔ʌn'tʃɪrfəl〕*adj.* 不快樂的

tie the knot 結婚　　*more than* 遠超過

Sat., Feb. 6　Fine later cloudy

The birthday of our English teacher

It was our English teacher's birthday today.
Although English is a hard subject, I like my English
teacher a lot, and so do my classmates. Unlike other
English teachers we've had before, our English teacher was nicer to us. She always told us stories of
her days when she was like us. She would even stay
in school sometimes to teach us some points in our
lessons that we didn't understand. She always encouraged us and told us to do our best. She is one
teacher who is really dedicated to her work. We all
admire her a lot.

Today, all of us pooled in our money to buy
her a cake and a gift. It was a surprise for her. We
even had a big card made that had all our names on
it. She said that she'll always remember us. After
we sang the Birthday Song we cut the cake and ate
it. That day our English teacher had a big smile on
her face during class. There is no other teacher like
our teacher. Because of her, I am now more confident
of my English.

二月六日　星期六　晴時多雲

英文老師的生日

今天是我們英文老師的生日。雖然英文這一科很難唸，但是我很喜歡英文老師，同學們也是。不像以前教我們的那些英文老師，她對我們要好多了。她常常告訴我們她在我們這個年紀時的事情。有時她甚至願意待在學校指導我們對課外有不懂的地方。她總是鼓勵我們，並要我們盡力而為。她是一位真正獻身於工作的老師。我們都很欽佩她。

今天，我們大家一起出錢為她買了一個蛋糕和一份禮物。對她來說真是一個驚喜。我們甚至做了一張大卡片並寫上所有人的名字。她說她會一直記得我們。在唱完生日快樂歌之後，我們切開蛋糕並吃了起來。一整天英文老師在課堂上始終笑容滿面。再也沒有其他的老師像她一樣了。由於她的緣故，使我對我的英文更具信心。

**　**

encourage 〔ɪnˈkɝɪdʒ〕 v. 鼓勵；激勵
do one's best 盡最大努力；盡力而為
dedicate 〔ˈdɛdə,ket〕 v. 獻身；致力
admire 〔ədˈmaɪr〕 v. 欽佩；歎賞
pool 〔pul〕 v. 將錢或物放在一起共同使用

《有關賀卡的常用語》

♠ May the joy and peace of Christmas always be with you!
願你聖誕平安喜樂，直到永遠！

♠ Happy holidays to you! 祝你假期愉快！

♀ May good fortune always be yours! 祝你永遠好運！

♀ Happy birthday to you, and many happy returns!
祝你生日快樂，永遠長壽！

Sun., Feb. 7　Overcast

The night before the examination

The clock struck eleven at night. The whole house was quiet. Everyone was in bed except me. Under the strong light, I looked gloomily before me at a huge pile of that disgusting stuff they call "books".

I was going to have my examination the next day. "When can I go to bed?" I asked myself. I did not answer. In fact I dared not.

The clock struck 12. "Oh, dear!" cried I, "Ten more books to read before I can go to bed!" We students are the most wretched creatures in the world.

二月七日　星期日　多雲

考試前夕

晚上十一點鐘，整個屋子靜悄悄的，除了我以外，每個人都睡了，在強烈的燈光下，我憂愁地望著那一堆擺在我面前，被稱作「書本」的討厭東西。

明天就要考試了，我問自己：「什麼時候才能上床睡覺呢？」我沒有回答，事實上我不敢。

鐘敲十二點了，我大叫：「天啊！還要唸十本書才能上牀睡覺！」我們學生眞是世界上最可憐的東西。

---

gloomily〔'glumɪlɪ〕 *adv.* 憂鬱地
disgusting〔dɪs'gʌstɪŋ〕 *adj.* 令人厭惡的
wretched〔'rɛtʃɪd〕 *adj.* 可憐的；不幸的

Sun., Feb. 14 Rainy

St. Valentine's Day

The boys were happy, because today was St. Valentine's Day. I saw " Y " early in the morning at school. I like " Y " more than any other boy student. I took chocolate with me to give to him, but...

At dinner I gave the chocolate to Father. He said, " They don't have the same custom in Europe and America. In Europe and America, boys give chocolate to girls. "

Ta-ming got several pieces of chocolate from Father. How funny !

二月十四日　星期日　雨

情　人　節

男孩們都很高興，因為今天是情人節。一早我在學校看到"Y"。我喜歡"Y"更勝於其他的男同學。我帶了巧克力糖給他，但是…。

晚餐時我把巧克力送給了父親。他說：「歐美沒有我們這樣的習俗。在歐洲和美洲，是男孩給女孩巧克力糖。」

大明從父親那兒得到了一些巧克力。真好玩！

St. Valentine's Day 情人節　　custom〔'kʌstəm〕 *n.* 習俗；風俗 chocolate〔'tʃɔkəlɪt〕 *n.* 巧克力糖

***Mon.*, *Feb.* 15**　*Rainy*

The spring rain

The spring rain has been falling gently since morning. Some swallows were busily flying about to and fro amidst the rain. The peach blossoms in the garden were beaten by the rain and fell off.

二月十五日　星期一　雨

春　雨

從清晨開始，春雨就輕輕柔柔地落了下來；一些燕子來來去去地忙著在雨中穿梭。花園裏盛開的桃花被雨擊傷，紛紛墜地。

---

to and fro 往復；來回

gently〔'dʒεntlɪ〕 *adv.* 輕輕地；逐漸地

swallow〔'swɑlo〕 *n.* 燕　　amidst〔ə'mɪdst〕 *prep.* 在其中

***Tues.*, *Feb.* 16**　*Overcast all day*

The Spring Cold

The Central Meteorological Observatory has announced that the cold season is over, but it is still cold. In the morning stayed in bed having nothing to do. Mother grew anxious and asked me whether I was sick, but I was all right except for a slight sentiment of melancholy.

In the afternoon finished reading the magazine I had bought from Caves Bookstore the other day.

Judging from the look of the sky, the warm spring does not seem likely to visit us so soon.

二月十六日　星期二　多雲

寒　冷

中央氣象臺預告說寒冷的季節結束了，然而天氣還是很冷。早上賴在床上沒事可做。媽媽變得擔心起來，問我是不是病了。我一切都好，只是有些輕微的愁緒罷了。

下午讀完了我前天從敦煌書局買的雜誌。

從天空的樣子看來，暖和的春天似乎不會來得太快。

** ───────────────────

meteorological〔,mitɪərə'lɒdʒɪkl,-,ɔrə-〕*adj.* 氣象的；氣象學的
observatory〔əb'zɜvə,torɪ〕*n.* 天文臺；氣象臺；瞭望臺
announce〔ə'naʊns〕*v.* 預知；廣播；通知

Wed., Feb. 17 Clear

New Year's review

Another year has gone by. Every year seems to go by faster than the last one. We had our annual feast at Aunty Joan's house. She made a wonderful Peiping duck this time.

二月十七日　星期三　晴

新年回顧

又是一年過去。每一年似乎都過得比上一年還快。我們在瓊恩嬸嬸家吃年夜飯。這回她做了一道美味可口的北平烤鴨。

** ───────────────────

go by 過去；結束　　annual〔'ænjʊəl〕*adj.* 一年一次的
feast〔fist〕*n.* 饗宴；節日　　Peiping〔'pe'pɪŋ,'be'pɪŋ〕*n.* 北平

Thurs., Feb. 18 *Fine*

Lucky money

I'm so happy today because I got $ 3,000 in "Lucky Money." Grandpa alone gave me $ 1,000. I must try to save this for college though and not waste it. But I think I'll allow myself to use part of it to buy a new dress tomorrow and then I'll put the rest in the bank.

二月十八日　星期四　晴

紅　包

今天我很高興，因為我拿了三千元的紅包。祖父一個人就給了我一千元。我必須儘量存起來以作上大學之用而不去花掉。不過我想我會讓自己明天用一部份錢去買件新衣服，然後其他的錢存到銀行裡去。

**

waste〔west〕*v.* 浪費　　　allow〔ə'laʊ〕*v.* 容許

Tues., Feb. 23 *Fine*

The leap year

As it is a leap year this year which comes once in four years, we have one additional day this month. To those who are born or die on this day, their birthdays or the anniversaries of their death come round only once every four years.

二月二十三日　星期二　晴

閏　年

因為今年是每四年一次的閏年，所以這個月多一天。對那些在這天出生或者死亡的人而言，他們的生日或逝世周年紀念四年才一次。

**

additional〔ə'dɪʃənl〕*adj.* 加添的；補充的

Thurs.,Feb. 25   Cloudy later a little rain

Being ill

I was confined to my bed the whole day today as by doctor's order. My teacher called up this morning to see what was wrong with me. My mother said that I was sick and was not going to school. My teacher said, that she will be sending over some of the homework for today so that I won't have to miss anything in class. There's no escape from schoolwork, even if I am sick. Maybe the only time I can get away from it is when I'm already buried six feet underground. My teacher said that I should get well soon and then said goodbye.

So, what else did I do today, aside from just sitting on my bed? Nothing really much. I drank a lot of juice that mother made and could eat nothing but rice gruel all day. I also slept a lot because of the medicine I took.

In the evening, Leni called to ask how I was. I told her that I'd probably be going back to school the day after tomorrow after I had some rest. She told me some things that went on in school today. She also gave me the assignments for the mathematics class. She said that the class was a little bit more quiet because I wasn't there. I didn't know whether this means they missed me or they were glad I wasn't there. Anyway I just shrugged off the thought.

二月二十五日　星期四　多雲有雨

生　病

　　我照著醫生的吩咐，今天整天都躺在床上，早上老師打電話來看看我出了什麼事，媽說我病了，不能上學。老師說她會把一些今天的功課送來給我，我就不會跟不上進度了。即使生病，也逃不掉學校的功課。也許我唯一能逃掉的一次是我埋在地下六尺深、入土為安的時候。老師說我很快就會痊癒的，然後就道再見了。

　　因此，除了光躺在床上，今天我做了些什麼？眞的沒什麼。我喝了許多媽媽弄的飲料，整天都只能吃稀飯。因爲吃藥的關係，我也睡得蠻久的。

　　傍晚，莉妮來看看我怎麼樣了，我告訴她也許我休息夠了之後，後天我就能上學了。她跟我說了些今天在學校所發生的事，也給了我數學作業。她說因爲我沒去，所以班上變得比較安靜。我不知道這意味著他們想念我，還是高興我的缺席。無論如何，我只是一笑置之。

❋❋────────────────────

confine〔kən'faɪn〕 *v.* 監禁；臥病
underground〔ˌʌndə'graʊnd〕 *adv.* 在地下
gruel 〔'gruəl〕 *n.* 粥　　***shrug off*** 一笑置之；不理

《表示痊癒的常用語》

♠ I recovered slowly after my long illness.
　我於久病後慢慢復元。

♠ He has recovered from his illness. 他已痊癒。

♠ I regained health quickly. 我很快恢復了健康。

♠ Though the wound is cured, it is not healed.
　此傷口雖經治療，但尙未痊癒。

Sat., Feb. 27　　***Fine***

Losing my temper

I nearly got into a fist fight with someone today. It all started like this. I wasn't feeling very good this day because I had just flunked my History test. I was really angry with the boys at my back because they got high marks although they cheated. I was just going to leave it at that but one of the boys started teasing me as a failure. They thought I was dumb because I didn't cheat like they did. Normally I would just leave them but they got to be too much this time. That's why I started arguing with them. But that didn't stop them until I got really mad and they challenged me to a duel. We were about to exchange blows when the principal saw us and took us to the office. I didn't tell on them but I got punished like the rest of them. It was really unfair.

Someday, I'm going to have my revenge. I'll just laugh when the day comes when the tables are turned against them. Yes, in fact I don't have to do anything at all. I know that one day they'll be the ones who are going to fail because they don't study that much. Then on that day, I'll get my sweet, sweet revenge.

二月二十七日　星期六　晴

發脾氣

　　我今天差點和某人打架。事情是這樣開始的，因爲歷史考不及格，我今天覺得不太痛快。我很氣後面的傢伙，因爲他們雖然作弊，却得到高分。我正想忘了這件事時，其中一個傢伙却嘲笑我是失敗者，他們認爲我很笨，因爲我沒有像他們一樣作弊。平常我會不理他們，但是他們這次太過分了。這就是我爲什麼開始和他們爭吵，但是這沒有制止他們，直到我憤怒到極點，他們向我挑釁要來一次決鬥。我們正要打起來時，校長正好看到，所以把我們帶到校長室。我沒有告發他們，但是和他們一樣受到處罰，眞不公平。

　　有朝一日，我要報復。當情勢對他們不利的那天來臨時，我要嘲笑他們。沒錯，實際上我什麼都不必做，我知道有一天他們會是失敗的人，因爲他們不用功。然後在那天，我會得到最甜美的報復。

《表示憤怒的常用語》

♤ He gave them an angry look. 他向他們怒目而視。

♤ Anger does no good. 念怒無濟於事。

♤ By their sins they provoked the wrath of God.
　　他們因犯罪而激起了上帝的憤怒。

♤ The atrocity caused widespread indignation.
　　那暴行引起了普遍的憤慨。

♤ She was in one of her wild furies.
　　她在一陣憤怒當中。

Sun., Feb. 28 Bright but windy

The Old Man and the Sea

Finished reading "The Old Man and the Sea" by Ernest Hemingway. This is one of Hemingway's best stories. Relatively easy to read, but very impressive, more impressive than Orwell's "Animal Farm".

This old fisherman gallantly fought against nature, but his human effort had its limit. Felt very sorry for him. This old man, however, learned the great truth in the end.

二月二十八日　星期日　晴朗有風
老人與海

讀完了海明威的老人與海。這是海明威最好的小說之一，比較容易讀，但相當深刻感人，比奧威爾的動物農莊還勝一籌。

老漁人勇敢地與自然搏鬥，然而人力却有其限制，我爲他深深地感到遺憾。但是，這個老人，最後却學到了偉大的眞理。

---

relatively (ˈrɛlətɪvlɪ) *adv.* 比較上；相對地
impressive (ɪmˈprɛsɪv) *adj.* 感人的；留給人深刻印象的
gallantly (ˈgæləntlɪ) *adv.* 英勇地；莊嚴地
fought (fɔt) *v.. pt.* & *pp.* of fight (faɪt) *v.* 戰鬥；抵抗

Mon., Feb. 29   Sunny

New fashions

A new fashion has arrived in Taipei. Young women now wear miniskirts.

Last Sunday I met a classmate wearing a miniskirt on the street. Her name was Lin Yi-ching. She looked cute. I said to Mom in the kitchen, "Will you buy a miniskirt for me?" She said, "You don't look nice in that kind of clothing."

I think her thinking is old-fashioned. I would like to buy a miniskirt with my own money.

二月二十九日　星期一　晴

流行服飾

一種最新流行的服裝樣式已經來到台北了，現在年輕的女孩們都穿迷你裙。

上個禮拜我在街上遇到一位穿著迷你裙的同學，她的名字是林宜靜。她看起來好可愛。我告訴在廚房忙碌的媽媽：「妳會不會買一件迷你裙給我？」她却說：「妳穿那樣不好看。」

我認為她的思想太守舊了。我要用我自己的錢去買一件迷你裙。

---

miniskirt〔'mɪnɪ,skɚt〕 *n.* 迷你裙
cute〔kjut〕 *adj.* 美麗嬌小而可愛的；聰明漂亮的
old-fashioned〔'old'fæʃənd〕 *adj.* 老式的；守舊的

Sun., Mar. 6　　*Fine*

Bargain sale

I went to a bargain sale this morning. Most of the stuff there was junk. The only thing I liked was an old chair they had; it was too expensive though. I met Sandra there, she didn't find anything worth buying either.

三月六日　星期日　晴

大　拍　賣

今天早上我去大廉價的地方逛。大部份的東西都很便宜。我唯一喜歡的一樣東西是一張舊椅子，但是它還是太貴了。在那兒我遇到珊德拉，她也沒有找到值得買的東西。

**

bargain sale 大廉價　　stuf〔stʌf〕*n.* 物品

Tues., Mar. 8　　*Rainy*

Women's Day

Today is "Women's Day." It made me think about being a woman. I like being a woman even though we have a harder life than men. When we come home from work we have to do the housework. Why must we do it? When men come home from work they fall on the couch and watch TV while we prepare dinner for them.

三月八日　星期二　雨

婦　女　節

今天是婦女節。這使我想到當女人的事。我喜歡身爲女人，即使女人的生活要比男人苦。當我們下班回家後，我們得做家事。我們爲什麼要做家事？當男人下班回家坐在沙發上看電視時，我們卻正在爲他們準備晚餐。

＊＊

even though 即使　　　***fall on*** 落在…上
couch 〔kaʊtʃ〕 *n.* 長沙發

Thurs., Mar. 10　Fine

Korean barbecue

New Year's atmosphere has completely disappeared. We no longer see little boys and girls in colorful costumes and adults exchanging lengthy New Year's greetings in the street.

At supper went to a Korean restaurant with Li. and had Korean barbecue. There were only a few people in the restaurant. Probably because of the cold weather!

三月十日　星期四　晴

韓國烤肉

新年的氣氛已經完全消失了。我們不再看到小男孩小女孩穿著色彩鮮艷的服裝，以及大人們在街上互相交換冗長的新年問候語。

晚餐時和李小姐到一家韓國餐館吃韓國烤肉。餐館裏只有一些人，或許是因爲天氣冷的緣故吧！

＊＊

atmosphere 〔'ætməs,fɪr〕 *n.* 氣氛；環境
barbecue 〔'barbɪ,kju〕 *n.* 烤肉　　　costume 〔'kastjum〕 *n.* 服裝
lengthy 〔'lɛŋkθɪ,-ŋθ-〕 *adj.* 冗長的

Sun., *Mar.* *13*　*Fine*

Cherry blossom viewers

According to the newspaper, nearly thirty thousand people visited Yang Ming Shan. Viewing cherry blossoms is all right, but what can we see and appreciate among the jostling crowds? If flower-viewing is their purpose, there may be many other places quieter and less crowded.

It is foolish to have to go to a certain place just because others go. Stayed indoors all day except lunch-time when I took my dog for a short walk.

三月十三日　星期日　晴

花　季

新聞報導說，去陽明山的遊客將近三萬人。賞櫻花是不錯，但是在擁擠的人潮中我們能看到和欣賞到些什麼呢？假如賞花是他們的目的，一定還有很多其他比較安靜，比較不擠的地方。

因為別人去那個地方玩，你就跟著去，這是很愚蠢的。我整天都待在家裏，只有在午餐時間才帶狗出去轉了一圈。

＊＊

view〔vju〕*v.*, *n.* 觀看；視察
appreciate〔ə'priʃɪ,et〕*v.* 重視；賞識；欣賞
jostling〔'dʒɑslɪŋ〕*adj.* 推擠的
purpose〔'pɝpəs〕*n.* 目的；用意

Mon., *Mar.* *14*　*Rainy later fine*

A warm spring day

It was pretty warm today, but I prefer spring to autumn. It is chiefly because spring is the fore-runner of happy summer. This coming Saturday we shall go on a spring excursion to Tam Shui. Very anxious to see Tam Shui as I have never been there. According to the weatherman, it will continue to be fine toward the weekend. But the weather forecast sometimes turns out to be wrong. I really hope it will be true this weekend.

三月十四日　星期一　雨後晴

春　暖

今天非常暖和，但我喜歡春天甚於秋天。主要是因爲春天是快樂夏天的前驅。這個星期六我們要舉辦一次到淡水的春季旅遊。好想去淡水，因爲我以前從沒去過。氣象報告說，一直到週末都會是好天氣。但是天氣預報有時候會是錯誤的，我眞心盼望對這個週末而言，它是正確的預報。

**

forerunner〔'for,rʌnɚ〕*n.* 預兆；先驅

excursion〔ɪk'skɝʒən, -ʃən〕*n.* 遠足；旅行

weatherman〔'wɛðɚ,mæn〕*n.* 擔任氣象預報的人或氣象局之官員

forecast〔'for,kæst〕*n.* 預測；預報

Tues., *Mar. 15 Fine*

Another fine day

I got up early today. I had a fitful sleep last night. When I opened the window the sun was shining and a soft gentle breeze was blowing into my face. I could hear some birds chirping in a nearby tree also. Immediately, I cleaned up and got dressed. Mother was already cooking breakfast when I got down. She was listening to the early morning report on the radio. Somehow, I just felt so light and carefree today. After breakfast, I hurried to the bus depot and caught my bus in the nick of time.

Everything went smoothly at school. I was even commended by my teacher for the fine work I did with my homework. She read my composition aloud to the class. I was a bit embarrassed but at the same time very flattered. My classmates even teased me about it and congratulated me on it. At four in the afternoon, I was ready to go back home. I had dinner and finished all my lessons. I'm going to bed now and I'll be saying my prayers. Today wasn't bad at all.

三月十五日　星期二　晴

又是晴天

今天我起得很早。昨晚睡得斷斷續續的。當我打開窗戶，陽光照射，微風輕輕吹在我的臉上，還能聽見一些小鳥在附近的樹上吱喳叫著。我很快地盥洗完畢，穿好衣服。當我下樓時，媽媽已經煮好早餐了。她正在聽收音機裏的晨間新聞。不知怎麼，今天我只感到輕快無比，無憂無慮。吃完早餐之後，我匆匆趕到公車站，正好搭上了車。

在學校的一切都進行順利，我甚至還因家庭作業做得很好而大受老師稱讚，她在班上大聲朗讀我的作文。我覺得有點不好意思，但又覺得受寵若驚。同學們甚至因此而揶揄我並恭喜我。下午四點，我準備回家了。吃完晚餐，做完功課，現在我要去睡覺和禱告了。今天眞不賴！

＊＊

chirp〔tʃɝp〕v. 吱喳而鳴（鳥）　　commend〔kə'mɛnd〕v. 稱讚
carefree〔'kɛr,fri〕*adj.* 無憂無慮的；快樂的
flatter〔'flætɚ〕v. 諂媚　　depot〔'dɛpo〕*n.* 公共汽車站
tease〔tiz〕v. 揶揄
in the nick of time 正是時候

《表示晴天的常用語》

♤ It is fine. 天氣很好。

♤ There is not a speck of cloud in the sky. 天空沒有一片雲。

♤ It's a nice sunny day. 陽光普照的好日子。

♤ It suddenly clears up. 天氣突然轉晴了。

♤ The weather has settled at last.
　　天氣終於穩定下來了。

Wed., Mar. 16   Fine

A camera

With brother took a walk in the suburbs with a camera in hand. It was very pleasant to walk among the trees which were flaming with fresh verdure. Took a few pictures at the rural scene.

三月十六日   星期三   晴

攝影之樂

拿著照相機，和哥哥到郊外散步。在熱烈地綻放著新綠的樹林中走動眞是件賞心悅事。我拍了些鄉村景緻的照片。

Thurs. Mar. 17   Rainy later fine

Salon's famous pictures

On my way home from school went to see the exhibition of Salon's famous pictures held at Taipei Art Museum. Most of the pictures were nude pictures and there were some which corrupt public morals. The discipline of the authorities seems to have lately become lenient.

三月十七日   星期四   雨後晴

看　畫　展

我放學回家的途中，跑去看在台北市立美術館舉行的沙龍名畫展。大部份的畫都是裸體畫，有些有導壞世風的傾向。政府當局的法令紀律最近似乎趨於和緩。

＊＊─────────────────

exhibition〔,ɛksə'brʃən〕 *n.* 展覽會；陳列品
nude〔njud〕 *adj.* 裸體的；裸體畫　　morals〔'mɔrəl〕 *n.* 風氣
corrupt〔kə'rʌpt〕 *v.* 使腐敗；敗壞

Fri., Mar. 18   Fine

A sports competition

This afternoon we had some time off from our class. We went out to watch our school team take part in a basketball match with another school. We were supposed to cheer for our school team. When we got to the court the game was already in full heat. We cheered so loudly that my voice became hoarse from shouting. Although our team lost in the end we were still very happy because they tried their best. All in all it was a very exciting match.

三月十八日   星期五   晴

運動競賽

今天下午我們的課有一些休息時間。於是我們跑出去看我們校隊和別校的籃球比賽。大家都認為我們要為我們的校隊加油。當我們到達場地時,比賽已經進行得如火如荼的了。我們大聲加油,以致於我的聲音都因喊叫而沙啞了。雖然最後我們這隊輸了,我們仍然很快樂,因為他們盡了全力。就整體而言,這是一場非常令人興奮的比賽。

---

cheer〔tʃɪr〕 v. 喝采;為…加油
court〔kɔrt〕 n. 場
hoarse〔hors〕 adj. 嘶啞的
all in all 就整體而言

Sat., Mar. 19 Fine

My indifference to English

Today while I was walking at the Taipei Railroad Station, a foreigner approached me. She seemed to be lost. She asked me if I could help her. I said O.K. But when she started talking I couldn't understand a single word she uttered. Ashamedly, I could only say " I don't know ", then I slowly walked away. My failure to communicate with her is the result of my indifference to English. The truth is I've been too lazy to study English. The result is although I've been studying English for three years now, I still can't understand English well enough.

三月十九日　星期六　晴

忽視英文的下場

　　今天當我走在台北火車站的時候，一個老外向我走過來。她好像迷路了。她問我可不可以幫助她。我說好。但是當她開始說話的時候，我却一個字也聽不懂。丟臉的是，我只能說「不知道」，然後慢慢地走開。我與她的溝通失敗是由於我忽視英文所造成的。事實上是我一直太懶了，以致於沒唸英文，而結果是雖然我到現在爲止已經讀了三年的英文，但却仍然無法把英文瞭解到相當好的程度。

＊＊────────────────────

indifference〔ɪnˈdɪfərəns〕 *n.* 不重視；漠不關心

ashamedly〔əˈʃemdlɪ〕 *adv.* 慚愧地；羞恥地

Sun., Mar. 22　Very fine

Today is Sunday

Today is Sunday. What did I do today? Let me
think... In the morning I went out for a walk with my
pet dog, Ralph. We went to the park. I played frisbee
with my brother, Joel. Ralph also played with us. Ralph
really knows how to catch a frisbee already. At around
eleven, we went to McDonalds to eat some ham-
burgers. Then we went back home. In the afternoon I
helped Dad clean the car. And then after that he helped assemble my model plane. At seven we had dinner
and then watched some TV. At nine, I went to bed. I
had to go to bed early so that I can go to school
early too.

三月二十二日　星期日　大晴

今天星期天

今天是星期天。我做了些什麼？讓我想想 ... 早上我和我的寵
物，小狗雷夫一起去散步。我們去公園。我和弟弟喬一起玩飛盤。
雷夫也跟我們一起玩。雷夫已經可以懂得如何去接飛盤了。大概十
一點的時候，我們去麥當勞吃漢堡。然後就回家了。下午我幫爸爸
洗車。洗完之後他幫我裝配我的模型飛機。七點吃晚飯，然後看了
一些電視節目。九點上牀睡覺。我必須早睡，以便明天可以早點
上學。

---

pet〔pɛt〕*n.* 寵愛的動物　　frisbee〔ˈfrɪzbi〕*n.* 飛盤
assemble〔əˈsɛmbḷ〕*v.* 裝配

Sat., Mar. 26   *Fine*

Understanding a movie

I went out with Cousin Yann-yann today. We went out to watch a movie. The title of the movie was "Dirty Dancing". When we got to the movie theatre, there were already a lot of people falling in line to buy tickets.

I told Yann-yann to wait in line while I went to buy some snacks and drinks. After we bought our tickets we went inside to find our seats. There were some people sitting in our seats so we showed them our tickets and they moved away. Then we started munching on the popcorn I bought.

The movie was very well done. I liked the dancing a lot. They could really all dance very well. We also liked the music, especially the song "The Time of my Life". The story was about a teenager's belief in her ideals. It was also a story about how cruel and corrupt the world may be.

In the end the ideals of the girl prevailed over all the disappointments and heartaches that she encountered. It was a good movie with a very positive message. The movie was really worth our money. It's one of the better films I've seen so far this year.

三月二十六日　星期六　晴

了解電影

今天我與燕燕表妹出去，我們去看電影，片名是「熱舞十七」。我們到達戲院時，已經有很多人在排隊買票了。

我叫燕燕在隊伍中等，而我跑去買一些零食和飲料。買完票後我們走進戲院找位子，有人坐在我們的位子上，於是我們拿票給他們看，他們才走開。然後我們就開始大吃我買來的爆米花。

這部電影拍得非常好，我很喜歡裏面的舞蹈，他們真的都跳得非常好。我們也很喜歡它的音樂，尤其是「美好時光」這首歌。故事敍說一位少女對其理想的信仰，並描述這個世界可能是多麼的殘酷腐敗。

結局時少女的理想戰勝她所遭遇的所有失望及悲痛。這是一部有積極寓意的好電影，實在值得我們花錢來看。這是今年到目前爲止我看過的佳片之一。

**————————————————————

in line 排成隊　　munch〔mʌntʃ〕 *v.* 用力咀嚼；大聲咀嚼
popcorn〔'pɑp,kɔrn〕 *n.* 玉米花
prevail over 戰勝
message〔'mɛsɪdʒ〕 *n.* （電影、戲劇、小說中的）寓意；教訓

《有關電影的常用語》

◇ We have been to a movie today. 我們今天看過一場電影。

◇ He worked for years in the movies. 他在電影界工作了幾年。

♤ James Dean is my favorite movie star.
詹姆斯狄恩是我最喜歡的電影明星。

♤ How often do you go to the movies?
你多久看一次電影？

Sun., Mar. 27 *Cloudy*

Going shopping

I did my favorite pastime today : Shopping. It was good that Dad came along with me and Mom. I don't like going shopping with my Mom too much. This is because I don't get to buy the things that I want. I usually end up just being the bag carrier. Dad is more generous, at least he lets me pick one thing that I really like and buys it for me.

I've gone shopping with Dad only a few times. And I've enjoyed each time I've gone out shopping with him. He didn't disappoint me either today.

We went to Sogo Department Store today. The white facade of the building and its unique architecture attracts anyone's attention very easily. The salesladies inside were very courteous. All of them kept on bowing and saying welcome to us. I found this a bit uncomfortable. After a while we learned to just ignore them.

Anyway the whole area of the department store was quite big. The things sold were also very expensive. It was hard to find something I really liked and wasn't expensive. Finally I chose a pair of shoes that were on sale. When we went home our feet were very sore and painful. This was my day at the Department Store.

三月二十七日　星期日　陰

逛街購物

　　我今天做了最喜愛的消遣：購物。有爸爸跟我和媽同行眞好。我不太喜歡和媽媽去購物，因爲我開始就買不到想要的東西。結果我通常只是提袋子的人。爸爸比較慷慨，至少他會讓我挑一樣我眞正喜歡的東西買給我。

　　我只跟爸爸去買過幾次東西，而每次跟他出去買東西都很快樂，他今天也沒有讓我失望。

　　我們今天到崇光百貨公司。大樓的白色正面及獨特的建築架構很容易吸引住任何人的注意力。裏面的售貨小姐很有禮貌，他們一直對我們鞠躬說歡迎。我覺得這樣有一點不自在。過了一會兒我們就學會了不要管他們。

　　總之，百貨公司的整個地區相當廣大，賣的東西也很貴，很難找到我眞正喜歡而又不貴的東西，最後我選了一雙拍賣中的鞋子。回家時我們的脚都非常酸痛。這就是我在百貨公司的一天。

---

get to 開始；著手　　　facade〔fə'sɑd〕*n.* 建築正面

be on sale 拍賣；廉價

《表示逛街的常用語》

♧My sister is out shopping. 我的妹妹出去買東西去了。

♧We shopped all morning for new coats.

　　我們整個上午都在買新衣服。

♧The shop was shut up. 那家店關了。

♧I like to go shopping. 我喜歡逛街。

Thurs., Mar. 31 *Sunny*

Losing my way

Today, being a sunny day, I went out to ride my bike. I rode to the countryside where I could breathe fresh air. This is something I miss living in Taipei. Taipei's pollution is so bad. I always smell the foul air of the city. And when I walk on the streets, I have to breathe the noxious fumes from the buses, motorcycles and cars. Today I had the chance to be away from it all.

As I was riding along the country road, I didn't notice that I was beginning to stray away from my route. Soon enough I was lost. I must have gone a hundred times in circles looking for the familiar road I used to travel on. It was getting dark and soon I couldn't see a thing. I was really scared. The wind was blowing cooler and cooler. Finally, in a far end of a street, I saw some light. I rode the bike as fast as I could. There was a telephone there and so I called up my mother to pick me up. Soon, she came and took me home. This was really a humbling experience.

三月三十一日　星期四　晴

迷　路

今天，天氣晴朗，我到外面騎腳踏車。我騎到鄉間，在那裏我可以呼吸新鮮的空氣。這是我住在台北所得不到的東西。台北的空氣污染太嚴重了。我總是嗅到都市污穢的空氣。在街上走時，我必須呼吸由公共汽車、摩托車及汽車排出的毒氣。今天我總算有機會遠離這一切。

由於沿著鄉間道路騎著，我沒注意到我開始叉離原路。很快我就迷路了。我必定是轉了一百次圈子尋找以前走過的熟路。天愈來愈黑，很快地我就一點東西都看不到了。我很害怕。風越吹越冷。最後，在一條路遠遠的盡頭，我看到一些亮光。我儘快地騎著腳踏車。那兒有一個電話亭，所以我打電話給媽媽要她來載我。很快地，媽媽就來帶我回家。這眞是一個可恥的經驗。

**──────────────

foul〔faʊl〕*adj.* 污穢的；惡臭的
noxious〔'nɑkʃəs〕*adj.* 有害的；有毒的
fume〔fjum〕*n.* （有害的、氣味難聞而強烈的）烟、氣體
stray〔stre〕*v.* 走入歧途　　　humbling〔'hʌmblɪŋ〕*adj.* 令人羞辱的

《表示害怕的常用語》

♧ He was scared by the thunder. 他爲雷聲所驚嚇。

♧ The noise frightened me. 那聲響使我害怕。

♤ They were appalled at the news. 他們被這消息嚇壞了。

♤ I was terrified of being left alone in the house.
　我害怕一個人留在家裏。

♤ She was startled out of her sleep. 她從睡夢中驚醒。

Fri., Apr. 1   Fine

All Fools' Day

Today is All Fools' Day. People play all kinds of tricks and practical jokes on their friends, and when the victim sees he has been taken in, they call him "April fool". Moderate tricks and jokes are all right, but in extreme cases people may suffer.

This practice was originally introduced from America, but I think we should reconsider it in our country.

四月一日　星期五　晴

愚　人　節

今天是愚人節。人們以各種方式捉弄他們的朋友，當受害者發覺他被捉弄了，他們就叫他"四月的傻瓜"。適度的惡作劇和開玩笑都還好，但在某些極端過份的情況下，人們會感到痛苦難受。

這個習俗最初是從美國傳來的，但我認爲若要在我國實行，還有待商榷。

---

trick〔trɪk〕*n.* 詭計；惡作劇　　　joke〔dʒok〕*n.* 玩笑；幽默
take in 欺騙　　victim〔'vɪktɪm〕*n.* 受害者；犧牲品
moderate〔'mɑdərɪt〕*adj.* 適度的；不過分的

Sat., Apr. 2　*Very Fine*

Candle light

After supper, sat before the desk to do my homework when the electric current failed and it became dark for two hours. Felt no longer like studying under the dim light of a candle, was obliged to go to bed.

四月二日　星期六　晴

停　電

晚餐後，我坐在書桌前寫作業，突然停電了，黑暗持續了兩個小時。在蠟燭微弱的光線之下，我不想再研讀下去了，只好迫不得已地上牀去睡覺。

＊＊────────────────

supper〔'sʌpə〕 *n.* 晚餐　　*electric current* 電流

dim〔dɪm〕 *adj.* 模糊的；微弱的；暗淡的　　candle〔'kændl〕 *n.* 燭光

oblige〔ə'blaɪdʒ〕 *v.* 強制；束縛　　*be obliged to* 不得不；必須

Wed., Apr. 6　*Cloudy, later fine*

My dream

In English class today we talked about our dreams. This was my speech:

I watched a shocking program on television. In Africa, many people need more food, clothes, and houses. The United Nations is helping them, but it needs our help. The United Nations does a great job! My dream is to work for the United Nations.

I felt happier today than yesterday.

四月六日　星期三　多雲時晴

夢　想

今天在英文課的時候,我們談論我們的夢想。以下是我所說的:

「我在電視上看到一個令人驚駭的節目,在非洲,許多人都需要更多的食物,衣服以及房屋。聯合國一直在援助他們,但仍需要我們的支持。聯合國從事的真是神聖的工作啊!我的夢想就是能在聯合國裡頭服務。」

我覺得今天比昨天還快樂。

**

shocking〔'ʃɑkɪŋ〕 *adj.* 可驚的;駭人的;震動的
The United Nations 聯合國

Thurs., Apr. 7　Fine

Calligraphy

Fewer and fewer people are coming to calligraphy class. Many of them find learning calligraphy too boring. The teacher says the same thing happens every term. People register for class not realizing the time and effort necessary to learn calligraphy.

四月七日　星期四　晴

毛　筆　字

上書法課的人越來越少。很多人覺得學書法太無聊了。老師說同樣的情形發生在每一期。人們登記上課却不了解學書法是需要時間和努力的。

**

calligraphy〔kə'lɪgrəfɪ〕 *n.* 書法　　boring〔'borɪŋ〕 *adj.* 令人厭倦的
register〔'rɛdʒɪstɚ〕 *v.* 登記

Fri., Apr. 8　Cloudy

A traffic accident near
the Palace Museum

As I was returning home late last Tuesday, a terrible accident near the National Palace Museum occurred. I was wondering why the traffic had piled up to such a mess. Our bus was moving at a snail's pace. When we reached the scene of the accident I saw a man's body covered with newspapers and blood was all over the street. Apparently, the man had been run over by a car. Nearby a car had its windshield smashed to pieces. I didn't see the driver, but probably the driver got hurt in the accident also. I thought, there was no way the driver could have escaped the accident by the way the windshield had been broken. There were a lot of people milling around the scene and the drivers of the cars that were passing by slowed their cars down too to watch the scene.

This accident sent a chill through my spine. I remember the many times when I was nearly hit by passing vehicles, but each time nothing happened. The dead man on the street near the National Palace Museum told me that that person could have been me.

四月八日　星期五　多雲

在故宮附近的車禍

　　上個禮拜二稍晚我正趕著回家，在故宮博物院附近發生了一場可怕的車禍。那時我還在奇怪，爲什麼交通變得這麼擁擠，塞成一團。我們的公車開得像蝸牛在爬。當我們到達車禍現場，我看到一個覆蓋了報紙的男人身體以及滿地的血。顯然地，那人是被一輛車子輾過去。附近的一輛車子擋風玻璃全碎了。我沒看到駕駛，不過他可能也在車禍中受了傷。我想，在擋風玻璃全碎的情況下，駕駛是沒有辦法躲過這場意外的。許多的人在現場四周爭相觀看，而從旁邊經過的駕駛人也減低了車速張望著。

　　這起車禍使我不禁悚然。我記得有好幾次差點被經過的車輛撞到，幸好每一次都沒發生什麼事。那個死在故宮博物院附近的人告訴了我，有一天我可能就像他一樣了。

＊＊

pile up 積成堆　　mess 〔mɛs〕 *n.* 雜亂的一團
run over 輾過；壓過
windshield 〔'wɪnd‚ʃild〕 *n.* 〔美〕（汽車之）擋風玻璃
smash 〔smæʃ〕 *v.* 破碎；粉碎　　mill 〔mɪl〕 *v.* 亂闖闖地推擠
chill 〔tʃɪl〕 *n.* 寒慄；寒顫　　spine 〔spaɪn〕 *n.* 脊骨
vehicle 〔'viːɪkl〕 *n.* 車輛

《有關交通的常用語》

♤ Traffic is heavy on this street. 這條街的交通流量很大。

♤ I was walking on a pedestrian crossing.
　　我走在行人穿越道上。

♤ The traffic on the speedway was suspended.
　　高速公路的交通中斷。

♤ I didn't see a traffic signal. 我沒看見交通號誌。

Sun., *Apr*. *10*   *Fine*

The weather forecast

Relying on the weather forecast through the radio, went to school without carrying my umbrella or raincoat with me. In the afternoon it began to rain all of a sudden so got home wet to the skin.

四月十日　星期日　晴

天氣預報

信賴收音機的天氣預報，我既沒帶傘，也沒帶雨衣就到學校去了。下午却突然下起雨，以致於我回家時全身都濕透了。

**

forecast〔'for,kæst〕*n.* 預測
raincoat〔'ren,kot〕*n.* 雨衣　　　　skin〔skɪn〕*n.* 皮膚

Mon., *Apr*. *11*   *Cloudy later rainy*

Mathematics

I got an A-plus on the math test again. It was so easy, I think I must be a genius. Maybe I can go study at Harvard and make brilliant discoveries and win the Nobel Prize. Sure, why not?

四月十一日　星期一　多雲有雨

數　學

數學考試我又得了一個A⁺。考試這麼容易，我想我一定是天才。也許我可以去哈佛大學唸書並且獲得重大的發現而贏得諾貝爾獎。當然，爲何不？

**

mathematics〔,mæθə'mætɪks〕*n.* （作單數用）數學（= *math.* ）
genius〔'dʒinjəs〕*n.* 天才　　brilliant〔'brɪljənt〕*adj.* 顯赫的

Tues., Apr. 12　Fair

At the beach

Perhaps today will be the hottest day of these days. The temperature was 28 degrees centigrade at two o'clock.

My family went swimming in Yeh Liu. We enjoyed the blue sea and white clouds. Both Mom and Dad are good swimmers. Brother and I enjoyed playing in the sand on the beach. We swam only a little. Swimming in the sea was more interesting than in the pool.

We were ready to go home at six and were all very tired. Then we saw the wonderful sunset above the level surface. What a touching scene! And it gradually sank below the horizon.

四月十二日　星期二　晴朗

海濱落日

今天大概是這些日子以來最熱的一天了。兩點的時候溫度竟然高達攝氏二十八度。

我們一家人去野柳游泳，享受碧藍的海洋與潔白的雲。爸爸媽媽都是游泳好手，哥哥和我則在海灘玩沙。我們只會游一點點。在海裏游泳比在游泳池裏有趣多了。

六點當我們準備回家，而且都很累的時候，看見水平面上美麗的夕陽，真是動人的一幕！然後它緩緩地沉到海裏去了。

✱✱

temperature〔'tɛmprətʃə〕 *n.* 溫度　　degree〔dɪ'gri〕 *n.* 溫度；程度
centigrade〔'sɛntə,gred〕 *adj.* 攝氏寒暑表的

Wed., Apr. 13　Fine

Letter from my pen pal

Pat is my pen pal in New Zealand. Today I received a letter from her with some pictures.

She said in her letter, " It is fall in New Zealand. Leaves are turning red and yellow. I'm going on a hike on Saturday. " Fall in New Zealand now?!

I went to the school library. I said to myself, " Oh! Summer in Taiwan is winter in Pat's country. Winter in Taiwan is summer in New Zealand. "

It was a surprise for me. Well then, I thought, " Will Santa Claus wear swimming trunks at Christmas? " I'll ask Pat about it in my next letter.

四月十三日　星期三　晴

一封筆友的來信

潘特是我在紐西蘭的筆友。今天我收到她寄來的信和一些照片。

她信上說：「紐西蘭現在是秋天，葉子正紛紛轉紅或變黃。星期六我要去健行。」紐西蘭現在是秋天嗎？

我到學校圖書館去，自言自語著：「噢！台灣的夏天就是潘特國家的冬天，台灣的冬天就是紐西蘭的夏天。」

我眞感到驚奇，然後我想：「聖誕老公公在聖誕節時會不會穿著冰褲呢？」我下封信裏頭要問問潘特。

---

pen pal 筆友　　hike〔haɪk〕*n.* 遠足；徒步旅行
surprise〔sə'praɪz〕*n.* 驚訝；驚奇

Thur., *Apr*. *14* *Fine*

Make up

The teacher allowed me to make up my test on English poetry, but I flunked it again. I'm no good with English poetry, I have enough trouble with Chinese poetry. Why am I wasting my time with this stuff? I want to be an engineer, not a poet. I have to learn to talk with computers, not people.

四月十四日　星期四　晴

補　考

老師答應我補考英詩，但我又一次沒考過。我對英詩不行，中文詩已經給我不少麻煩了。我為什麼要浪費時間在這些廢物上？我要做工程師，不是詩人。我必須學習與電腦交談而不是和人談。

＊＊─────────────────

make up 補考　　poetry〔'po·ɪtrɪ,'po·ətrɪ〕 *n*. 詩

flunk〔flʌŋk〕 *v*. 考試不及格　　stuff〔stʌf〕 *n*. 廢物；劣品

Sat., *Apr*. *16* *Fine*

A dictionary

Mother and Father gave me a dictionary. Of all the things in this world why did it have to be a dictionary? I wanted a Sony walkman or a new dress, but no, they gave me a dictionary. I suppose they expect me to study all the time, but there's more to life than studying. I want to have some fun.

四月十六日　星期六　晴

字　典

爸媽給我一本字典。什麼都行，為什麼卻是一本字典？我想要一台新力牌隨身聽或是一件新衣，但不是，他們給我字典。我想他們希望我一直唸書，可是人生有比唸書更重要的事。我要有些娛樂。

Mon., Apr. 18　*Rainy later fine*

A kind woman

This morning, the weather was fine and cool. I got up at six and went to school as usual. On my way to school, the sky suddenly turned pitch dark. Later, it started to rain cats and dogs. Since I did not expect it would rain, I had no umbrella or raincoat with me. I was anxious to find shelter, but to my disappointment, there were no buildings in sight. I thought I would catch a cold because I was almost drenched to the skin.

Fortunately, a kind woman came near me and shared her umbrella with me. She was kindness itself when she walked me all the way to school. I felt very warm for this woman. Without doubt there is much benevolence and sympathy in our society. I am very obliged to that kind woman for her kindness. I will never forget this experience in my life.

四月十八日　星期一　雨後轉晴

一個好心的女人

今天早上是個涼爽的晴天。我如往常般在六點起床上學。上學途中，天色突然變黑，沒一會，便下起了傾盆大雨。由於我沒料到會下雨，所以我根本沒帶傘或是雨衣。我急著想找地方躲雨，但失望的是，觸目所及沒有一棟建築物。我想我會感冒，因為我快淫透了。

幸好，有一個好心的女人走近我並和我一起撑她的傘。當她陪我一路走到學校時，我覺得她簡直就是仁慈的化身。她使我感到好溫暖。無疑地，在我們的社會中仍有許多善良和有同情心的人。我非常感激那位好心腸的女人。我一輩子都不會忘記這段經歷的。

---

pitch〔pɪtʃ〕*n.* 瀝青　　　***rain cats and dogs*** 下起傾盆大雨
in sight 在望；看得見　　　**drench**〔drentʃ〕*v.* 浸；浸透
be obliged to sb. 感激某人

《表示行爲的常用語》

♠ His good behavior deserves praise.
　　他的好品行值得稱讚。

♡ She always conducts herself like a lady.
　　她的舉止經常有如淑女。

♠ This action speaks volumes for his probity.
　　此一行動極足以證明他的正直。

♢ God helps those who help themselves.
　　天助自助者。

♢ To say the least, he was very rash.
　　不是我愛說，他實在很鹵莽。

Thurs., Apr. 21　Cloudy

An unfair test

My teacher gave a surprise quiz today. All of us couldn't answer the questions on the quiz. This was because he had not yet taught this lesson yet. So I complained to my teacher about it. I said the test was unfair because we didn't know anything about it yet. The teacher was surprised that I stood up to complain of such a thing. I hope that the teacher didn't get me wrong for my complaining. But sometimes the pressure that the teachers give us becomes too much to handle. I don't mind taking tests but when the teacher is unfair I think it is only right that someone says so.

四日二十一日　星期四　多雲

不公平的考試

老師今天舉行一次出人意外的小考，大家都不會寫。因為他還沒教到這課。所以我向老師抱怨這件事。我說這次小考是不公平的，因為我們一點都不曉得。老師對於我站起來，抱怨這種事情，感到很驚訝。希望老師不要因為我的抱怨而誤會我。但有時候老師給我們的壓力會變得太大，以致於我們無法承受。我不介意考試，但當老師不公平時，我認為有人說出來並沒有錯。

---

quiz〔kwɪz〕*n.* （非正式的）測驗
pressure〔'prɛʃɚ〕*n.* 壓力

Sun., *Apr.* **24**   *Fine*

A meeting

I woke up early this morning to take a bath.
Usually I get up late because I've got such lazy
bones. But since my friend Janice and I had a date
I had to get up early. After I finished my shower I got dressed and went straight to the park.
After waiting for a long time, Janice still didn't
show up. I was really angry.

Then, I noticed there was a boy who looked as
if he was in the same shoes that I was. After an
hour, he approached me and smiled. He asked me if I
would like to drink something with him. I found
him interesting to talk with. We soon took to each
other.

In the evening, Janice gave me a phone call and
said she was sorry, I said it was alright. Though
I was angry that Janice didn't show up, I was also
glad because I got to know a new friend – James.
It was a blessing in disguise.

四月二十四日　星期日　晴

相　遇

　　早上我起得很早，洗了個澡。通常我都起得很晚，因為我是**個懶骨頭**。但因為我和朋友珍妮絲有個約會，因此必須早起。在淋浴之後，我穿好衣服，直接走到公園，等了好久，珍妮絲仍然沒有來。我真的很生氣。

　　然後，我注意到有個男孩看起來好像與我面臨相同的情況。一小時後，他向我走過來，微笑著。他問我願不願意跟他去喝點**飲料什麼**的。我發覺跟他聊天很有趣。我們很快就喜歡彼此了。

　　傍晚，珍妮絲打電話來道歉，我說沒關係。雖然我生氣珍妮絲放我鴿子，但我也蠻樂的，因為我認識了一個新朋友——**詹姆斯**。真是塞翁失馬，焉知非福啊！

**───────────────────

take to 喜歡

Mon., Apr. 25　　*Fine*

A baseball game

An ideal day for a baseball game. Went to Taipei Municipal Baseball Diamond to see the first game between the Giants **and** Hang-Yeh. The Giants won by a score of three to one.

四月二十五日　星期一　晴

棒　球　賽

　　今天是比賽棒球的理想天氣。我去台北市立棒球場看巨人隊和紅葉隊的第一次比賽。巨人隊以三比一的分數獲勝。

**───────────────────

match〔mætʃ〕 *n.* 比賽　　*Taipei Municipal Baseball Diamond* 台北市立棒球場

Sun., Apr. 31   Fine

Goodbyes

Today my friend, Yueh-shiun left for America. His short vacation here has ended and now he has to go back to continue his studies in New York. I took him to the airport to say my last goodbyes. By now he is flying over the Pacific Ocean on his way to the United States. I could only feel a tinge of sadness because a good friend has gone away. His diligence has always inspired me to study harder myself. Although we are far apart now, I believe that we will see each other again. Now, there are a little more than one hundred days to the entrance examination. I will prepare for it and also enjoy my beautiful summer vacation.

四月三十一日　星期日　晴

道　別

今天，我的朋友月鄉去了美國。他在此地短暫的假期已經結束，而現在，他必須回去美國，繼續那邊的學業。我帶他到機場，道最後一聲再見。此時他正飛越太平洋，往美國的旅途上。我只覺得有些感傷，因爲一個好友離開了。他的勤勉總是激勵我自己更努力用功，雖然我們現在分開了，相信我們會再見面的。現在，還有一百多天就要聯考了，我要準備考試，而且好好地度過美麗的暑假。

---

tinge〔tɪndʒ〕*n.* 少許　　diligence〔'dɪlədʒəns〕*n.* 勤勉

夏日 2.

SUMMER 記事

To Daffodils

Robert Herrick

We have short time to stay, as you,
We have as short a Spring;
As quick a grown to meet decay
As you, or any thing.
We die,
As your hours do, and dry Away
Like to the Summer's rain;
Or as the pearls of morning's dew,
Ne'er to be found again.

致 水 仙

我們駐留的時光匆促，如妳們，
也擁有同樣短暫的青春；
同樣快速的成長之後，面臨衰老，
像妳們，或者任何事物，
我們死去
就如同妳們的凋萎，枯乾一般；
像夏日的驟雨，
或者清晨的露珠，
突然消逝，再也難尋。

—錄自赫里克。
（英國詩人,1591-1674）

Sun., May 1   Cloudy

A barber shop

It's hot and close in early summer. Mother said my hair needed to be cut. That would make me spirited-looking. Went to the neighbouring barber's but, as it was crowded with customers, was kept waiting as long as two hours. It is now a rush period for barbers.

五月一日　星期日　多雲

理髮店

　　初夏的天氣十分悶熱，媽媽說我的頭髮該剪了，那會使我整個人看起來有精神些。於是我去理髮，但是理髮店裏却擠滿了顧客，所以我足足等了兩個小時之久。現在正是理髮業者的旺季。

---

barber〔'bɑrbɚ〕 *n.* 理髮匠
rush〔rʌʃ〕 *n.* 熱潮；搶購

Wed., May 4　　*Fine*

Judo

On my way home from school, went to the tao-kuan with Mr. Wang to see "Judo". Since the war-end, Judo has been getting more and more popular with foreigners. It is said that the Olympics will have Judo in their program in the near future.

五月四日　　星期三　　晴

柔　道

　　從學校回家的路上，我和王先生一起去道館看柔道。自從戰爭結束之後，柔道受到越來越多的外國人的歡迎。聽說奧林匹克運動會在不久的將來會把柔道列入比賽的項目中呢。

——————————————————————————
the Olympics 奧運　　　judo〔'dʒudo〕 *n.* 【日】柔道

Fri., May 6　　*Fine*

A friend as an intern

What I need is sleep. I never thought being an intern would be so gruelling. I had a chat with Martha. We both agreed we wouldn't be doctors if we could do it all over again.

五月六日　　星期五　　晴

實習醫生

　　我所需要的是睡眠。我從來沒想到當駐院的實習醫生會這麼累人。我和瑪莎談過，我們兩個都同意，如果能從頭再來過，我們不會當醫生的。

——————————————————————————
intern〔'ɪntɜn〕 *n.* 【美】住在醫院中之見習醫生
gruelling〔'gruəlɪŋ〕 *adj.* 令人筋疲力竭的　　*have a chat with* 與～閒聊

Sun., *May 8*　*Cloudy*

Mother's Day

Today was Mother's Day. I got up earlier than usual. We worked for Mother all day. Dad and brother painted the terrace. Younger sister cleaned the rooms. Then she went to a flower shop and bought carnations. I cooked chicken curry and rice.

Mom smiled and said to us: " I feel very happy today. " After supper, we sang songs.

五月八日　星期日　雲

母　親　節

今天是母親節。我比平常早起。整天我們都為母親做事。爸爸和哥哥漆屋頂，妹妹打掃房間，然後跑去花店買康乃馨。我則煮咖哩雞和飯。

母親笑著對我們說：「我今天好快樂。」晚餐後，我們大家唱了歌。

---

usual〔ˈjuʒʊəl〕*adj.* 通常的；平素的
terrace〔ˈtɛrɪs, -əs〕*n.* 房屋之平頂
carnation〔kɑrˈneʃən〕*n.* 荷蘭石竹，俗稱康乃馨
curry〔ˈkɝɪ〕*n.* 咖哩粉；咖哩醬所調製的食品

Mon., May 9 Clear

A watermelon

Got a present of a watermelon cooled down in the well from my next-door neighbour. As I was very thirsty, enjoyed it very much. They say the watermelons have turned out very well this summer due to the dry weather.

五月九日　星期一　晴

西　瓜

隔壁鄰居送我一個用井水冰過的西瓜。因為我十分口渴,因此吃得津津有味,據說因為這個夏天氣候乾燥,所以西瓜生長得特別好。

**

watermelon 〔'wɔtə‚mɛlən〕 *n.* 西瓜 ; 西瓜藤
well 〔wɛl〕 *n.* 井 ; 泉

Tues., May 10 Fine

Preventive injection

As typhus is prevalent all the pupils in the neighbouring primary school were given a preventive injection for typhus. At night a cinema show was held on the school ground as a precautionary measure against the plague.

五月十日　星期二　晴

預防注射

因為斑疹傷寒正在流行,鄰近小學的學生都實施了斑疹傷寒的預防注射。晚上學校空地放映一場有關針對遏阻疫病的預防措施的電影。

**

typhus 〔'taɪfəs〕 *n.* 斑疹傷寒症　　pupil 〔'pjupl〕 *n.* 學生
preventive 〔prɪ'vɛntɪv〕 *adj.* 預防的
cinema 〔'sɪnəmə〕 *n.* 電影 (之統稱) ; 電影院
plague 〔pleg〕 *n.* 瘟疫

Mon., *May 16* *Fine*

Changing clothes

Changed into my summer clothes. Many people wear white summer clothes. Ice cream parlour are crowded with people eating ice-cream or drinking cooled cola. The street scene has at last come to look like summer.

Father, who is also in summer clothes, is working in the garden. Gardening is his hobby. He says that by gardening we make friends with nature.

五月十六日　星期一　晴

換　夏　服

我已經換穿夏天的服裝了，許多人都穿白色的夏裝。冰淇淋店擠滿了吃冰淇淋，喝冰可樂的人們。街景終於漸漸有個夏天的樣子了。

爸爸也穿了夏裝，在花園裏工作。園藝是他的嗜好。他說藉著園藝，我們可以和大自然交朋友。

---

parlour〔ˈparlə〕*n.* 店舖
cola〔ˈkolə〕*n.* 可樂（可樂樹子所做的飲料）
gardening〔ˈgardṇɪŋ〕*n.* 園藝
hobby〔ˈhabɪ〕*n.* 嗜好；癖好

Thurs., *May* **19** *Rainy*

A black-edged card

Received a black-edged card this morning. Upon reading it, was quite surprised at the sad news of my friend Steven's death. He was a young man of great promise, planning to study abroad in the United States this summer. Could hardly believe the death of Steven whom I had met last month. Made a telephone call to his mother and found out that he had been killed in a traffic accident three days before. Felt all the more keenly that all is vanity in life.

五月十九日　星期四　雨

悼　念

今早收到一份訃聞，立刻拆開來讀，才對我朋友史蒂芬死亡的壞消息感到萬分驚訝。他是一位極有前途的年輕人，正計劃今年暑假去美國留學。眞不敢相信上個月我才見過史蒂芬，而今他却死了。我打電話問他母親之後才知道他三天前死於車禍。現在才强烈地感悟到人生虛幻無常的道理。

---

black-edged〔'blæk,ɛdʒɪd〕 *adj.* 喪事的；哀悼的
promise〔'pramɪs〕 *n.* 有希望；成功的預兆；有前途
study abroad 出國唸書　　call〔kɔl〕*v.*,*n.* 打電話

Tues., May 24 Fine

My bad habit

I have a bad habit and that is to watch TV while I study my lessons. My parents have always reprimanded me for this fault of mine, but I've never listened. I've never been a very serious student. Somehow I just get by. I guess I'm what you might call your typical average student in school. Today was the same as the other days. When I came home from school, I kicked off my shoes, ate some snacks and took a shower. After I had dinner, I did my usual habit. I took some books out and sat in front of the TV set, turned it on and started studying.

By ten, I was finished with all my assignments. I know this bad habit of mine can't go on forever. I've got to change at one time or another. But when you're into a habit it's so hard to change. I really should be doing better in school. Next year I'll be taking part in the College Entrance Examination. I better have better studying habits or else I won't be able to get into a good college. Maybe tomorrow I'll start trying to just study and not watch TV.

五月二十四日　星期二　晴

我的壞習慣

　　我有一個壞習慣，那就是邊讀書邊看電視。父母總是嚴厲申斥我這個毛病，但我從來不聽。我向來不是個很認眞的學生，不知怎麼我就是剛好勉強及格。我猜我就是那種你們稱之爲典型的學校裏的中等生。今天和往常一樣，回家後，我踢掉鞋子，吃了一些點心然後沖個澡。吃完晚飯後，我照著平常的習慣。我拿出幾本書來，坐在電視機前，打開電視，開始讀書。

　　在十點前，我完成所有作業。我知道我這壞習慣不能一直持續下去，我遲早得改掉。但是，當你養成壞習慣之後，就很難改掉了。我的確應該在學校表現得好一點。明年我就要參加大學聯考了，我最好養成良好的讀書習慣，否則我就不能進入理想的大學。也許明天我要開始試著只讀書，不看電視。

* *

reprimand〔,rɛprə'mænd〕*v.* 嚴斥；申戒
get by 勉強及格

《表現自己的常用語》

♤ I am poor in speaking. 我很不會說話。

♤ I don't like pessimism. 我不喜悲觀。

♤ I have an optimistic view of all things.
　我對每件事都很樂觀。

♤ I very easily laugh at the slightest thing.
　我很容易爲一點小事發笑。

♤ I am active and I like to be the leader in everything.
　我很積極並且我每件事都喜歡當領袖。

Fri., May 27   Cloudy

Crying about my girlfriend

Today is a cloudy day. My mood today is as gloomy as today is. The reason being I still can't get over losing my girlfriend. I just kept on thinking of her the whole day. I found it hard to concentrate in school all day. I couldn't eat or sleep much too. I tried calling her up, but she wouldn't even answer the phone.

I can't forget the other day, when we last met. She said she couldn't see me anymore for her family was moving to America. She said it would be better if I forget about her but how can I forget about her? She has been my inspiration in everything. I felt my heart sink when she told me this. No matter what I said or how I pleaded she just wouldn't listen to me. I said we could still write letters but she still said no. I really miss her so much. I don't know if I'm ever going to get over this. I hope she'll realize how much I love her. My friend said that it'll take time for me to get over it. I hope it comes soon because I can't stand missing her so much.

五月二十七日　星期五　多雲

爲女友而哭泣

今天是陰天，我今天的心情就像天氣一樣陰鬱。理由是我仍然無法克服失去女友的痛苦。我整天都一直在想她。我發現整天在學校要集中精神很困難。我吃不下也睡不著。我設法打電話給她，但是她就是不接電話。

我忘不了前天我們最後一次見面時，她說她再也不能見到我，因爲她們家要搬到美國。她說我最好忘了她，但是我怎麼忘得了她？她是我的一切靈感，她告訴我這件事時，我的心情很沮喪。不管我說什麼或如何懇求她，她就是不聽我說。我說我們仍然可以寫信，但是她還是說不。我實在是很想念她。我不知道我到底能不能克服這個傷痛。我希望她能了解我有多愛她。朋友說我要克服這個傷痛得花一段時間。希望那個時刻快點來到，因爲我受不了如此想念她。

＊＊————————————————————————

get over 恢復；克服

《表示哭泣的常用語》

♤ She wept over her sad fate. 她爲她的悲慘命運而哭泣。

♤ I wept bitter tears. 我痛哭。

♤ I cried myself to sleep. 我哭倦而睡。

♤ He sobbed his heart out. 他哭得死去活來。

♤ The tears rolled down her cheeks. 淚珠從她的面頰流下。

♤ Don't snivel. 別啜泣了。

♤ She blubbers out her sins. 她哭訴她的罪惡。

Sat., May 28   Fine

A birthday present

I got up late this morning. Mother told me to dress up in a hurry or I would be late for school. So I didn't eat any breakfast. Luckily I got to school on time.

Today is my sister's birthday. Last night I asked her what she wanted for a present. She said she wanted a new doll. So, after I got off from school today, I went to a gift shop to buy her a gift. Mother also gave me some money to buy a cake. I bought my sister a chocolate cake. Afterwards, I bought her also some flowers. Girls in Taiwan like flowers very much. I hope she'll have a good time tonight.

五月二十八日　星期六　晴

生日禮物

今天早晨起晚了，媽媽叫我趕快穿好衣服，否則上學要遲到了。因此我沒有吃早餐。還好我準時到校。

今天是妹妹的生日，我昨晚問她想要什麼禮物。她說要一個新的洋娃娃。所以今天放學後，我到禮品店買禮物給她。媽媽還給了我些錢買蛋糕，我替妹妹買了個巧克力蛋糕。然後我還買了些花給她。台灣的女孩子很喜歡花。希望她今天晚上愉快。

Sun., May 29 Fair

Family swimming

It is a holiday today, and the weather is very nice. My family went to the beach in the afternoon. The moment we got there we changed into our swimsuits right away. My father and I could swim very well while my mother and brother could play in the water. One hour later, all of us felt hungry and we bought some hot dogs to eat. After that we played in the sand. We built a sand castle. The castle was complete with spires and a moat. It was really an achievement. On our way home, my brother and I fell asleep. We were very tired but we had a very good time.

五月二十九日　星期日　晴

與家人游泳

今天是假日，而且天氣非常好。我們家下午到海邊，到達那裏後我們立即換上泳裝。爸爸和我游得很好，而媽媽和弟弟却只能在水裏玩。一小時後，我們都覺得餓了，因而買了些熱狗來吃。然後我們在沙灘上玩。我們用沙造了一座城堡。城堡很完整，有塔頂還有濠溝。眞是一項傑作。回家的路上，弟弟和我都睡著了。我們很疲倦，但却玩得很愉快。

** spire〔spaɪr〕*n.* 塔尖　　moat〔mot〕*n.* 濠溝

Mon.*, *May 30*　*Cloudy

My classes in a day

The weather today was unpredictable. In the morning it was warm, then suddenly in the afternoon it
started to get cold. That's why I didn't wear suf-
ficient clothes today. I think I'm catching a cold.
Today I had English, Chinese, Math and Geography for
my classes. In our English class we had to read
Shakespeare. It was already difficult to understand present-day English and more so old English.
But our teacher said Shakespeare was one of the
greatest writers in the world so we had to read his
works. Tonight I think I'm going to have a headache
just trying to read Shakespeare.

五月三十日　　星期一　　陰

一日的課程

今天的天氣變幻莫測。早晨天氣還很溫暖，下午就突然開
始變冷。因此我今天沒有穿足夠的衣服。我想我感冒了。今天
有英文、國文、數學和地理課。英文課上我們要唸莎士比亞，
要懂現代的英文已經夠難了，而古英文就更難了。但是老師說
莎士比亞是世界最偉大的作家之一，所以我們必須讀他的作品。
我想今晚我要爲設法唸莎士比亞而頭痛了。

** unpredictable 〔͵ʌnprɪˈdɪktəbḷ〕 *adj*. 不可預測的

Tues., May 31　Fine

A horrible scene

I am sick today. My mother brought me to the hospital for a check-up. The doctor said I just had the flu and that I just needed some rest. He wrote the prescription and then he said not to forget to drink the medicine three times a day. Mother scolded me for getting sick. She said I had better take better care of myself. I could only nod my head. On our way out, we happened to pass by the emergency room. I heard a child screaming inside, so I took a look. There was blood all over the head of the kid and the doctor was stitching his head. He was screaming loudly and was clutching to his mother. The mother was also crying and was trying to calm the child. Then, my mother turned my head, so I wouldn't see the scene. It was too late. I felt like vomitting after seeing that.

On the way home, in the taxi, I couldn't help remembering the scene. I wondered what happened to the child. Maybe he fell down from a high place and got hurt. Then it occurred to me how precious a mother's love is for her child. I think I shouldn't let my mother worry about me. That's why I think I should take better care of myself from now on.

五月三十一日　星期二　晴

可 怕 的 一 幕

　　今天我病了。我媽帶我去醫院檢查。醫生說我只是得了流行性
感冒,只需要多休息。他開了藥方,然後說別忘了一天吃三次藥。媽
媽怪我為什麼生病。她說我最好小心照顧自己。我唯有點頭說好。
要出去的路上,我們正好經過急診室。我聽到裏面有個小孩在叫,
於是看了一下。那小孩滿頭的血,大夫正在幫他縫頭上的傷口。他
一直大叫並且緊抱著他媽媽。他媽媽也在哭,同時試著讓他安靜下
來。這時,媽媽把我的頭轉了一個方向,好讓我沒法再看到那一幕。
可是已經太遲了。看到之後,我只覺得想吐。

　　在回家的計程車上,我沒法不去回憶那一幕情景。不知道那孩
子是發生了什麼事。也許他是從一個高處摔下來受的傷吧。這使我
察覺到一個母親對她的子女的愛有多偉大。我想,我不該讓我媽為
我擔心的。這也是為什麼我覺得從現在開始應該自己好好照顧自己
的原因。

---

check-up〔ˈtʃɛkˌʌp〕 *n.* 健康檢查　　flu〔flu〕 *n.* 【俗】流行性感冒
prescription〔prɪˈskrɪpʃən〕 *n.* 藥方　　scold〔skold〕 *v.* 叱責;責罵
emergency〔ɪˈmɝdʒənsɪ〕 *n.* 緊急處理;急診　　stitch〔stɪtʃ〕 *v.* 縫
clutch〔klʌtʃ〕 *v.* 緊抱住;抓住　　vomit〔ˈvɑmɪt〕 *v.* 嘔吐

Fri., June 3   Cloudy

A wrist -watch

My wrist-watch being too slow, have had it mended. This time, on the other hand, it seems rather to gain. It is over six years since I bought it, so it is natural that it doesn't work so well.

六月三日　星期五　雲

手　錶

我的手錶走得太慢，曾經把它送去修理。這一次，相反的，它好像又走得太快了。我買這隻錶已有六年多了，所以難怪它會出毛病。

*** **

wrist〔rɪst〕*n.* 腕；腕關節　　mend〔mɛnd〕*v.* 修理
gain〔gen〕*v.* 增進；進步

Mon., Jun. 6   Fine

A woman's voice

At dead of night, was awakened by the noisy ring of the telephone bell, so put the receiver at once to my ear. "Hello! Is this Mr. Chang?" said the charming voice of a young woman. I hung up coldly, saying it was a wrong call.

六月六日　星期一　晴

一個女人的聲音

在靜寂的午夜，我被一陣電話鈴聲吵醒，於是立刻把話筒拿近耳邊。「喂！是張先生嗎？」是一個年輕女子的迷人聲音。我告訴她打錯了，並冷冷地掛斷電話。

✱✱————————————————————————

awaken〔ə'wekən〕n. 喚醒　　applied〔ə'plaɪd〕v. 使用的過去式
receiver〔rɪ'sivɚ〕n. 電話的話筒
hello〔hə'lo〕interj. 喂（特指打電話時用）

Wed., Jun. 8　Fine

Pimple

I'm afraid to look in the mirror. I think I got a new pimple on my nose. What am I going to do? How can I go on living? Maybe I can just stay home all day and not go out until the pimples are all gone.

六月八日　星期三　晴

青　春　痘

我怕照鏡子。我想我的鼻子上長了個新的青春痘。我該怎麼辦？我怎麼能這樣活下去？也許我可以整天待在家裡不出去，直到所有的青春痘都消去為止。

✱✱————————————————————————

pimple〔'pɪmpl̩〕n. 青春痘

Sat., Jun. 11 *Cloudy and a little rainy*

Language is power

Today is the last day before graduation. Everyone was very happy today. There were no lessons to be learned today. The whole day, our teachers just let us do anything that we wanted. Our last period for this day was English. He told us about his various experiences as an English teacher and why he decided to become an English teacher. He said English was right now becoming more important everyday. That is why we had to learn English well. The reason behind this was, he said, that we will come into contact with more and more things which need English. He said although going to college is one of the major reasons why we are learning English there is much more to it than just that. He said although he knows that we find learning English very hard he knows that we will find it useful one day.

Finally, he congratulated all of us and wished us all good luck. We also thanked him for being our teacher. After a few minutes the bell rang and classes were over. We were all very happy today and all of us exchanged addresses and telephone numbers and reminded one another to keep in touch. For me, I was both happy and sad. I was happy because finally I won't have to face

examinations everyday anymore and I could finally say
I made it. I was sad because I was leaving behind my
friends and teachers whom I shared so much with for
the past few years.

六月十一日　星期六　多雲有雨

語言即力量

今天是畢業前的最後一天。每個人都很快樂。今天不必上課。整天，我們老師只是讓我們隨心所欲地做我們想做的事。今天最後一堂課是英文。他告訴我們他做為一個英文老師所遭遇的各種經驗，和他為什麼決定當一位英文老師。他說英文現在在每天的生活中都愈來愈重要。這就是我們為什麼必須把英文學好的原因。他說，除此之外，我們會接觸到越來越多的事物需要用英文。他說雖然上大學是我們現在學英文的主因之一，但還有比那更多的因素。他說雖然他知道我們發覺英文很困難，但他也知道我們將來會發現它很有用的。

最後，他恭禧我們大家，希望我們都很幸運。我們也謝謝他擔任我們的老師。幾分鐘之後，鈴聲響了，課程結束了。今天我們都很快樂，大家交換了住址、電話號碼，互相提醒要保持連絡。至於我，我是又悲又喜。喜的是我終於不必再每天應付考試了，我終於能說我辦到了。悲的是要離開過去這些年來和我分享這麼多東西的朋友和老師們。

---

graduation〔͵grædʒuˊeʃən〕*n.* 畢業

Sun., Jun. 12 *Fine*

Graduation party

It was a nice graduation party. Everybody was sad that high school is over. I'm not, I hated high school, I'm glad it's over. I'm gonna miss some of the people though, I hope we'll keep in touch.

六月十二日　星期日　晴

畢業晚會

這是個很棒的畢業晚會。每個人都感傷於高中生活的結束。我則不然。我恨高中生活。我很高興它結束了。但是我會懷念某些人的，希望我們會保持聯絡。

**

graduation〔‚grædʒʊ'eʃən〕 *n.* 畢業　　***keep in touch*** 保持聯絡

Tues., Jun. 14 *Rainy*

A cat's love

At midnight was awakened by the quarrel of cats and could sleep no more. Got through my home lesson in English composition. It is now the time when the cats will fall in love with each other.

六月十四日　星期二　雨

野貓之愛

三更半夜被貓兒的吵架聲吵醒，無法入睡，我就起來把英文作文的作業做完。現在是貓兒們互相愛慕的時刻了。

**

quarrel〔'kwɔrəl〕 *n.* 爭吵　　composition〔‚kɑmpə'zɪʃən〕 *n.* 作文
fall in love with 戀愛

Wed., Jun. 15　Fine later cloudy

Doctor Wang's advice

I had a bad headache today. Although I attended school as usual I had a hard time concentrating on my work. In fact I couldn't understand what the teacher was saying. I even dozed off in class. Doctor Wang examined me this afternoon, he advised me to have enough sleep. He said: "As long as you take a day off and stay in bed you'll recover in no time at all. " I suppose Dr. Wang must have forgotten that I'm a 12th grader, I have to prepare for the JCEE.. I thought to myself, he must be kidding.

六月十五日　星期三　晴時多雲

王醫生的勸告

今天我頭痛得厲害。雖然我照常上學，但我却無法集中精神。事實上，我聽不懂老師在說些什麼，我甚至在課堂上打瞌睡。王醫生下午來檢查，勸我多休息，他說：「只要你休息一天，躺在牀上，你馬上就會痊癒。」我認爲王醫生一定忘了我是高三學生，必須準備大學聯考，我在內心想，他一定是在開玩笑！

---

doze off 打瞌睡　　recover 〔ˌrɪˈkʌvɚ〕 *v.* 復元；痊癒
kid 〔kɪd〕 *v.* 開玩笑；嘲弄
JCEE = Joint College Entrance Examination

Thurs., Jun. 16　　*Rainy later fine*

Before the bell rang

　　We had a test in mathematics today. It was a very long and hard test. I must have used up ten pages of scratch paper trying to figure out the solutions to the problems I was faced with. I almost didn't finish my test. In the last five minutes of our period I hastily answered the remaining portions of the test. I was able to submit my paper before the bell rang. I don't know if I answered correctly or not the last few items, but I guess I'll find out soon enough tomorrow when my teacher hands out the results of our tests.

六月十六日　　星期四　　雨後轉晴

鈴響之前

　　今天數學課有考試。真是漫長而且困難的考試。我用掉了十張便條紙才能試著計算出我所面對的問題。我幾乎沒有寫完。最後五分鐘我匆忙地回答了剩下的部分。在鈴響之前我能及時交出答案紙。不知道我最後幾題回答得對或錯,但我猜明天老師發考卷的時候我很快就能知道。

**

scratch paper 便條紙;計算紙
portion〔'porʃən〕 *n.* 部分
submit〔səb'mɪt〕 *v.* 提出;呈交
item〔'aɪtəm〕 *n.* 項目

Sat., *Jun. 18*　*Rainy*

The rainy season

I don't believe the weather reports any more. This morning it looked like rain. A newscaster on T.V. said, "Today will be cloudy in the morning, but clear later." So I did not take my umbrella to school. However, the rain began to fall, and I got all wet on my way home.

When I got angry, Grandma said, "The rainy season is a gift from Heaven." I do not like the rainy season, though.

六月十八日　星期六　雨

梅雨時節

我再也不相信氣象報告了。今天早晨天氣看起來像要下雨，電視新聞說，「今天早晨多雲，但晚一點會放晴。」因此，我沒帶傘到學校。然而卻下起雨來，於是我在回家路上全身都被淋溼了。

我生氣時，祖母說：「雨季是上天給的禮物。」僅管如此，我還是不喜歡雨季。

---

weather report 氣象報告
newscaster〔'njuz,kæstɚ〕*n.* 新聞廣播員

Sun., Jun. 19　*Fine*

The month of marriage

This is the month of marriage. Don't know what relation exists between the season and marriage, but the number of marriages is much greater from early winter into spring than in other seasons. The god of marriage will be surely busy.

Today Mother and I went to my cousin Lily's wedding. She looked happy and very beautiful in her white dress. We had something to give her. It was a pretty painting.

Lily was a June bride. Mother said, " In Europe, June is the month of pretty flowers. Almost all young girls want to marry during this month, because a June bride will be the happiest."

In Taiwan, weddings are not popular in June, for it's the rainy season.

I hope Lily will have a very happy marriage.

六月十九日　星期日　晴

紅色炸彈

本月是結婚的月份。不曉得季節與結婚有什麼關係，但是從初多到春天，結婚的人數比其它季節多了很多。婚姻之神一定很忙。

今天我和媽媽去參加莉莉表姐的婚禮。她穿著白色禮服看起來幸福而美麗。我們有東西送她，是一幅美麗的畫。

莉莉是六月新娘，媽媽說，「在歐洲，六月是漂亮的花季。因為六月新娘將是最幸福的新娘，因此幾乎所有的少女都想在這個月中結婚。」

在台灣，婚禮在六月就沒那麼盛行了，因為六月是雨季。

我希望莉莉有幸福的婚姻。

**

marriage〔'mærɪdʒ〕 *n.* 婚姻；結婚　　exist〔ɪg'zɪst〕 *v.* 存在；有
cousin〔'kʌzn̩〕 *n.* 堂兄弟；堂姊妹；表兄弟；表姊妹
wedding〔'wɛdɪŋ〕 *n.* 結婚；婚禮　　bride〔braɪd〕 *n.* 新娘

《表示祝賀的常用語》

♤ I offer my heartiest congratulations. 謹致衷心的祝賀。

♠ Tons and tons of congratulations. 萬分恭禧。

♠ I'm so happy for you. 我很替你高興。

♤ You are a lucky one indeed. 你真幸運。

♤ Mere words can hardly express our joy.
　我們的喜悅，真是筆墨難以形容。

♠ You deserve all the credit in the world.
　你值得世上所有的榮耀。

Thurs., Jun. 23   *Rainy later fine*

The evening glow

In the evening it cleared up, and there was
a red sky. We shall have fine weather tomorrow
after a long spell of rain. Took out my shoes to
polish them and found that they were covered
with mildew.

After supper helped Father clear the weeds
out of the garden. Thanks to that, shall have a
sound sleep tonight. Watched amateur singers
competing on television until 10 o'clock and went
to bed.

六月二十三日　星期四　雨後晴

夕　照

傍晚天氣放晴，天空呈現一片紅色。在一段長時間的雨
季之後，我們明天就要有好天氣了。把鞋子拿出來擦，發現
上面覆有霉。

晚餐後幫爸爸清除花園裏的雜草。就因爲這樣，我們今
晚將會熟睡。看電視的業餘歌唱比賽到十點，然後上牀睡覺。

***

spell〔spɛl〕 *n.* 一段時期；一陣子　　***thanks to*** 由於；因
mildew〔'mɪl,dju〕 *n.* 霉　　amateur〔'æmə,tʃʊr〕 *adj.* 業餘的
compete〔kəm'pit〕 *v.* 比賽；競爭

Fri., Jun. 24 Clear

The final countdown

June 28, a week before the Joint College Entrance
Examination. The night tonight is clear. It is exactly
a week before the event that I have been waiting for
a year now. I'm feeling nervous and restless. Mother
told me today to take care of myself. She said it
was important that I should be in the right state
of mind on that fateful day. I'm already having
trouble sleeping. I get all these nightmares at night
that I stay awake at night. I can't even look at my
textbooks anymore. Well, tonight is the start of
the final countdown. I'll just give my best shot at
this examination. A week from now everything will
be all over.

六月二十四日　　星期五　　晴

最後倒數的時刻

六月二十八，大學聯考前一個禮拜。今晚的夜色很純淨。
現在距我一年來一直等待的事正好一個禮拜。我覺得緊張不安，
媽媽今天叫我好好照顧自己，她說在那個重要的一天保持頭腦清
醒非常重要。我無法入睡，整晚我都在做惡夢，所以我整夜醒著。
我甚至連課本都看不下。嗯，今晚是倒數計時的開始。考試時
我只要全力以赴。一個禮拜後，一切都會結束。

＊＊ countdown〔'kaʊnt,daʊn〕*n.* 倒數計時

Sun., Jun. 26   *Rainy*

Looking for a job

The job interview went terribly today. The guy said he'll call me tomorrow with his decision. I'm sure it'll be a rejection. I was so nervous and I didn't know half the questions he was asking me. I've got to be better prepared next time.

六月二十六日   星期日   雨

求　職

今天的面談眞糟。那個人說他明天會打電話告訴我他的決定。我確信他會拒絕我。我太緊張了，而且他問我的問題我有一半都不知道。我最好還是爲下一次的面談求職做準備吧。

**──────────────

interview〔'ɪntə,vju〕 *n.* 會見；接見

Wed., Jun. 29   *Rainy*

Table manners

In the hour of English, Mr. Brown, our teacher, told us about table manners which made our mouth water. Someone said "Practice rather than theory" and we had a hearty laugh over it.

六月二十九日   星期三   雨

用餐禮節

英文課時，布朗先生，我們的老師，告訴我們關於餐桌禮儀的事，使得我們垂涎三尺。有人說「實踐重於理論」而使我們都縱情大笑起來。

**──────────────

make one's mouth water 使人垂涎   practice〔'præktɪs〕 *n.* 實行
theory〔'θɪərɪ〕 *n.* 理論   hearty〔'hɑrtɪ〕 *adj.* 縱情的；豪爽的

Thurs., Jun. 30　Fine

The night before the College
Entrance Examination

It's twelve o'clock at night and the clock has just struck twelve. Here I am banging my head on the wall trying to get everything I've learned for the past three years into my head. Everyone is asleep and I am alone here in my room studying. Oh, how I wish all of these would end. I've gone through my lessons over and over again. What else is there to memorize? I've drunk two cups of coffee already, yet I am getting drowsy.

I'll remember this day forever whether I should pass the exam or not. God forbids it though that I shouldn't. I've worked so much these past years for this goal of mine. My parents are counting on me a lot to get into a university. I just can't fail them nor myself. My parents have worked so hard for us children. If I should pass the examination tomorrow, this is the best way I could repay them. Well, I'd better get back to the books, no use wasting my energies here.

六月三十日　星期四　晴

大學聯考的前一天晚上

已經是夜裏十二點了，鐘剛敲了十二下。我把頭去撞牆，試著記起過去三年的苦讀，所學到的一切。每個人都入睡了，我自己一個人在房間裏唸書。天啊，眞希望這一切快點結束。我一遍又一遍地複習。還有什麼要背的嗎？我已經喝了兩杯咖啡了，却漸漸昏昏欲睡。

不管我會不會考上，我都將永遠記得今天。但上帝也會要我考上的。過去這些年來我這麼努力，只爲了我這個目標。我的父母對於我上大學抱著很大的希望，我就是不能讓他們，或者自己失望。父母爲了我們孩子，工作十分辛苦。如果我上榜了，就是對他們最好的回報。呃，我最好把心思放回到書本上，別白白把時間浪費在這兒了。

＊＊

bang〔bæŋ〕*v.* 重擊　　memorize〔'mɛmə,raɪz〕*v.* 記於心
drowsy〔'draʊzɪ〕*adj.* 昏昏欲睡的　　goal〔gol〕*n.* 目標
repay〔rɪ'pe〕*v.* 報答

《有關聯考的常用語》

♤ I am busy preparing for the entrance examination.
　我忙著準備聯考。

♤ I got 80 marks in physics. 我物理得八十分。

♤ I studied hard simply to enter this university.
　我努力讀書只爲了進這所大學。

♤ The results of the examination were published yesterday.
　考試的成績已於昨天公布。

Fri., Jul. 1 Fine

An earthquake

At night, when I was doing my homework in mathematics, an earthquake suddenly occurred and all the members of my family rushed out of the door. If, as in the case of the weather forecast, we can foretell the coming of the shock, it would be splendid.

七月一日　星期五　晴

地　震

晚上我在做數學作業的時候，突然發生地震；家裏所有人都衝出門外。如果，我們可以像預測天氣一樣預知地震的來臨，那一定很棒。

＊＊

earthquake〔'ɝθ͵kwek〕*n.* 地震　　***rush out*** 衝出

weather forecast 氣象預報　　foretell〔for'tɛl, fɔr-〕*v.* 預測

splendid〔'splɛndɪd〕*adj.* 絕妙的；極佳的　　shock〔ʃɑk〕*n.* 地震

Sat., Jul. 2 Fine

Michael with thin moustache

I bumped into Michael today. He still has that stupid-looking thin moustache. He won't believe me that he looks better without it. I keep telling him to grow a thick moustache if he's determined to have one.

七月二日　星期六　晴

微髭的麥克

　　我意外碰到了麥克。他仍然留著那看來很可笑的稀疏鬍子。他不會再相信我說他不留鬍子會好看些的話了。是我一直告訴他如果想留鬍子就留個濃密點的。

＊＊────────────────────

　　moustache〔′mʌstæʃ, mə′stæʃ〕 *n.* 髭（＝mustache）

Sun., Jul. 3　*Cloudy*

Ping-pong

The examination being over, feel greatly relieved. Was unable to go out owing to the cursed rain, so played ping-pong with sisters. To my regret, was beaten three times in succession.

七月三日　星期日　多雲

打乒乓球

　　考完試後，覺得很輕鬆。因爲可惡的雨，無法出去，所以與姊姊打乒乓球。可恨的是，我連續敗了三次。

＊＊────────────────────

　　cursed〔kɜst〕 *adj.* 可憎的；可厭的
　　ping-pong〔′pɪŋ,pɑŋ〕 *n.* 乒乓；桌球　　***in succession*** 連續

Mon., Jul. 4　*Rainy*

Mother's helper

Mother's still sick. The doctor says she just needs rest so I've been doing all the housework. Today I baked her a cake which she said is the best cake she has ever eaten. I hope she gets well soon.

七月四日　星期一　雨

母親有疾

　　母親仍在生病。醫生說她需要多休息，所以我幫忙做所有的家事。今天我爲她烤了一個蛋糕，她說這是她所吃過味道最好的蛋糕了。我希望她能早日康復。

**

　　housework〔'haus‚wɜk〕 *n.* 家事；家務
　　bake〔bek〕 *v.* 烘；焙

Tues., Jul. 5　Cloudy later fine

The Entrance Examination

　　The season for the entrance examination has at last come. How we wish there were not such an annoyance as an entrance examination and the time would come when we can enter any school we choose!

七月五日　星期二　多雲時晴

聯考大事

　　聯考的季節終於來了。我們多麼希望能夠沒有聯考這種煩惱，很快地我們可以進入我們所選擇的任何學校。

**

　　entrance examination 入學考試（指聯考）
　　annoyance〔ə'nɔɪəns〕 *n.* 煩惱

《 有關考試的常用語 》

♤ I looked over my examination papers. 我檢查試卷。

♤ I write my paper with a pencil (in ink).

　　我用鉛筆（鋼筆）作答。

Thurs., Jul. 7 *Rainy*

To cherish what I have

On the way to school today, I met an old friend of mine. He is now a waiter in a restaurant. He said his father had died and since there was no one to take care of the family he had to quit school, and go out and make a living. I couldn't find the right words to tell him how sorry I was to hear that. There was really nothing much I could do to help. When we said goodbye to each other I felt ashamed of what I had.

I am glad that I still have my family. I don't have to worry about financial problems and I can continue going to school. I should make the best of what I have because nothing will last forever. What I have today might not be mine anymore tomorrow. So I should live each day to its fullest. In whatever I do, I should do my best. I should also love those people around me more. It's so sad to know how cruel fate can be. No matter how good you are there are no guarantees in life that everything will go your way, are there?

七月七日　星期四　雨

珍惜我所擁有的

今天在上學途中，遇見我一個老朋友。他現在在一家餐廳當服務生。他說他爸死了。沒有人照料家裏，因此他必須休學，出去討生活。我找不到適當的話來告訴他，聽到這件事我有多難過，我眞的無力去多做一點什麼，當我們分手後，我深爲自己所擁有的感到羞愧。

我很高興我還有家人，所以不用擔心經濟問題，而且我也能繼續上學。我應該好好利用我現在所擁有的，因爲沒有任何事是永恆的。今天我有的也許明天就沒有了。因此我應該每一天都活得很充實。不管做什麼，都該盡全力去做。我也應該多愛我周圍的人，了解命運可以有多悲慘眞是敎人傷心。不管你多好，生活却不能保證你諸事順遂美好，不是嗎？

**

living〔'lɪvɪŋ〕 *n.* 生計；生活
make the best (***most***) ***of*** 善爲利用
guarantee〔,gærən'ti〕 *n.* 擔保；保證

《表示悲傷的常用語》

◊ I am sad for his death. 我爲他的死而悲傷。

◊ I learned the sad news by telegram.
　我由電報中得悉這項噩耗。

◊ He felt sorrow over the lost money.
　他爲了丢錢而悲苦。

◊ Her grief when he died was unbearable.
　當他死時，她的哀傷是不勝負擔的。

Fri., Jul. 8   *Cloudy later fine*

Some bad news

Today, something terrible happened. I lost my club's money. I was at a loss explaining my predicament to our club president today. Well, this is what happened. I got up this morning, there was nothing unusual about the day. The money of our club was entrusted to me because I was the club treasurer. The amount was quite substantial, something like two thousand NT dollars. It was the money collected from the membership fees of our club. We usually use this money to finance some projects that the club decides to do. For example, last year we took a field trip to the beach. This year, we were planning to go to the mountains. Anyway, I think I was just too careless about how I handled the money. Before I left home, I remember that I placed the money inside my pocket. When I got to the school and dipped inside my pocket, I found that the money was gone. I looked everywhere, but the money was nowhere to be found.

When I told our club president, I was really flustered. My face was just all red. He said that I had to come up with the money one way or another, or else I would be in hot water. Maybe I'll just have to take it from my savings account or scrimp from my allowance. I told him to first keep this as a secret between us and not tell our club members.

> He said yes, provided that I come up with the money by next month. Well, that's the bad news for the day.

七月八日　星期五　多雲時晴

壞　消　息

　　今天，發生了可怕的事情。我把社團的錢搞丟了。今天我不知道如何向社長說明我的處境。事情是這樣的：今天早晨起床並沒有什麼不對勁的。因為我是社裏的總務，所以社團的錢交給我保管。數量相當龐大，大約有新台幣二千元，是由社團會員費收得的款項。我們經常用這筆錢來資助社團決定的某些計劃。例如，去年我們舉辦到海邊郊遊。今年，我們計劃到山上。總之，我想我處理這筆錢的方式太不小心了。出門前，我記得我把錢放入口袋。到了學校我把手伸入口袋時，發現錢不見了。我到處找，但就是找不到錢。

　　在告訴社長時，我很緊張，我的臉都紅了。他說我必須設法拿出這筆錢，否則我將會惹來麻煩。也許我得從存款中取出這筆錢，或者從零用錢中節省。我叫他先將這件事當作我們之間的秘密，不要告訴社團團員。他說好，假如我能在下個月前拿出這筆錢來就行。哎！這就是今天的壞消息。

**――

at a loss 迷惑　　predicament〔prɪˊdɪkəmənt〕*n.* 處境；困境
entrust〔ɪnˊtrʌst〕*v.* 交託　　treasurer〔ˊtrɛʒərə〕*n.* 財務
substantial〔səbˊstænʃəl〕*adj.* 大的　　dip〔dɪp〕伸入
fluster〔ˊflʌstə〕*v.* 使緊張；慌亂
come up with 取出　　*be in hot water* 陷入困境；惹來麻煩
scrimp〔skrɪmp〕*v.* 節省；節縮

Sun., Jul. 10   *Fine*

Graduation excursion

I had a nice time today. We went to the beach and had a picnic. We exchanged plans about our future. Everybody laughed when I told them I wanted to be a farmer. I don't care, I think farmers have a good life.

七月十日　　星期日　晴

畢業旅行

我今天過得很愉快。我們到海邊去野餐。我們互換對未來的計劃。當我告訴他們我要做農夫時，每個人都笑了。我不在乎，我認爲農夫的生活很好。

＊＊─────────────────────────

excursion〔ɪk'skɜ˞ʒən, -ʃən〕*n.* 遠足　　exchange〔ɪks'tʃendʒ〕*v.* 交換

Mon., Jul. 11   *Fine*

Aspirin

This morning had a bad headache, so absented myself from school and cooled my head with an ice-bag. As the temperature was 39 degrees, took a dose of aspirin to sweat out the cold and went to bed.

七月十一日　　星期一　晴

阿斯匹靈

今天早上我的頭很痛，因此我向學校請假，並且用冰袋來冰我的頭。當溫度燒到三十九度時，我吃了一片阿斯匹靈以幫助發汗並上床睡覺。

＊＊─────────────────────────

headache〔'hɛd͵ek〕*n.* 頭痛　　***absent oneself from*** 請假；缺席
temperature〔'tɛmprətʃɚ〕*n.* 溫度　　***sweat out a cold*** 發汗治傷風

Wed., Jul. 13 Fine

A mosquito net

As many mosquitoes appeared tonight, burned a mosquito coil to keep them away and hung up a mosquito net. A mosquito net is an uncomfortable thing, but it is quite pleasant to see its folds swayed softly by the cool evening breeze.

Lying in the mosquito net, recollected an English essay on a mosquito, which I had read long before. The hero of the essay chases a mosquito in the train but, failing to catch it, acquits it of its crime.

七月十三日　星期三　晴

蚊　帳

由於今晚出現許多蚊子，所以點了蚊香來驅逐牠們，並且掛上蚊帳。蚊帳是一種令人不舒適的東西，但是，見其摺層在傍晚涼爽的微風中輕輕搖曳却很愉快。

躺在蚊帳中，我想起很久以前讀過一篇有關蚊子的英文散文，文中主角在火車上追逐一隻蚊子，但却無法捉到這隻蚊子，因此宣告蚊子無罪。

---

mosquito coil 蚊香　　*mosquito net* 蚊帳
fold〔fold〕*n.* 摺層；摺縫　　recollect〔ˌrıkəˈlɛkt〕*v.* 記起
hero〔ˈhıro〕*n.* 男主角；英雄　　acquit〔əˈkwıt〕*v.* 宣告無罪

Thurs., Jul. 14   Fine later cloudy

My first contribution

The newspaper actually printed my essay! Millions of people will see it. This is my first step in becoming a world famous author.

Mom and Dad are proud of me. I've told all my friends and teachers about it. Just think, 10 years from now when I go to the library I'll still be able to find my essay. I'm immortal!

七月十四日　星期四　晴時多雲

初次投稿

報紙真的刊登我的文章了！數百萬人將看到這篇文章。這是我邁向世界聞名作家的第一步。

爸媽以我為榮。我已經把這件事告訴所有的朋友及老師。想想看，十年後我到圖書館時還能夠找到我的文章。我永遠都不會被遺忘了。

---

contribution〔͵kɑntrə'bjuʃən〕 *n.* 投稿
print〔prɪnt〕 *v.* 刊出
immortal〔ɪ'mɔrtḷ〕 *adj.* 不朽的

Sun., Jul. 17　Fine

Staying at home on Sunday

There's not much to write today. I just spent a boring day at home. My parents were out in Taichung, and I was left all alone here in the house today.

I tried calling some friends up, but they were all busy or gone. In the morning, with nothing else better to do, I decided to take up some of my books for review. Before noon though, I had already finished the books and done some of my homework, too. I had lunch outside and came back home at about one.

In the afternoon, I could only watch some MTV. This spiced up my day a bit. Then I was back to my books. At around three, I decided to call Frank to see if he wanted to see some movies. Well, still no luck. All I could do was just continue studying my lessons.

My parents came back home at around seven. I had my dinner. After watching some more TV, I then decided to call it a day. I took my bath, fixed my bed, dried my hair, brushed my teeth, got my things ready for the next day and that was it. What a very, very boring day.

七月十七日　星期日　晴

星期天待在家裏

　　今天沒什麼可寫的，我只是在家裏渡過了無聊的一天。爸媽外出到台中，今天我一個人被留在家裏。

　　我打了電話給一些朋友，但是他們不是很忙就是外出了。早上由於沒什麼好做的，我決定複習一些功課，然而在中午前，我已經看完書並且做了一些家庭作業。我在外面吃午餐，大約一點時回家。

　　下午，我只能看一些MTV，爲我這一天添加了一點情趣。然後我又回到書本上。大約三點時，我決定打電話給法蘭克看他要不要看電影。哎，運氣還是不好。我只好繼續讀書。

　　爸媽在七點左右回來。吃了晚餐，看了一些電視節目之後，我決定結束一天的工作。我洗澡，舖牀，弄乾頭髮，刷牙，把隔天的東西準備好，就是這樣。眞是窮極無聊的一天！

＊＊────────────────────

　　take up 開始；從事於…；著手　　spice〔spaɪs〕*v*. 添增情趣
　　call it a day 結束一日之工作

《表示無聊的常用語》

♤ I am bored to death. 我無聊死了。

♤ He's a perfect bore. 對他實在是厭膩透了。

♤ It irked me to wait. 我討厭等候。

♤ It is an irksome task. 眞是令人厭煩的工作。

♤ He wearied me with idle talk.

　　他無聊的話使我厭煩。

Mon., Jul. 25 *Rainy*

A bad cold

I'm down with a cold today. I feel terrible.
Being sick is no fun at all. Here I am bundled up
in three or four blankets in my bed. Today is also
a school day. How I wish I could time my colds to
be the weekends, so I wouldn't have to miss any lessons
in school. Not that I like my lessons that much
but I just worry about having to catch up on so
many missed lessons. Besides, I also miss my
friends.

You know, it's only when you are sick that you
think about the good things in life. My doctor
says I can't eat any sweets or fried foods. I'm
right now craving for some ice cream, fried chick-
en and a Big Mac. Once I get well, I promise
to treat myself to all the things I want.
And there is no one who is going to stop me. How
miserable life can get. Mother is right now in the
kitchen preparing some Chinese medicine for me to
drink. Oh, how I hate the bitter taste of it. Yuck!
I just can't wait till I get well.

七月二十五日　星期一　雨

重　感　冒

今天我患了感冒，覺得眞糟。生病一點都不好玩，我躺在床上裹著三四條毛毯，今天也是上學的日子。多希望我能選擇在周末感冒，這樣就不必缺課了。並非我這麼喜歡上課，而是我擔心要補許多堂課。另外，我也蠻想念我的朋友們。

知道嗎？只有當你生病的時候，才會想念生活中美好的事物。我的醫生要我別吃甜的和油炸的食物。但現在我就渴望著能有一些冰淇淋、炸雞、麥香堡之類的食物。一旦我好了，我會讓自己得到一切想要的東西。没有人能阻止得了。生活眞悲慘。媽媽正在厨房裏弄一些中藥給我喝。我多討厭那種苦味啊！我眞是等不及要趕快痊癒了。

---

bundle up 裹暖；包紮　　blanket 〔ˈblæŋkɪt〕 *n.* 毛毯
craving 〔ˈkrevɪŋ〕 *adj.* 渴望的　　miserable 〔ˈmɪzərəbl̩〕 *adj.* 悲慘的
bitter 〔ˈbɪtə〕 *adj.* 苦的

《有關生病的常用語》

♠ I have a fever. 我發燒。

♢ I feel a chill. 我感到一陣寒冷。

♠ He takes my temperature. 他量我的體溫。

♠ The pulse beats fast. 脈搏跳得很快。

♠ I feel ill. 我覺得不舒服。

♢ I have a cold. 我感冒了。

♢ I have a sore throat. 我喉嚨痛。

Thurs., Jul. 28　Rainy

My kingdom

This morning, I cleaned my aquarium. First I
took out all the fish and all the plants and the decorations. Then I slowly pumped out the water. Later, I
scooped out the sand and started to wash them with
water. When this was all done I started to scrub off
the slime that was clinging to the glass off the
aquarium. With my aquarium being sparkling clean
I started placing back the sand, the water, the plants
and decorations and the fish. When all was done, I
turned on the lights of the aquarium and looked at it
with satisfaction. To me my aquarium is like my own
little kingdom where I am king.

七月二十八日　星期四　雨

我的王國

今早我清洗了我的水族箱。首先我取出所有的魚、植物和裝飾
物。然後慢慢地抽出水來。後來，我舀出沙子開始用水清洗。這些
都做完之後，我開始擦洗掉黏在水族箱玻璃上的黏液。等到水族箱
變得乾淨發亮後，我開始放回沙子、水、植物、裝飾物和魚。做完之後，
我把水族箱的燈打開，心滿意足地注視著它。對我來說，我的水族
箱像是我自己的一個小王國，而我是裏面的國王。

---

aquarium〔əˈkwɛrɪəm〕 *n.* 水族箱　　pump〔pʌmp〕 *v.* 抽水
scoop〔skup〕 *v.* 舀取　　　scrub〔skrʌb〕 *v.* 擦洗
slime〔slaɪm〕 *n.* 黏泥

Youth is not a time of life ; it is
a state of mind ; it is not a matter
of ripe rosy cheeks, red lips and
supple knees ; it is a temper of the
will, a quality of the imagination, a
vigor of the emotions ; it is the
freshness of the deep springs of life.

— *MacArthur*

青春並非人生的一個時期，而是一種
心智的狀態；不是成熟玫瑰色的臉頰、
紅潤的嘴唇與靈巧的姿態，而是一種
意志的氣質、想像的才能、情感的活
力；是生命深泉中湧出的清新。

深秋小札 3.

AUTUMN

Ode to Autumn

John Keats

Season of mists and mellow fruitfulness,

　Close bosom- friend of the maturing sun;

Conspiring with him how to load and bless

　With fruit the vines that round the thatch-eaves run;

To bend with apples the mossed cottage- trees,

　And fill all fruit with ripeness to the core;

　　To swell the gourd, and plump the hazel shells

　With a sweet kernel; to set budding more,

And still more, later flowers for the bees,

Until they think warm days will never cease,

　　For Summer has o'er-brimmed their clammy cells.

秋之頌詩

霧與果實豐饒的季節
是圓熟太陽親密的知己，
他們共謀如何去裝載與祈福
那些攀繞草屋簷的葡萄藤果
以及壓在青苔叢生的茅屋頂上的蘋果。
使所有的果實都熟透，
葫蘆膨脹，榛穀豐滿，
擁有甜美的核心，愈來愈會發芽，
然後開花，讓蜜蜂擷採
直到它們認為溫暖的日子永不歇止，
因為盛夏已經溢滿它們冷濕的窩巢。

—錄自濟慈。
（英國詩人，1795-1821）

MONTH 8 August

Wed., Aug. 10 Rainy

A bad road

The roads in the suburbs are very bad, owing to the con-
tinual rainy days. We find puddles on the road here and there
and it is troublesome for us to pick our way. Foreigners may
well speak ill of our bad roads.

八月十日　星期三　雨

路況惡劣

由於持續的雨天，郊區的道路路況相當不好。在路上到處可以
發現泥坑，而且我們很難選擇道路走。外國人可有足夠的理由毀謗
我們的破馬路了。

＊＊

suburbs 〔'sʌbɜ·bz〕 *n.pl.* 城郊之住宅區
owing to 由於　　puddle 〔'pʌdl〕 *n.* 泥坑
may well 有好的理由　　*speak ill of* 說壞話

Thurs., Aug. 11 Clear

Full of rural life

Called on Mr. Yeh who moved to Taichung. Though his house
stands a little far away from the station, it commands a fine
view. The place is full of rural life with a farm and rice fields
in the neighbourhood.

八月十一日　星期四　晴

野趣漫漫

去拜訪葉先生，他搬到台中去了。雖然他的房子離車站有點距離，但是它俯臨著一片美好的景致。這地方充滿了鄉村生活的情趣，附近有一個農場和一片稻田。

**

call on 拜訪　　command〔kəˈmænd〕*v.* 臨視；俯視
rural〔ˈrʊrəl〕*adj.* 鄉村的

Sat., Aug. 13　Fine

My parents' advice

Before my parents left me today, they told me not to leave the house. I didn't plan to go out but after a while I started getting bored. My friend called me and asked if I wanted to take a ride with him on his motorbike. Without giving much thought to it, I said O.K. While we were on the highway an accident happened. Because my friend was riding too fast he lost control of his motorbike and we were both thrown off of his motorbike. I was bruised and hurt a little bit. How I regret disobeying my parents. Because of it I got into an accident.

八月十三日　星期六　晴

父母的忠言

今天爸媽在出去之前，告訴我待在家裡別亂跑。我沒打算要出去，但過了一會之後，我開始覺得無聊。朋友打電話來問我要不要騎他的摩托車，跟他去兜兜風。不及細想，我就答應了。當我們在公路上時，車禍發生了。因為我的朋友騎得太快，以致於摩托車失去控制，我們兩個都摔了出去。我瘀傷，而且受了一點輕傷。我好後悔沒聽父母的話。因為這樣，我才發生意外的。

**

bruise〔bruz〕*v.* 瘀傷　　disobey〔ˌdɪsəˈbe〕*v.* 不服從

Sun., Aug. 14   Fine

Going fishing

Uncle Lin took us out fishing today, me and my brother Richard. For some reason I don't know, my brother kept on catching fish while I just sat there waiting for some fish to bite my line. After he had caught five fish, I finally caught a small fish. I was a little embarrassed. But later on, I finally had a fish biting my line. I thought it was going to be a big fish for I had a hard time bringing it up. Finally when the fish surfaced it turned out to be an old shoe. Uncle Lin and Richard could only laugh at me. My whole face turned red. When I went home I had one fish with me and Richard had nine fish to his credit.

八月十四日　星期日　晴

釣　魚

　　林叔叔今天帶我們去釣魚，我和哥哥理查兩人。不知道什麼原因，當我還坐在那兒等魚上鈎的時候，哥哥不斷地釣到魚。在他釣了五條魚之後，我終於釣到了一隻小魚。我有些不好意思。但後來，終於有魚咬住我的魚線了。我認為它會是條大魚，因為我很難將它拉上來。最後當魚露出表面時，才發覺它是**一隻舊鞋子**。**林叔叔**和理查只能嘲笑我了。我整個臉都漲紅了。當我回家的時候，我只有一隻魚，而理查卻光榮地有著九條魚。

---

to one's credit 能成為某人的光榮

Mon., Aug. 15　Cloudy

Air pollution

The weather bureau issued a warning today that the air quality in Taiwan was very bad. When I went to school this morning, the air was not as clear as it used to be. It was dirty. Although I had taken a bath that morning I felt really dirty with all the dust and fumes covering me. Because it was hot today, the air pollution made us all even more uncomfortable. When I went home, I had to take another shower because I felt dirty and sticky. I wish there was something I could do about this air pollution. I think that there are just too many vehicles on the streets of Taipei. In the meantime I can only grin and bear it.

八月十五日　星期六　多雲

空氣污染

今天氣象局發出警告說台灣的空氣品質十分惡劣。當我今早上學時，空氣不像以前那樣清新了。它是髒的。雖然我早上洗過澡，我仍覺得覆在我身上的灰塵和臭氣實在骯髒。因為今天很熱，空氣污染使得我們大家都更不舒服。當我回家時，我必須再淋一次浴，因為我覺得又髒又黏。我希望我能為空氣污染做些什麼。我認為只是台北市的街道上有太多的車子了，同時我也只能逆來順受罷了。

---

issue〔ˈɪʃʊ〕*v.* 發出
fume〔fjum〕*n.*（有害的、氣味難聞而強烈的）烟、氣體等
sticky〔ˈstɪkɪ〕*adj.* 黏的；濕熱的　　vehicle〔ˈvihɪkl̩〕*n.* 車輛

Tues., Aug. 16　　*Fine later cloudy*

A black cat

Today a black cat crossed my path. When a black cat crosses your path you are supposed to experience some bad luck. I was worried about that today although I know this is but a superstition. That thought kept nagging me the whole day. Luckily nothing untoward happened to me today. In fact I can say today was lucky for me for I got a ninety-five on my Chinese test. But I couldn't leave off my guard until the day finally came to an end this evening. Whether true or not I still don't want to have a black cat crossing my path ever.

八月十六日　　星期二　　晴時多雲

一隻黑貓

今天一隻黑色的貓擋住了我的路。當一隻黑貓擋住你的去路時，你便將遭遇噩運。因此今天我一直擔心著，雖然我知道這不過是迷信而已。這種想法搞得我整天痛苦不安。幸好今天我沒發生什麼不幸的事。事實上，我可以說今天對我而言是幸運的，因為我的國文考了九十五分。然而我直到今晚一天終於結束時，才敢鬆懈下來。不管是真是假，今後我仍然不願意有黑貓擋住我的路。

---

superstition〔͵supə'stɪʃən〕*n.* 迷信

nag〔næg〕*v.* 煩擾；造成痛苦、不適等

untoward〔ʌn'tord〕*adj.* 不順利的；不幸的　　　*leave off* 戒除

Wed., Aug. 17　　*Fine*

An unforgettable experience

Last week, I went to see the concert of my favorite singer, Paul Young. Because I didn't have enough money I could only buy a seat which was the farthest from the stage. The night of the concert, I wore my best. I hoped to get the autograph of my favorite pop idol. When Paul Young started singing " Everytime You Go Away , " everyone in the audience went crazy. Some even started crying. Because we were too far off from the stage, we couldn't see Paul Young very clearly. I wasn't able to get the autograph of Paul Young, either. But still, I was glad that he came to Taiwan to give a concert. This will be my most unforgettable experience.

八月十七日　　星期三　　晴

難忘的經驗

上個星期，我去聽我最喜愛的歌星保羅楊的演唱會。因為我錢不夠，所以只能買到離舞台最遠的位置。演唱會那天晚上，我穿了最好的衣服。我希望能拿到我最喜愛的流行音樂偶像的親筆簽名。當保羅楊開始唱「每次當你離去時」這首歌時，每一位觀衆都要瘋狂了。有些人甚至哭了起來。因為我們離舞台太遠了，以致於無法很清楚地看到保羅楊本人。我也沒法得到他的親筆簽名。但我仍然很高興他來台舉行演唱會。這將是我最難忘的經驗。

---

autograph〔'ɔtə,græf〕*n.* 親筆簽名　　pop〔pɑp〕*n.* 通俗音樂

Thurs., *Aug*. *18* *Rainy*

Under one umbrella

On my way home from school, was very much embarrassed by a sudden shower, for I had no umbrella with me. Asked for the loan of an umbrella at Linda's. Sandy and I came home together under one umbrella.

八月十八日　　星期四　　雨

傘　下

在從學校回家的路上，由於突來的陣雨，使得我非常窘，因為我沒有帶傘。在琳達家借了一把傘，珊蒂和我兩個人，撐一把傘一起回家。

**———————————————————

embarrass〔ɪmˈbærəs〕*v.* 使困窘　　loan〔lon〕*n.* 借

Fri., *Aug*. *19*　*Rainy later fine*

Giving directions

An American asked me directions on the street today. I was so excited I almost had a heart attack. I can't believe that of all the people on the street that this American would pick me to ask for directions. I was so nervous that my mouth became dry and couldn't utter a word. I tried drawing a map for him but my hand was shaking too much. I became so embarrassed that, to his surprise, I ran away.

At least I can still brag to my friends that a real live American tried to talk with me.

八月十九日　星期五　雨後晴

指　路

今天一個美國人在街上向我問路。我太興奮了，幾乎要心臟病發作。我不敢相信在街上那麼多人中，這個美國人會挑我來問路。我太緊張了，所以嘴巴變得乾燥，說不出話來。我想畫一張地圖給他，但是手抖得太厲害了。我很尷尬，因此出乎他意料之外地，我跑掉了。

但至少我還能向朋友吹噓，說一個活生生的美國人想跟我談話。

**

heart attack 心臟病發作　　utter〔ˈʌtə〕v. 發出；說出
brag〔bræg〕v. 吹噓

Sat., *Aug*. *20* *Fine*

The essay on Milton

Read the essay on Milton which I borrowed from Professor Li, but could hardly go even a line without consulting the dictionary. At this rate it will take more than a month to read it through.

八月二十日　星期六　晴

論密爾頓的隨筆

閱讀向李教授借來的有關密爾頓的論文，但是如果沒有查字典，連一行都幾乎進行不下去。照這種情況下去，想把它讀完要花不只一個月的時間。

**

consult〔kənˈsʌlt〕v. 參考；查閱
at this rate 照此情形下去

Mon., Aug. 22   Fine

Autumn

Autumn is my favorite season. In autumn everything starts to come alive after the long, hot lazy summer. The temperature cools and there's a feel in the air that now it's time to work. I especially like the roasted yams and peanuts that start appearing on vendors' carts. I like to buy them on the way home from school.

八月二十二日　星期一　晴

秋　天

秋天是我最喜歡的季節。秋天裏，萬物經過漫長、炎熱慵懶的夏天，開始變得有生氣。氣溫涼爽，而且空氣中讓您感覺現在是工作的最好時機。我特別喜歡開始出現在小販車上的烤蕃薯和花生，我喜歡在放學回家的路上買這兩種食物。

**————————————————

yam〔jæm〕*n.* 蕃薯　　vendor〔'vɛndɚ〕*n.* 小販
cart〔kɑrt〕*n.* 手拉車

Tues., Aug. 23 *Windy*

A typhoon

Could not sleep well last night. Following the warning of a typhoon yesterday evening, a severe typhoon passed through the Hengchun district around midnight. The velocity of the wind was over 30 meters per second, and, the lights having failed, it was pitch-dark. Fortunately, however, it is said that no serious damage was done except for some floods which visited mountain districts. But it must have been a horrible experience for those living in the Hengchun area.

八月二日　星期二　有風

颱風來了

昨晚無法安睡。緊接著昨天傍晚的颱風警報後，一個強烈颱風約在半夜時通過恒春地區。風速超過每秒 30 公尺,而且,由於停電，四週漆黑。然而，慶幸的是，據報除了山區的一些洪水以外，沒有造成重大的損害。但是對於那些住在恒春地區的人，一定是個可怕的經驗。

**——————————————————————

severe〔səˊvɪr〕*adj.* 劇烈的；嚴重的　　district〔ˊdɪstrɪkt〕*n.* 區域；地方
velocity〔vəˊlɑsətɪ〕*n.* 速度；速率
pitch-dark〔ˊpɪtʃˊdɑrk〕*adj.* 極黑的；漆黑的

Wed., Aug. 24　Fine

Swimming pool

It was so hot in the morning that I was wet with perspiration. Went to Youth Park with my brothers to avoid the heat and to swim. The swimming pool was crowded with people, but the water was comparatively clear and cool. We stayed there until the sunset before we came back home. It is still very hot in the evening. Everybody complains of the heat.

八月二十四日　星期三　晴

游泳池畔

早晨天氣很熱，我汗流浹背。和弟弟到青年公園避暑游泳。游泳池裏擠滿了人，但池水仍清澈涼爽。我們留在那裏直到太陽下山才回家。傍晚仍然很熱，每個人都抱怨熱天。

**——————————————————————

perspiration〔ˌpɝspəˊreʃən〕*n.* 汗；流汗
comparatively〔kəmˊpærətɪvlɪ〕*adv.* 相當地
complain〔kəmˊplen〕*v.* 抱怨　　heat〔hit〕*n.* 熱天

Fri., Aug. 26   Fine

After Classes

After classes today, because I was feeling a little bit tired I decided to eat some noodles at a sidewalk stand that sold noodles. I also ordered some soy-bean curd or tofu. A lot of other students were eating there too. So it took me quite some time before I was served. I usually do not go straight home after class. I usually first go for a walk in order to soothe my nerves after an exam-filled day. Or I buy something to eat. Usually I go to a bookstore in order to read the latest magazines or just look at the books. On other days, I also go to a record store to buy cassette tapes of my favorite singer or rock group. On some days some of my friends go with me but there are days when I just go alone.

After I finished my noodles I started to walk towards the bus stop. I saw some of my classmates on the way and we said hello to each other. Today, I didn't have to wait for the bus for a long time. After five bus stops I was walking on my way home. A brick almost hit me while I was passing a construction site, luckily it missed me by just a foot. After that I started to walk faster as it gave me a scare. There was no one there when I got home. After relaxing for a few minutes I started to take out my books from my school bag. Studying until twelve my mother came into my room and told me to go to sleep already. I said I would in a few more minutes. After I finish writing here then I'll go to bed. Tomorrow's another day.

八月二十六日　星期五　晴

放學後

今天放學後，由於覺得有點累，所以決定在路邊賣麵的攤子吃一些麵，我還叫了點豆腐。一大堆其他學生也在那裏吃，所以我等了一段時間，才有人來招呼我。放學後我通常沒有直接回家，我通常會先散個步，好在排滿考試的一天後鬆弛一下精神。或者我會買一些東西吃。我通常是到書店去看最近的雜誌或者看看書。其他時候，我還會去唱片行買喜歡的歌手或搖滾樂團的錄音帶，有時候一些朋友會和我一起去，但是有時我自己一個人去。

吃完麵後，我走向公車站，在路上我看到一些同學，我們互相問候。今天，我不用等公車等很久。過了五站後，我已走在回家的路上。經過一個建築工地時，一塊磚頭差點打到我，幸好只差了一步。然後我開始走快一點，因爲它嚇到我了。到家時沒有人在家，休息幾分鐘後，我開始把書從書包裏拿出來。一直讀到十二點，媽媽進來房裏告訴我該睡了。我說再過幾分鐘會去睡。寫完這裏我就要上牀睡覺了，明天又是另外一天。

**────────────────

sidewalk stand 人行道旁的路邊攤　　*soy-bean curd* 豆腐
cassette tape 卡式錄音帶

≪有關吃的常用語≫

♤ Doesn't it smell delicious！好香的味道！

♤ He ate a big dinner（supper）. 他吃了一頓大餐（晚餐）。

♤ We eat our soup first. 我們先喝湯。

♡ Those apples are really very tasty.
　　那些蘋果眞是美味可口。

Sat., Aug. 27   *Sunny*

The end of the world

"Why does the sun go on shining?" This is
how I feel today. This morning in class, we had
a test in math. I got a "0". My god! I felt
like it was the end of the world. I wanted to cry
at that time. I just wanted to leave school. I
just hate to go to math class. I have not had a
good report card in math ever since I started
learning that subject. I don't know why my answers
don't match the ones given to me by my teacher.
I am always wrong.

Once I made a resolution to study it well, but
I still kept on failing. The more I failed the
more disappointed I became. Though I know math
is a useful subject, I don't know why everyone
has to study it in high school. I'm sure if there
were no math courses in high school, we students
would be much happier.

Oh! I can just say that today is my darkest
day.

八月二十七日　星期六　晴

世界末日

「爲什麼太陽還繼續照耀？」這是我今天的感受。今早在班上，有個數學測驗，我考了個零鴨蛋，天啊！我覺得像世界末日。當時眞想哭。只想離開學校，我只是討厭去上數學課。自從開始學數學之後，我的成績單上就没出現過好成績。我不懂爲什麼我的答案，就是跟老師給我的解答不一樣，我老是出錯。

我曾經下決心要好好唸數學，但我仍然一直嘗到失敗的滋味。我愈失敗就愈失望。雖然我知道這門課很有用，但我不明白爲什麼每個高中生都要唸數學。我敢確定假如高中没有數學課，我們學生會快樂多了。

噢！我只能說今天是我最黑暗的日子。

---

resolution〔‚rɛzəˈljuʃən〕*n.* 決心　　***report card*** 學生的成績報告單
disappointed〔‚dɪsəˈpɔɪntɪd〕*adj.* 失望的；沮喪的

《表示失敗的常用語》

◊ His failure disappointed me. 他的失敗使我很失望。

◊ Success came after many failures.
經過多次失敗，成功終於到來。

◊ We tried but failed. 我們嘗試過，可是失敗了。

◊ After some consideration, the teacher failed him.
經過一番考慮之後，老師給他不及格。

◊ Failing election, he will return to his law practice.
如果競選失敗，他將重操律師舊業。

Sun., Aug. 28 Fine

Barbecue

Today we went out on a picnic. Dad had told us about it last night. We woke up earlier than usual today. Mom also prepared some food to bring with us. She made some barbecue for the picnic. It didn't take long for us to reach the place we were going to. Once there, we leaped out of the car to take a look at the natural surroundings. Dad started setting up the barbecue grill while Mom took out the food. I felt like we were part of the scene for the "Sound of Music", when we all sang while Dad played the guitar. By eleven, Dad was already starting the barbecue. The barbecue was very good.

There was a small stream nearby. We could wade our feet in the stream and feel the cold water. There were also some fish in the stream. They were very small. We tried to catch some but because the stream was very rocky we couldn't catch any. We also saw mushrooms. Dad said that we shouldn't touch them because they may be poisonous. I collected some beautiful rocks that I saw beside the stream. These rocks will be my remembrance of this day. At four o'clock we started to head for home. We cleaned the place where we had picnicked and put the garbage where it belonged. It was a very tiring day. We all slept in the car while Dad drove. This was how my day was today.

八月二十八日　星期日　晴

烤　肉

　　今天我們出去野餐。爸爸昨晚就告訴我們了。我們今天比平常早起。媽媽也準備了一些食物讓我們帶去。她做了野餐吃的烤肉。沒花多少時間我們就到達目的地了。一到那兒，我們就跳下車，欣賞大自然的周遭景物。當媽媽拿出食物時，爸爸也正好開始架好烤肉架。當爸爸彈著吉他，而我們都唱著歌時，我覺得我們就好像「真善美」電影中的一幕。十一點時，爸爸已經開始烤肉了。烤肉十分美味。

　　附近有一條小溪。我們可以把腳放進溪裏，感受水的冷列。溪裏也有些魚。魚都很小。我們想試著抓他們，但因為溪流裏面有很多岩石，所以我們一條也沒抓到。我們也看到了蘑菇。爸爸說我們不該摸因為它們可能是有毒的。我收集了些我在溪邊看到的美麗岩石。這些石頭將是我今天的回憶。四點時，我們啟程回家。我們把剛剛野餐的地方弄乾淨，把垃圾放到丟垃圾的地方。這真是令人疲倦的一天。當爸爸開車時，我們都在車上睡著了。我今天就是這麼過的。

----

barbecue〔ˈbɑrbɪˌkju〕n., v. 加作料炙烤的肉片或魚

grill〔grɪl〕n. 烤架　　mushroom〔ˈmʌʃrum〕n. 蕈；菌；蘑菇

poisonous〔ˈpɔɪznəs〕adj. 有毒的　　garbage〔ˈgɑrbɪdʒ〕n. 垃圾

《有關野餐的常用語》

♤ We went on a picnic. 我們去郊外野餐。

♤ They went on a picnic to the lake. 他們去湖邊郊遊。

♤ She took part in a picnic in the woods.

　　她參加了森林中的野餐。

Mon., Aug. 29　Fine

Our family trip

It was an exciting day today. Today was the first time for me to go abroad with my family. Last night, I went to bed late because I had to pack my things. It was a good thing that mother first looked at my things. She took out a lot of things that she said I would not be needing on the trip. She even laughed at some of the things I was bringing. I mean how was I supposed to know what to bring on a trip. This was my first trip abroad mind you. She must've taken out half of the things I was carrying in my suitcase. The trip will last for only a week. Next time I go abroad I'll remember to just travel light.

八月二十九日　星期一　晴

全家旅行

今天是個令人興奮的日子。今天我第一次將要和家人到國外旅行。我昨晚因為必須整理行李，所以晚睡了。好在媽媽先檢查了我的東西，她拿出很多東西，說我在旅行中用不到，她甚至嘲笑我要帶的某些東西。我是說我怎麼知道旅行該帶哪些東西。你知道這是我第一次出國旅行。她一定拿出了我一半的行李。這趟旅行只有一個禮拜，下次出國我要記得只帶一點行李。

***

travel light 帶很少的行李旅行

Thurs., Sept. 1　Fine

Being late

I must have slept too little last night because when the alarm clock went off this morning I didn't hear it and I slept until it was nearly seven o'clock. When I got up I was surprised to see that the sun was already high up. Then I felt my blood racing to my heart. I quickly jumped out of my bed and shouted "Oh, my god, I'm going to be late." Hurriedly, I put on my uniform, shoveled all my books into my bag, and in a flash was out of the house. I ran as fast as I could to the bus stop, but there was no bus. My mind was deciding whether to go by taxi or wait for the bus for another five minutes. I decided to wait. Fortunately before the five minutes were up a bus came. There were a lot of people on the bus. I was the last person who was able to squeeze into the bus. I was praying while on the bus that the bus driver would go faster, but it went on chugging along its route.

At last, the bus stopped at my school. I got off and rushed into my classroom. Before I could catch my breath, the teacher took one look at me and then told me to stand in the corner. Everyone looked at me too. All my effort was useless. I think that I've learned my lesson today. Next time I'll just take my time if I'm late.

九月一日　星期四　晴

遲　到

　　昨晚我一定睡太少了，因爲今早鬧鐘響的時候，我竟然沒有聽見，而一直睡到將近七點才起牀。起來時才發覺太陽已經高照。我一時心跳加速，急忙跳下牀，大喊著：「天啊！我要遲到了。」匆忙穿好制服，把全部的書都塞進書包，閃電般跑出來，儘快地跑到公車站，卻不見公車的踪影。我不知道該搭計程車呢，還是再等五分鐘。最後我決定等。很幸運地，還沒到五分鐘，公車就來了，滿載著乘客。我是能夠擠進去的最後一個人。在車上我一直祈禱司機開快一點，但是車子仍然沿著路線軋軋地走。

　　最後，車子停在我的學校了，我下車，趕快跑進教室。還沒來得及喘氣，老師就瞪著我，罰我站在角落。每個人也都看著我，所有的努力都白費了，我想今天我是得到教訓了，下回如果我遲到，我就乾脆慢慢地走。

---

go off 響　　uniform 〔'junə‚fɔrm〕 *n.* 制服
shovel 〔'ʃʌvl〕 *v.* 大量地投送　　squeeze 〔skwiz〕 *v.* 擠
chug〔tʃʌg〕*v.* 軋軋而行　　route〔raut‚rut〕*n.* 道路
take one's time 慢慢做

Fri., Sept. 2 Fine

Moonlight

In the evening went up the Tamsui river in a boat with several friends. The moon-light was as bright as day and the night was calm; only the splash of our oars broke the silence. It was indeed very splendid.

九月二日　星期五　晴

賞　月

傍晚和幾位朋友乘船沿淡水河直上。月光和白日一樣明亮,夜極寧靜；只有船槳濺起的陣陣水聲劃破寂靜。實在是太美妙了！

＊＊————————————————————————

splash〔splæʃ〕*n.* 激濺聲　　oar〔or〕*n.* 櫓；槳
splendid〔'splɛndɪd〕*adj.* 輝煌的；絕妙的

Sat., Sept. 3 Fine

An omelet

Mother being out, sister cooked an omelet for our supper. Tried to eat it, but failed to enjoy it as it was too salty to eat. Even my empty stomach flatly refused to take it in.

九月三日　星期六　晴

蛋　捲

因為媽媽出去了,姊姊煎蛋捲給我們當晚餐。我試著去吃它,但因為它太鹹了而無法吃下。即使是我餓扁的空胃也拒絕它的進入。

＊＊————————————————————————

omelet〔'ɑmlɪt,'ɑmǝlɪt〕*n.* 煎蛋捲　　*fail to* 無法
salty〔'sɔltɪ〕*adj.* 有鹹味的；含鹽的
flatly〔'flætlɪ〕*adv.* 斷然；絕對地

Mon., Sept. 5　Fine

English

Damn it！I hate English！Why can't the rest of the world learn Chinese？But if I want to go to America and get my Ph.D., I must get a high score on the TOEFL, so I must keep study-ing. Why does life have to be so hard？

九月五日　星期一　晴

英　文

該死！我恨英文！爲什麼世界上其他的人不學中文呢？但是如果我要去美國拿博士學位，我必須在托福考試獲得高分；因此，我得繼續唸英文。爲何人生要這麼痛苦呢？

✱✱ ─────────────────────

damn〔dæm〕*v.* 咒罵　　Ph.D. 博士學位
TOEFL 托福（＝Test of English as a Foreign Language）

Wed., Sept. 7　Fine

A burglar

In the afternoon, took a walk to Youth Park with Mr. Lin, stepping on the fallen leaves. The park in the late autumn presented a dreary sight. But maple trees alone were still showing off their gorgeous red leaves.

In the evening, a cold wind began to blow hard. According to the evening newscast, a burglar broke into a jewelry shop this afternoon and, threatening the people with a pistol, he made away with 100,000 NT dollars in cash. As such a burglar is dangerous, we must take great care.

九月七日　星期三　晴

搶劫犯

午後和林先生到青年公園散步，我們踩在落葉上。晚秋的公園呈現出一片淒涼的景色。只有楓樹還在展現他們燦爛的紅葉。

傍晚，涼風開始狂吹。據傍晚的新聞報導，今天下午有一個竊賊闖入一家珠寶店，並用槍威脅民衆；他拿走了現金十萬元。因爲這種竊賊很危險，所以我們必須極度小心。

**

burglar〔'bɜˋglɚ〕 *n.* 夜賊；竊賊　　dreary〔'drɪrɪ〕 *adj.* 淒涼的
gorgeous〔'gɔrdʒəs〕 *adj.* 華麗的；燦爛的
jewelry〔'dʒuəlrɪ〕 *n.* 珠寶　　***take care*** 小心；謹愼

Thurs., Sept. 8　Fine later rainy

A nickname

The opening ceremony was held in the lecture hall at 8 a.m. A new teacher of Chinese classics was introduced to us. He was a short and fat man so we all nicknamed him " An easy-going daddy . "

九月八日　星期四　晴後雨

綽　號

開學典禮早上八點在禮堂舉行。介紹一位新的中國古典文學老師給我們。他是一個又矮又胖的男人，因此我們給他取個綽號叫「好好先生。」

**

ceremony〔'sɛrə,monɪ〕 *n.* 典禮　　***the classics*** 古典文學
nickname〔'nɪk,nem〕 *v.* 加綽號
easy-going〔'izɪ'goɪŋ〕 *adj.* 隨遇而安的；做事懶散的

***Fri.*, *Sept.* 9** *Fine*

A souvenir

My aunt who returned from Ta-Hsi has given us as a souvenir a box of dried bean curd. They were sweet-scented and very nice. They say that the Ta-Hsi dried bean curd is the most famous one in Taiwan.

九月九日　星期五　晴

紀念品

從大溪回來的嬸嬸給了我們一盒土產的豆腐乾。甜甜的，非常好吃。他們說大溪豆乾是台灣最有名的豆乾。

**

　　souvenir〔'suvə,nɪr〕*n.* 土產　　***dried bean curd*** 豆乾
　　scented〔'sɛntɪd〕*adj.* 加有香料的

***Sun.*, *Sept.* 11** *Fine*

A decayed tooth

Having suffered from a toothache since last night, went to the dentist in the neighbourhood to have my teeth examined. He told me that one of my grinders was badly decayed, so had it filled with cement.

九月十一日　星期日　晴

蛀　牙

因從昨晚開始就一直為牙痛所苦，到附近的牙科醫生那裏去檢查牙齒，他告訴我，我有一個臼齒蛀得很嚴重，因此他用黏固粉將它補起來。

**

　　decay〔dɪ'ke〕*v.* 腐蝕；蛀爛　　dentist〔'dɛntɪst〕*n.* 牙科醫生
　　grinder〔'graɪndə〕*n.* 臼齒　　cement〔sə'mɛnt〕*n.* 黏固粉；水泥

Tues., *Sept*. **13** *Rainy later fine*

A goldfish

In the evening went to a pet shop with sisters and bought ten goldfish. When the weather is hot, it is pleasant to see the goldfish swimming peaceably in the glass-globe, making it their world.

九月十三日　星期二　雨後晴

金　魚

傍晚和姊姊到一家寵物店，買了十條金魚。天氣熱時，看金魚安詳地在玻璃缸中游來游去，把魚缸當成牠們的世界，眞是令人愉快。

＊＊───────────────────

peaceably〔'pisəblɪ〕*adv.*安詳地　　　glass-globe〔'glæs,glob〕*n.*玻璃缸

Wed., *Sept*. **14**　*Fine*

A goldfish basin

Awoke from my nap and found that a homeless cat had stolen in and eaten up all the goldfish, breaking the basin to pieces. Indignation penetrated to my heart's core.

九月十四日　星期三　晴

碎了的魚缸

小睡醒來，發現一隻無家可歸的貓潛入吃了所有的金魚，並把魚缸打成粉碎。憤怒穿透了我的心胸。

＊＊───────────────────

nap〔næp〕*n.*小睡　　　steal〔stil〕*v.*潛行
indignation〔,ɪndɪg'neʃən〕*n.*憤怒
penetrate〔'pɛnə,tret〕*v.*穿入；透過　core〔kor〕*n.*中心或最重要的部分

Sun., Sept. 18 Fine

An orphanage

I visited an orphanage today. The visit was part of our school's program to make us more aware of the less fortunate. We rode on the school bus on the way to the orphanage. Everyone was happy along the way. After about thirty minutes the orphanage came into view. It was a white washed building with a very wide yard in front of it. The yard was carpeted with grass and was planted with trees and flowering plants. There was also a playground with see-saws, swings and slides. Our teacher introduced us to the director of the orphanage and then he led us inside the orphanage. The children inside the orphanage were already waiting for us in a big hall when we got there. At first we didn't know what to do. Then, our teacher told us to distribute the gifts we had brought with us for them. Most of the gifts were either clothes, toys or candies.

After that we started playing with them. We also played some games together. Then, we ate lunch together. In the afternoon the children performed some songs and dances for us. After each number everyone clapped heartily. When it was time to go I couldn't help feeling a bit sad. To me, these children became like my younger brothers and sisters. I wanted to bring them home with me

so that they could have a family but I couldn't. I felt
really sorry for them because they didn't have parents
like we do.　I think when I graduate from school, I
would like to help these unfortunate children more.

九月十八日　星期日　晴

孤　兒　院

今天我去拜訪孤兒院，這是學校的活動之一，好讓我們更了解較不幸的人。我們搭校車到孤兒院去，一路上，每個人都很高興。大約三十分鐘孤兒院就在眼前了。那是一幢粉刷成白色的建築，前面有一個非常寬大的院子。院子上舖滿綠草並種著樹木及花朵。還有一個遊樂場，上面有蹺蹺板、盪鞦韆和溜滑梯。老師介紹我們給孤兒院院長，然後帶我們進去孤兒院。我們到那裏時，裏面的孩子都已經在一個大廳等我們了。起初我們不知道要做什麼，後來老師叫我們把帶來的禮物分送給他們，大部分的禮物是衣服、玩具或是糖果。

然後，我們開始和他們玩，我們還一起玩了一些遊戲。接著我們一塊兒吃午餐。下午，小孩們表演一些唱遊給我們看，每一首曲子表演完後我們都熱烈鼓掌。離去時我禁不住感到一絲悲傷。對我而言，這些小孩變得像我的小弟弟小妹妹，我想帶他們一起回家好讓他們有個家庭，但是我却沒辦法。我真為他們感到難過，因為他們不像我們一樣擁有父母。我想等我畢業後，我願意多幫助這些不幸的孩子們。

---

orphanage〔'ɔrfənɪdʒ〕*n.* 孤兒院
playground〔'ple͵graʊnd〕*n.* 運動場；遊樂場
see-saw〔'si͵sɔ〕*n.* 蹺蹺板

Mon., Sept. 26   Cloudy

Not my day

Today was simply not my day. Everything just went wrong. How unlucky could I get today. In the morning, I soiled my dress while I was eating my breakfast. The hotdog I was eating slipped from my plate and landed on my dress. It was really clumsy of me, but that was because I was in a real hurry to go to school. I had to go and get changed, of course, so I was late for school.

In school, in my history class, we had an examination. I did badly in that examination because I couldn't remember what I studied last night. To make matters worse, I had a silly fight with my best friend over a certain topic. I said some stupid words too. Now, I have to say sorry to Carol. Oh, I just couldn't wait to get back home today. Once home, I relaxed myself by taking a hot shower. Now, I'm glad the day is over. Whew! What a day.

九月二十六日　星期一　多雲

倒楣的一天

今天實在是倒楣的一天。每件事都不對勁。我今天眞是倒楣透了。早晨吃早餐時，我把衣服弄髒了。我的熱狗從盤中滑出來掉到衣服上。我實在是很笨，但這是因爲我急著要趕到學校去。我不得不去換衣服，不用說，我上學遲到了。

在學校，歷史課時舉行考試，我考得很糟，因爲我記不得昨晚唸的東西。更糟的是，我因某一個話題而與我最好的朋友發生無謂的爭吵，我還說了一些蠢話。現在，我得向卡洛說抱歉。我整天都迫不及待地想回家，一回到家，我就沖個熱水澡讓自己輕鬆一下。現在，我眞高興這一天結束了。哎呀！這是什麼日子嘛！

**

slip〔slɪp〕 *v*. 滑；溜　　　soil〔sɔɪl〕 *v*. 弄髒
clumsy〔'klʌmzɪ〕 *adj*. 笨拙的
to make matters worse 使事情更爲糟糕

《有關爭鬥的常用語》

♤ Doctors fight disease. 醫生們與疾病作戰。

♤ That was a combat between two persons.
　　兩人相鬥。

♤ The prisoner struggled fiercely with the police before
　　being arrested.
　　這犯人在被捕之前同警察作猛烈的抗爭。

♤ Quarrels are often followed by fights.
　　爭吵之後往往是打鬥。

Tues., Sept. 27   *Cloudy*

My nightmare

Yesterday I had a headache, so I was absent from school. I fell asleep and I didn't wake up until eight at night. In that sleep I dreamt a horrible dream. I found myself riding a bike down a dark woody trail. As I approached a small bridge, suddenly I spotted a lady sobbing. Out of curiosity I approached the lady. The lady had her back towards me. When I greeted her, she continued weeping without turning to face me. When I touched her on the shoulders and asked her what was troubling her, it was then that I was shocked out of my wits. I saw a face that had no eyes, eyebrows or even a mouth. I shrieked in terror and crawled my way out of the place. At that moment I woke up and didn't bother to fall asleep again.

九月二十七日　星期二　陰

惡夢

我昨天頭痛，因此沒到學校去。我睡著了，一直到晚上八點才起來。睡覺時我做了一個可怕的夢。我發現自己騎著脚踏車沿一條黑暗的林中小路而下。接近一座小橋時，我突然看到一位小姐在啜泣。由於好奇我走向這位小姐，她背對著我。我向她打招呼時，她一直哭而臉沒有轉向我。當我拍她的肩膀，問她什麼事困擾她時，這時我嚇呆了。我看到一張沒有眼睛、眉毛，甚至嘴巴都沒有的臉。我害怕地尖叫，並且一路爬出那個地方。這時我醒來，也別想再睡了。

---

shriek〔ʃrik〕*v., n.* 尖銳的叫聲

Wed., *Sept*. *28*   *Sunny*

A day of no exams

Today was no different from the days I've had
before. It was sunny and I got up early. I met my
classmate on the way to school. Once I got to
school I was already tired out because there were
so many people on the bus and the driver drove
at full speed.

Anyway, today was a special day because we
didn't have examinations in school. At five classes
were over and I went out with some friends to eat
noodles. Now I must go to bed in order to get up
early again tomorrow.

九月二十八日　星期三　晴

沒有考試的日子

今天和往常沒有兩樣。天氣晴朗，我早上很早起床。我在上學
途中遇到同學，一到學校我就已經累壞了，因為車上太多人了，而
且司機又開快車。

無論如何，今天是個特別的日子，因為學校沒有考試。五點下
課，我和幾位同學出去吃麵。現在，我得上牀睡覺，明天好再度早
起。

Fri., Sept. 30 Rainy

Self-confidence

Self-confidence someone said is the foundation of doing great things. I was thinking about this today. I guess it's true. I find that so many people fail to realize their potential and take advantage of the opportunities that come knocking at their doors because they lack self-confidence. This is such a pity. Although that's so easy to say it's really difficult to do.

Often I find people with budding talent for something but they do not dare go out and try to develop that talent because they lack self-confidence. Having no self-confidence will get you nowhere because you will be too timid to try anything. But self-confidence comes only when you know yourself. You should know both your weaknesses and strengths. Only after this can you forge ahead with doing great things.

I find this especially true with the great ones that I see around me. One key ingredient in their success is their self-confidence. Self-confidence has a way of affecting others around you to believe in you. This in turn reinforces your self-confidence further. I think to be successful in life you need to have first self-confidence to start with.

九月三十日　星期五　雨

自 信 心

有人說自信心是成就偉大事業的基礎。今天我一直想著這個問題，我想這是對的。我發現許多人因爲缺乏自信而不能了解自己的潛力並利用其前來叩門的機會。這實在是一件憾事。雖然說起來容易，做起來却很困難。

我常常發現對某件事有發展能力的人因爲缺乏自信心而不敢出來嘗試發展自己的才能。没有自信心你就不會成功，因爲你太膽怯，以致於不敢嘗試任何事情。但是唯有了解自己，自信心才會產生，你應該了解自己的弱點之後，你才能慢慢邁向成功。

我發現這點對我周遭所見的大人物而言特別眞實，他們成功的一個重要因素爲其自信心。自信能夠影響週遭的人，使他們信任你，這必然也會更加強你的自信。我認爲想在生命中成功，就必須先有自信心來作爲起步。

＊＊　─────────────────────

forge〔fɔrdʒ〕*v.* 徐緩推進

ingredient〔ɪn'gridɪənt〕*n.* 成份；組成份子

in turn 必然也　　　reinforce〔,rim'fors〕*v.* 增加

《 表示自信的常用語 》

♤ I have great confidence in my success.

我極有自信能成功。

♤ He has a confident manner of speaking in public.

他演說時有一種自信的態度。

♤ He went into the contest with the assurance of a born fighter.

他參加比賽，自信天生爲拳師。

MONTH 10 October

Sat., Oct. 1　　Fine

A fire

A fire broke out near by. Four houses were burnt to the ground. The wind was strong, and the water supply was poor. It was said that the fire was probably caused by careless handling of a kerosene heater. Have to check all the kerosene heaters in my house. My house luckily escaped the fire, but we should take more precautions against fire in the future.

十月一日　星期六　晴朗

火　災

　　附近著火了，有四幢房子都燒得精光，風很大，而水的供應又不足。聽說起火的原因大概是煤油爐的使用不愼所引起的。我必須檢查房子裏所有的煤油爐。我們的房子僥倖逃過一刼，但以後我們應該要採取更多的預防措施。

---

break out 大規模地出現　　careless 〔'kɛrlɪs〕*adj.* 粗心的；疏忽的
kerosene 〔'kɛrə,sin,,kɛrə'sin〕*n.* 煤油；火油（亦作 kerosine）
heater 〔'hitə〕*n.* 火爐；加熱器
precaution 〔prɪ'kɔʃən〕*n.* 預防（法）；事先之準備

Sun., Oct. 2　Fine

Before the desk

Today is a holiday, Sunday. When I woke up at six, it occurred to me that the weather outside was fine and I could go out playing all day. But then, I saw the books on my desk and I remembered I had some readings to do. So, there was nothing to do but study. Oh well, I said, here goes another day of studying. I picked up my book and skimmed through the pages. Then I took a piece of paper and pencil and started writing my schedule for the day. Most probably I would not follow the schedule but I needed it to force me to sit in front of my desk.

At one sitting I was able to finish two chapters of my history book. It was about American history. Then I took a break to stretch my legs and do a little bit of exercise. I went to the kitchen and drank a glass of milk. Mom was busy preparing for lunch. The smell of food made me hungry. Mom said I'd better wait till everything was cooked or else I would ruin my appetite. So I went back to my books. Later in the day I did my Mathematics homework. This took me a longer time. But finally I was able to finish everything. Then I left my things on the table and went to watch some TV.

十月二日　星期日　晴

書　桌　前

　　今天是假日，星期日。六點起牀的時候，我發現外面天氣很好，可以整天在外面玩。然而，我看見書桌上的書，想起來還有書要唸。因此，只有唸書啦！噢，又是一個讀書天。我拿起書本，草草翻了翻看，然後拿起紙筆，開始寫下一天的時間表。我很可能不會去遵照時間表辦事，但我却需要它來強迫我坐在書桌前。

　　我一口氣讀了兩章歷史，有關美國史的。然後我休息了一會兒，來伸伸腿，做些簡單的運動。我跑到厨房喝了杯牛奶。媽正忙著煮中飯，食物的香味使我餓得要命。媽敎我最好等到一切都準備好再說，免得搞壞胃口。所以我又跑去唸我的書。後來我做了數學作業，花了不少時間。但我終於可以完成所有的事了。然後我把東西留在桌上，跑去看了一會電視節目。

---

skim〔skɪm〕v. 草草閱讀　　　schedule〔'skɛdʒul〕n. 時間表；目錄
at one sitting 一口氣　　appetite〔'æpə,taɪt〕n. 食慾

Mon., Oct. 3　Cloudy

The new school term

The new school term has commenced today. At 8 o'clock in the morning, the opening ceremony was held in the lecture hall. The principal gave us conventional instruction to how to behave ourselves during the new term.

十月三日　星期一　多雲

新　學　期

　　今天是新學期的開始。早上八點鐘，開學典禮在演講廳舉行。校長照舊告訴我們在新學期中要如何的守規矩。

Wed., Oct. 5　Fine later cloudy

A morning-glory

When I got up this morning, found two beautiful purple morning-glories blooming with silvery dew on the petals. The morning-glories reminded me of its exact English name. A morning-glory is the morning glory.

十月五日　星期三　晴時多雲

牽牛花

我早晨起床的時候，發現了兩朵開得很漂亮的紫色牽牛花，花瓣上還滾著銀白色的露珠。它使我想起它的英文名字，牽牛花就象徵著早晨的光輝。

** ─────────────────────

　　morning-glory 〔'mɔrnɪŋ,glorɪ〕 *n.* 牽牛花
　　dew 〔dju〕 *n.* 露　　petal 〔'pɛtl〕 *n.* 花瓣

Thurs., Oct. 6 Fine

Cosmos

Owing to the last night's typhoon the walls of my house were blown down and the cosmos in the garden which I had carefully reared was spoilt. The paper says that the street trees at Jen Ai Road were almost uprooted.

十月六日　星期四　晴

波斯菊之死

由於昨晚的颱風，我家房子的圍牆都被吹倒了，花園裏一直受我細心培養的波斯菊也損失慘重。報上說仁愛路的人行道樹幾乎都被連根拔起。

Mon., Oct. 10   *Fine*

Double-Tenth Day

Today is Double-Tenth Day. It is neither too hot nor too cold. The sky is cobalt blue, and a fresh breeze blows from the south.

According to the evening newscast, there were quite a few people who did not fly the national flag over their doors. This is quite vicious. It is not too much to say that these people are wanting in patriotism. We put up a national flag newly washed and pressed at our gate.

十月十日　星期一　晴

國　慶　日

今天是國慶日，天氣不太熱，也不很冷，天空是深藍色，吹著涼爽的南風。

傍晚的新聞廣播說，有少數人沒有在家門口懸掛著飛揚的國旗，這實在是不對。說這些人缺乏愛國心一點也不過份。我們在大門口升起一面嶄新的，剛剛才熨過的國旗。

---

cobalt〔′kobɔlt〕 *n.* 由鈷製的深藍色顏色   ***fresh breeze*** 涼爽的風
vicious〔′vɪʃəs〕 *adj.* 邪惡；不正確的；墮落的
patriotism〔′petrɪətɪzəm〕 *n.* 愛國心；愛國的精神
press〔prɛs〕 *v.* 壓平；熨衣服

Fri., Oct. 14　Clear

Influenza

The advent of Autumn seems only nominal and the heat is still quite severe. As the air is very dry, many people are suffering from influenza. Decided to put on a respirator in the car or in the crowd in order to prevent infection.

十月十四　星期五　晴

流行性感冒

秋天的來臨似乎只是名義上的，天氣仍然極度炎熱。因為空氣很乾燥，很多人都爲感冒所苦。我決定在車上，或者在人群之中都要戴上口罩，以免被傳染。

---

advent〔'ædvɛnt〕*n.* 來臨；到來　　nominal〔'nɑmənḷ〕*adj.* 名義上的
influenza〔ˌɪnflʊ'ɛnzə〕*n.* 流行性感冒
respirator〔'rɛspəˌretɚ〕*n.* 口罩

Sat., Oct. 15　Rainy

A personal letter

A post-card came from Mr. Wang, informing me of his removal. He is such a careless fellow as to mark " Personal " on a postcard. He will surely bow to an invisible person in a telephone conversation when the talking is over.

十月十五日　星期六　雨

信　簡

收到王先生通知我他搬家了的明信片。他真是一個糊塗的傢伙，竟然在明信片上註明「限本人拆閱」。當他講完電話時，他也一定會對著電話這頭看不見的人鞠躬呢！

---

post card 明信片　removal〔rɪ'muvḷ〕*n.* 遷移；排除

Sun., Oct. 16   Fine

Going to the doctor's

We only go to the doctor when we are sick.
So the doctor makes money only if we are sick.
Consequently isn't it in the doctor's interest
to wish everybody were sick so he can make a lot
of money? I think doctors should only make money
if we are healthy, this way it would be in
his interest to keep us healthy. A national insur-
ance program, I think, would achieve this result
since doctors can then be encouraged to prevent
sicknesses from occurring.

十月十六日   星期日   晴

看 醫 生

我們只有在生病時才去看醫生，所以只有我們生病，醫生
才能賺錢。因此，以醫生的利益，他豈不就是希望每個人都生
病，好讓他能大賺錢了？我則認為如果醫生只在我們身體健康
時才能賺錢那就好了，這樣他就會為他的利益著想，而幫我們
保持健康了。我認為一套全國保險計畫可以達到這個成效，因
為這樣醫生就會受到鼓勵而防止疾病發生。

---

in one's interest 為⋯計；為對⋯有利
insurance〔ɪnˈʃʊrəns〕 *n.* 保險

Tues., Oct. 18　Fine

A book exhibition

Dropped in at National Central Library
to see the National Book Exhibition which will
close today. Surprised at the fact that so many
kinds of books are published in our country.
Thought the children's books with many pages of
colorful illustrations were made very nicely.
Bought a copy of the Chinese version of English
and American Short Stories at a 20 per cent
discount. Am going to read this through in this
good season for reading.

十月十八日　星期二　晴

書　展

信步走到中央圖書館看即將在今天結束的全國書展。驚奇
地發現我們國家竟然印行了這麼多種書籍。我覺得附有多頁彩
色插圖的兒童書籍印製得相當精美。我買了一本打八折的英
美短篇小說中文本。我要在這個讀書的好季節裡將它讀完。

---

drop〔drɑp〕 *v.* 不期而至；過訪
illustration 〔ɪˌləsˈtreʃən, ɪˌlʌsˈtreʃən〕 *n.* 插圖；圖解
version〔ˈvɝʃən, ˈvɝʒən〕 *n.* 譯本；翻譯
discount〔ˈdɪskaʊnt〕 *n.* 折扣

Sun., Oct. 23　Cloudy later fine

A sunny day

I had a very funny experience today. When I woke up today I felt something was amiss. It was cool and the sun was shining. When I looked to my side I saw that my brothers weren't in their beds anymore. Then suddenly the thought occurred to me they must have left for school already. So I started to panic. I put on my uniform as fast as I could. Then after that I got out of my room. Then I saw the clock, it said four o'clock. I was lost. How could it be four o'clock? Then I thought maybe I woke up too early but it was impossible because the sun was already out. Then I realized we had no classes today. What a fool I was.

十月二十三日　星期日　多雲時晴

晴　天

我今天有一個非常好玩的經歷。今天起床時，我覺得有些不對勁，天氣很涼但卻太陽高照。我看向身旁時，發現弟弟已經不在牀上了。然後我突然想到，他們一定是已經到學校去了，因此我開始惶恐。我儘快穿上制服，然後跑出房間，看看鐘，時鐘上指著四點，我迷糊了，怎麼會是四點？接著我想，或許我起太早了，但是不可能，因爲太陽已經出來了。後來我才明白我們今天沒課，我眞是個傻瓜。

---

amiss〔ə'mıs〕 *adj.* 錯誤的　　panic〔'pænık〕 *adj.,v.* 驚惶

Mon., Oct. 24　Fine

Missing an appointment

Today I was supposed to go to Fanny's birthday party. But before I could leave the house I received a phone call from my Mom telling me to go to the hospital because Father was ill. I soon rushed to the hospital. I forgot to let Fanny know that I couldn't go to her party.

When I got home, it was already deep in the moment. Suddenly I remembered that I had to give Fanny a phone call. I called her up and said I was sorry. To my surprise she did not feel angry at all but admired me for being a good girl. It is really worthwhile to have a friend like Fanny.

Good night, my dear diary.

十月二十四日　星期一　晴

失　約

今天我原應去參加芬妮的生日舞會，但是出門前我接到一通媽媽打來的電話，要我去醫院，因為爸爸病了。我很快地趕到醫院去，忘了通知芬妮，我無法去參加她的舞會。

回家時，已經很晚了。我突然想起必須打個電話給芬妮，我打電話給她向她道歉。令我驚訝的是，她一點都不生氣，反而誇獎我是個好女孩。有一個像芬妮這樣的朋友，真是值得。

晚安，我親愛的日記。

Tues., Oct. 25 *Cloudy*

My lucky day

Today is my lucky day. While I was walking in the streets I happened to find a five hundred dollar bill. Someone must have lost it. It was just lying on the pavement waiting for someone to pick it up. I waited for a few minutes to see if someone would come to get it. After a few minutes a man came by and was looking here and there. He asked me if I had seen a five hundred dollar bill. I said yes and then gave the money to him. He was so happy to see the money and he thanked me. He then gave me a hundred dollars and told me to keep it. I said no at first, but he insisted so I said thank you. Although I didn't keep the five hundred dollars for myself I still feel better because I did someone a good turn.

十月二十五日　星期二　多雲

幸運的日子

今天是我的幸運日。當我走在街上時我碰巧撿到了五百元大鈔。一定有人掉了。它剛好在人行道上等著人去撿。我等了幾分鐘，想看看有沒有人來拿。幾分鐘之後有個人走過來，四處張望。他問我有沒有看見一張五百元的鈔票。我說有，然後把錢給他。他見到錢好高興，對我說謝謝。然後他給了我一百塊錢，教我保存好。剛開始我拒絕了，但他一直堅持，因此我向他道謝。雖然我自己沒有得到那五百元，我仍然覺得安心多了，因為我幫了別人一次忙。

---

pavement〔'pevmənt〕*n.* 人行道　　*do a person a good turn* 幫某人一次忙

Wed., Oct. 26　Fine

Of stones and disorder

As usual I got up at six o'clock and went to the bus station at 6 : 30. On my way to the school near the Presidential Building I saw many persons in green coats and they were shouting something. The traffic routes leading to that area were blocked because of the demonstration of these people. Because of this I was late for school and I was a little bit angry.

After a day at the school, I went home. I turned on the television and I saw the demonstrations I saw this morning. On the footage of the film at one point the demonstrators got disorderly and some men started throwing stones at the police who were trying to keep the order. This really got me mad.

I think these people are abusing the meaning of the words freedom and democracy. Throwing stones is a behaviour deserving only of barbarians. Of course I want more democracy and freedom but certainly I don't want to see the chaos and inconvenience these people are causing to the general public.

十月二十六日　星期三　晴

經由石頭與混亂

和往常一樣我早上六點鐘起床，六點半到車站。上學途中，在總統府附近我看到許多穿綠色外衣的人在叫喊。到那個地區的交通路線因爲這些人的示威活動而阻塞了。因此我上學也遲到了，而且我有點生氣。

上了一天課後，我回家了。我打開電視機看到早晨所見的示威運動。影片的連續畫面中有一幕示威者變得混亂無秩序，有些人開始向設法維持秩序的警察丟石頭，這實在令我惱怒。

我認爲這些人是在濫用自由和民主兩字的意義。丟石頭是一種只有野蠻人才會有的行爲。當然我想要更多的民主和自由，但我決不想看到這些人帶給公衆的混亂及不便。

＊＊────────────────────

demonstration〔͵dɛmən'streʃən〕*n.* 示威運動
footage〔'futɪdʒ〕*n.*（影片之）連續鏡頭
barbarian〔bɑr'bɛrɪən〕*n.* 野蠻人

《表示民主與自由的常用語》

♤ Freedom of speech does not mean liberty to gossip or tell lies. 言論自由非指說別人閒話或說謊的自由。

♤ All men are now free in America.
現在在美國人人都是自由的。

♤ Is there more democracy in Australia than in Great Britain? 在澳洲是否比英國更爲自由平等？

♤ Schools in the United States are democratic.
美國的學校是民主的。

Sat., Oct. 29　Fine

Italian tourists

I had a chance to practice my English today. I did so with two Italian tourists. While waiting at the bus stop, two Italian tourists approached me and asked me for directions to the Chiang Kai-shek Memorial Hall. They said they had lost their way. With nothing else better to do, I decided to take them there myself. On the way there, they told me that this was their first time in Taiwan. It was also interesting to know that the two Italian tourists mistook Taiwan for Thailand. They said, a lot of people in Italy didn't even know where Taiwan was, or what Taiwan was. This then was my chance today to speak in English.

十月二十九日　星期六　晴

義大利遊客

今天我有個機會練習英文，我和兩名義大利遊客練習。在車站等車時，兩名義大利遊客走向我，問我到中正紀念堂怎麼走。他們說他們迷路了。由於沒什麼其他事好做，我決定親自帶他們到那裏去。途中，他們告訴我，這是他們第一次到台灣來。知道這兩個義大利遊客把台灣誤以為是泰國，我覺得很有趣。他們說在義大利很多人甚至不知道台灣在哪裏，或者台灣是什麼。這就是我今天練習英文的機會。

Winter Day

John Greenleaf Whittier

The sun that brief December day

Rose cheerless over hills of gray,

And, darkly circled, gave at noon

A sadder light than waning moon.

Slow tracing down the thickening sky

Its mute and ominous prophecy,

A portent seeming less than threat,

It sank from sight before it set.

冬　日

短暫的十二月天，太陽

陰鬱地升起照耀灰色的山頭，

在中午時分，模糊地環行天空，

顯露比月缺時還憂愁的亮光。

它沉默而不祥的預言

緩緩走下濃密的蒼穹，

彷彿惡兆決非恐嚇

太陽在沉沒之前，已從眼前殞落。

—錄自惠蒂爾。

（美國詩人，1807-1892）

冬天 4.

WINTER

行脚

Blow, Blow, Thou Winter Wind
William Shakespeare

Blow, blow, thou winter wind,

Thou art not so unkind

As man's ingratitude;

Thy tooth is not so keen

Because thou art not seen,

Although thy breath be rude.

Heigh ho! sing heigh ho! unto the green holly:

Most friendship is feigning, most loving mere folly:

Then, heigh ho! the holly!

This life is most jolly.

吹呀，吹吧，北風

吹呀，吹吧，北風

你並非如此殘酷無情

如人類負義一般；

你的牙齒並不尖銳

因為你不被看見，

雖然你的呼吸粗暴強勁。

歡唱吧！歡唱！為那亮綠的冬青：

友情大都虛僞，愛情多只愚昧：

來吧！歡唱！那冬青！

此種生命最是歡愉。

－錄自威廉‧莎士比亞。

（英國詩人及劇作家，1564-1616）

Tues., *Nov.* **1** *Cloudy*

Manager Ku

Manager Ku told me that because I'm such a good worker that I'd be getting a promotion and a raise. Manager Ku says that hard work is the key to success. I like Manager Ku, I think he's very smart.

十一月一日　星期二　多雲

顧經理

顧經理告訴我，由於我工作表現良好，所以我將升級並且加薪。顧經理說，努力工作是成功的關鍵。我喜歡顧經理，我覺得他很能幹。

❋❋────────────────────

promotion〔prə'moʃən〕*n.* 晉升；升遷

raise〔rez〕*n.* （待遇等之）提高　　key〔ki〕*n.* 重要的人或物

smart〔smart〕*adj.* 精明能幹的

Wed., *Nov.* **2** *Rainy*

A bamboo shoot

The double-cherry blossoms in the garden were all scattered by the recent rain. Was much surprised to find that a bamboo shoot, which put its head out of the ground four or five days ago, has grown taller than the wall.

十一月二日　星期三　雨

竹　筍

　　花園裡的重瓣櫻花在最近的一場雨中落了一地。我很驚訝的發現四、五天以前冒出地面的竹筍，已經長得比牆還高了。

** ─────────────────────

blossom〔'blɑsəm〕*n.* 花　　　scatter〔'skætɚ〕*v.* 分散；離散
shoot〔ʃut〕*n.* 芽；苗

Thurs., Nov. 3　Clear

A heavy burden

　　The examination was over yesterday and I felt as if I had a heavy burden taken off my shoulders. I am eagerly awaiting the day when the result is made public. In the evening I went to a puppet show.

十一月三日　星期四　晴

負　擔

　　考試終於在昨天結束了，我彷彿自肩頭卸下一大負擔。熱切地等待成績揭曉的日子。傍晚跑去看布袋戲來消遣。

** ─────────────────────

burden〔'bɚdn̩〕*n.* 負荷；重擔　　　eagerly〔'igɚlɪ〕*adv.* 熱心地；切望地
puppet〔'pʌpɪt〕*n.* 木偶

Sat., Nov. 5　Fine

" Gone with the Wind "

　　" Gone with the Wind " is such a wonderful movie. I went to see it again today. It's my third time seeing it. Why can't real life be as interesting and exciting as in the movies? I want to be a heroine like Scarlet and lead an interesting, exciting life

十一月五日　星期六　晴

美麗的電影

「亂世佳人」這部電影太好看了。今天我又跑去看。這是我第三次看這部片子。為什麼真實生活無法像電影中一樣的有趣和刺激呢？我要做一個像郝思嘉的女英雄，並且過著有趣、刺激的生活。

＊＊────────────────

heroine〔ˊhɛro‧m〕*n.* 女英雄

Sun., Nov. 6　Fine

A nightless city

Went to Shih Lin by bus. It was in as great a bustle as Chung Hua Road is in Taichung. The illuminations of theatres and movie-shows made the streets a nightless city.

十一月六日　星期日　晴

不夜城

搭公車去士林，那兒的夜市亂哄哄的，就像台中的中華夜市一樣。電影院以及放映影片的亮光使得街道成為一個不夜城。

＊＊────────────────

bustle〔ˊbʌsḷ〕*n.* 緊張而喧擾的活動　　*be in a bustle* 忙亂；雜沓
illumination〔ɪ͵luməˊneʃən,ɪ͵lju-〕*n.* 照明；亮度

Tues., Nov. 8　Rainy

Nervous debility

My head feels dull today as I could not sleep soundly last night owing to the crying of the neighbor's baby. I often wake up at a trifle nowadays. I fear I am suffering from nervous debility.

十一月八日　星期二　雨

神經衰弱

　　今天我的頭沉沉鈍鈍的，因爲鄰居小嬰兒的哭聲，所以昨夜沒能好好酣睡一場。現在經常因爲一點小事就醒來。眞怕我患了神經衰弱症。

------

dull〔dʌl〕*adj.* 麻木的；遲鈍的　　soundly〔'saʊndlɪ〕*adv.* 酣暢地；安穩地
trifle〔'traɪfl〕*n.* 少許；疏忽　　*a trifle* 稍微；有點
nervous〔'nɝvəs〕*adj.* 神經的　　debility〔dɪ'bɪlətɪ〕*n.* 衰弱；虛弱

Sun., Nov. 13　Fine

A fishing-pond

When I called on Mr. Pi, he was out fishing. Angling is his favorite hobby, and on Sundays, for which he waits impatiently, he goes to a public fishing-pond which he always patronizes and enjoys his favorite sport all day long.

十一月十三日　星期日　晴

釣魚趣味

　　當我去找畢先生時，他已經出去釣魚了。釣魚是他最喜愛的嗜好，他總是對釣魚迫不及待，每逢星期天，他會去常去的那處公共釣魚池，整天享受著他的釣魚運動。

------

angling〔'æŋglɪŋ〕*n.* 釣魚；釣魚術
impatiently〔ɪm'peʃəntlɪ〕*adv.* 不耐煩；焦急
patronize〔'petrən,aɪz〕*v.* 光顧；照顧

Tues., Nov. 15　Cloudy

In my dream

Last night, I dreamed I became a very beautiful bird. I dreamed that I was in a forest. In the forest, there were a lot of animals. Then, an old bird told us, "We have a very beautiful forest, we should therefore protect it from pollution". All the animals agreed with him.

But the second day, people came into our forest. Many animals were caught. The people wanted to build houses and parks in our forest. Many old trees were felled. And then suddenly, nothing was left standing.

I was so shocked and then I bursted out crying. I woke up at midnight. It was only a dream.

十一月十五日　星期二　陰

在夢中

昨晚我夢見我變成一隻非常漂亮的鳥。我夢到我在一座森林，森林裏有很多動物。然後有一隻老鳥告訴我們，「我們有一座非常美麗的森林，因此我們應該保護它，免得受到污染。」所有的動物都贊成他。

但是第二天，人們進入我們的森林，許多動物被逮捕。這些人要在我們的森林地上建造房子和公園。許多年老的樹木被砍下，然後，突然間，一切都被夷平了。

我很震驚，接著突然大哭起來。我在半夜醒來，原來只是個夢。

** fell〔fɛl〕*v.* 砍伐

Sat., Nov. 19   *Cloudy*

Fast friendship

Today is the start of the weekend. It being summer, I decided to spend a few hours in a department store to cool myself. Little did I know that I was heading for a very new experience. While I was walking around the store, I happened to see a foreigner trying to explain himself to a saleslady. I was curious about what was going on for the saleslady couldn't understand what the man was talking about. Mustering my courage then, I decided to step in and help the man explain himself. Fortunately I could understand what the man was talking about, so I just translated it back into Chinese. After the man got his message across, he smiled at me. He then invited me to have something to eat with him. I tried to refuse but finally I gave in.

I felt good for being able to help him and talk with him. He said that he was a student like myself and he was touring Taiwan by himself. He told me about the experiences he has had so far touring the country. He told me too, that he was just staying for a few more days. After we ate he thanked me and said goodbye. This is the first time I've met a foreigner. Although I won't be seeing him again it is good to be able to meet someone like him from another country.

十一月十九日　星期六　多雲

速成的友誼

　　今天是週末的開始。由於是夏天，我決定花幾個小時逛百貨公司，讓自己清涼一下。我完全沒想到我將會有非常新鮮的經歷。當我在百貨公司閒逛時，我看到一位外國人試著向售貨小姐說明自己的意思。我對正在發生的事感到很好奇，因為售貨小姐聽不懂這個人在說什麼。我鼓起勇氣，然後，決心走向前幫助這個人表達他的意思。還好我聽得懂這個人說什麼，所以就把他說的話翻成中文。傳達了他的意思後，這個人對我微笑，然後邀請我和他去吃一點東西。我試著拒絕，最後還是同意了。

　　能夠幫助他而且和他聊天，我感到非常愉快。他說他和我一樣是學生，他一個人在台灣旅行。他告訴我他旅行至今在此地所經歷的事物。他還告訴我，他只要再留幾天而已。吃完後，他向我道謝並說再見。這是我第一次遇到外國人，雖然我不會再遇見他，但是能遇到像他這樣來自另一個國家的人真好。

**────────────────────

muster〔 ′mʌstɚ 〕*v.* 鼓起；振作

across〔 ə′krɔs 〕*adj.* 被瞭解　　***give in*** 同意

《有關交友的常用語》

♤ He has been a good friend to me. 他一向是我的好朋友。

♤ The friendship will last forever. 這友情將持續永遠。

♤ She was my intimate friend. 她是我的密友。

♤ Their acquaintanceship lasted many years.

　　他們的交往維持了許多年。

Sun., Nov. **20** *Fine*

Books

I had to struggle to get up this morning. I didn't
want to let sleep steal the better half of my day though,
so painfully I removed my blanket and sat up straight
and with my eyes still half-closed slowly put on my
slippers. I could feel my body resisting the orders
that my mind was giving. But I had to get up or else I
would have wasted another day sleeping. Later on
when I was sufficiently awake I turned on the radio and
went into the bathroom. I turned on the shower and
waited for the hot water to come out. In a minute I was
fully undressed and I got into the shower. The spray
coming out of the shower head was really what I needed
to start my day.

After I finished breakfast, I went on to read some
books. I read some short stories. I like reading short
stories because they are easy to read and I can finish
a whole story within a few minutes. My teacher told us
that aside from our regular homework, we should also
do some outside reading. Thus I chose to read short
stories. It doesn't take much of my time. Books open
a lot of doors for us. Aside from entertaining us we
can also learn from books. When I read books I can go
to places I've never been to and meet persons I've
never met or will never have a chance of meeting. It
also broadens my mind as it tells me ways to do

things that I would have never thought of doing. Finally it leads us to know ourselves better. After reading
five short stories I was ready to go back to my schoolwork.

十一月二十日　星期日　晴

書　籍

今天早上我必須掙扎著起床。雖然我不想讓睡眠偷走一天較好的
大半時光，我還是極為痛苦地才把氈子拿開，把身子坐直，而且
眼睛還半閉著，慢慢穿上拖鞋。我可以感覺到身體在抗拒大腦發
出的命令，但是我必須起床，否則我又會浪費一天的時間來睡覺了。
稍後當我充分清醒時，我打開收音機，走進浴室。我打開蓮篷頭等
待熱水流出來，不到一分鐘，我已經脫光衣服，然後走進水中。
從蓮篷頭噴出來的水正是我這一天的開始所需要的東西。

吃完早餐後，我繼續讀書，讀了一些短篇小說。我喜歡讀短篇
小說，因為短篇小說容易閱讀，而且我可以在幾分鐘內讀完整個故
事。老師告訴我們除了正常的功課外，我們還應該唸一些課外讀物。
因此，我選擇閱讀短篇小說，這不用花費我很多時間。書本為我們
開啟很多扇門，除了愉悅我們外，我們還可以從書中學習。閱讀時，
我可以到從未去過的地方，見到從未遇過或永遠沒有機會遇到的人。
書本還可以開闊我的心胸，因為它告訴我許多我從未想到過的做事
方法。最後它引導我們更了解自己。讀完五則短篇小說後，我已準
備好回到學校功課上了。

---

blanket〔'blæŋkɪt〕*n.* 毛毯；氈　　slipper〔'slɪpɚ〕*n.* 拖鞋
spray〔spre〕*n.* 水沫　*aside from* 除…以外
entertain〔ˌɛntɚ'ten〕*v.* 娛樂　　broaden〔'brɔdn̩〕*v.* 增廣

Mon., Nov. 21   *Cloudy later fine*

Telling a funny story

Today our class held a contest. The contest was called : " Telling a funny story. " It was fun because it gave a chance for us to show our sense of humor. The class itself judged which story was the funniest. From this contest, I found some of my classmates had the ability to make others laugh and laughing relieved our anxieties. After a good laugh we had a better and brighter view of the world.

This morning I was worrying about today's tests, for I had not prepared for them very well. But, after the contest I was able to relax. Now, I think that in order to get through our troubles what we need is only to take it easy. Am I right?

十一月二十一日　星期一　多雲時晴

說笑話

今天班上舉行一項比賽，這項比賽叫做：「說笑話」。這很有趣，因為它給我們機會，讓我們表現幽默感。同學自己評判那個故事最有趣。從這項比賽中，我發現某些同學能夠讓其他人笑，而笑可以解除我們的憂慮。大笑之後，我們對世界有較好及較光明的看法。

早晨我很擔心今天的比賽，因為我沒有準備得非常充份。但是比賽後，我卻能夠輕鬆。現在，我認為想克服困難需要的只是放輕鬆。我的想法對嗎？

Tues., Nov. 22 Fine

Good manners

This morning, I went to school as usual. There were so many people on the bus, I felt like a sardine in a tin can. There was nothing I could do but stand up. Everyone was pressing against each other. I just hate crowded buses. As the bus screeched to a halt everyone standing up was carried along with the motion of the bus. Then some people got off. At last I was able to breathe some air. The smell of human odors mixed together was already getting to me. There was an old woman who was getting on the bus. She looked frail and was maybe in her 60's. No one wanted to budge, until a young student stood up and offered his seat to her. The boy was very courteous and gallant for his age, I thought. The old woman appreciatively said thank you then.

If everyone in our society were like this student, I think our society would be a peaceful and harmonious one. Sadly though everyone is so busy nowadays that courtesy is beginning to lose its significance.

十一月二十二日　星期二　晴

良好的禮儀

今天早晨我和以往一樣去上學。公車裡都是人，使我覺得像是在沙丁魚罐頭裡一樣。沒辦法，我只有站著。大家都互相擠來擠去。我最討厭擁擠的公車了。當車子刹車時，所有站著的乘客都被車子的突然動作帶得往前移。後來有些人下車了。我終於可以呼吸一些空氣，但撲鼻而來即是人們混合的一股氣味。有一位老太太上了車，她看來很脆弱，而且大概有六十多歲了。沒有人肯動，直到一個年輕的學生站起來把位子讓給她。我想，那男孩雖年紀輕輕，卻彬彬有禮。後來那位老太太向他道謝。

如果我們社會上的每個人都能像這個學生一樣，我相信社會將更為和諧安寧。然而悲哀的是現在每個人都很忙碌，以致於禮儀已開始失去它的意義了。

------

sardine〔sɑr'din〕 *n.* 沙丁魚　　screech〔skritʃ〕 *v.* 發出尖銳的聲音
halt〔hɔlt〕 *n.* 停止前進　　*get off* 下車　　frail〔frel〕 *adj.* 脆弱的
budge〔bʌdʒ〕 *v.* 移動　　courteous〔'kɝtɪəs〕 *adj.* 有禮貌的
gallant〔'gælənt〕 *adj.* 慇勤的　　courtesy〔'kɝtəsɪ〕 *n.* 禮貌；禮儀

《有關公車的常用語》

♠ The bus was crowded. 公車很擠。

♠ I could not get a seat. 我找不到位置。

♠ The buses run every five minutes during the rush hours.
　公車在交通顛峯時間每隔五分鐘一班。

♠ I commute by bus. 我通車。

♠ I go to school by bus. 我搭公車到學校。

Thurs., Nov. 24　Fine

Making a new friend

Today I made a new friend. His name is Joseph. He studies in the same school as I do but we're not classmates. We were waiting for our lunch in a line. The line was a long one. Then the guy in front of me started fidgeting around. As he turned around, he said "Hi" to me. Then I said " Hi " too. Then we started talking. After a few minutes, he introduced himself as " Joseph ". After we had our lunch boxes, we sat together and continued talking.

He's a very interesting guy. He says he likes to play basketball a lot and he has his own computer. I said I had my own computer, too. It was given to me by my dad on my birthday. He said if I had time maybe we could exchange programs. I said yes. I'll be seeing him next weekend in his home. He wants to show his computer to me. It was such a coincidence to meet someone like him who shares my interest in computers. Well, that's all for now. I have to do my assignment.

十一月二十四日　星期四　晴

交新朋友

　　今天我交了一個新朋友，他的名字叫約瑟夫。他和我唸同一個
學校，但我們並不同班。我們正好一起排隊要吃午餐。隊伍很長。
然後，我前面的傢伙開始不耐煩地亂動。當他轉過身來時，他向我
說「嗨」。我也對他說「嗨」。接著，我們便談了起來。幾分鐘
後，他自我介紹說他叫「約瑟夫」。在我們拿到餐盒後，我們便坐
在一塊兒繼續談。

　　他是個很有趣的傢伙。他說他非常喜歡打籃球，而且擁有自己
的電腦。我說我自己也有一台電腦。那是我爸爸給我的生日禮物。
他說如果我有空，我們可以互相交換程式，我說好。下週末我將去
他家看他，他要給我看他的電腦。遇到像他這樣一個能和我共享對
電腦方面的興趣的人實在是太巧了。好了，目前為止就是這些了。
我還有功課要做呢。

**

fidget〔ˈfɪdʒɪt〕*v*. 煩燥不安；煩亂
coincidence〔koˈɪnsədəns〕*n*. 巧合；偶合
program〔ˈprogræm〕*n*. 電腦程式

《有關人物的常用語》

♤ He is a man of character. 他是一個有個性的人。

♠ He is a man of few words. 他是一個沈默寡言的人。

♤ He is quite a reliable man. 他真是一個可信賴的人。

♠ In short, he is an irresponsible man.
　　扼要地說，他是一個不負責任的人。

♤ Well-educated people never look down upon the poor.
　　有教養的人從不會輕視窮人。

Mon., Nov. **28**　*Fine*

A second-hand book

November is drawing to a close and now and then a cold wind blows. The leaves of the trees are falling like rain. Came across Mr. Lin from Taichung. He was hunting up second-hand books as usual.

十一月二十八日　星期一　晴

舊　書

十一月已經瀕臨結束，而且偶而冷風會吹起。樹葉紛落如雨。遇見家住台中的林先生，他仍像以往一般地仔細尋找舊書。

**————————————————

　　draw〔drɔ〕*v.* 拉；曳；拖；起草　　*come across* 偶遇　　*hunt up* 仔細尋找

Wed., Nov. **30**　*Fine and windy*

Motorcycle racing

What an exciting race it was tonight！ I saw two motorcycles crash into each other head-on. There were fire trucks, police cars, and ambulances everywhere. I never realized these races could be so exciting. I'm gonna go more often, These races beat watching TV any day.

十一月三十日　星期三　晴有風

飇　車

今晚的比賽真是刺激！我看到兩輛摩托車正面相撞。到處都是消防車、警車及救護車。我以前從不了解這飇車會如此的刺激。我以後要更常去看，這些飇車活動可要勝過看電視呢。

**————————————————

　　crash into 衝撞；碰撞　　　head-on〔'hɛd'ɑn, -'ɑn〕*adv*. 正面地

Thurs., Dec. 1　Cloudy later fine

Notes on Chinese classics

The first term examination is drawing near. In the after-noon, called at Mr. Ku's lodging to borrow his notes on Chinese classics. He was taking a nap at full length, with his head pillowed on the dictionary.

十二月一日　星期四　多雲時晴

中國經書的筆記

第一次期考即將來臨。下午,我拜訪顧先生的住處去向他借中國經書的筆記。他正全身伸直了在睡午覺,而把頭枕在字典上。

＊＊

Chinese classics 中國之古經典 (如四書五經之類)
draw near 接近　　lodging〔'lɑdʒɪŋ〕n. 寓所
take a nap 午睡

Fri., Dec. 2　Fine

A crowded car

As it is getting near the end of the year public buses are crowded during the rush hours in the morning and evening. Every bus is overcrowded. Old folks and women as well as children have to take cars at the risk of their lives.

十二月二日　星期五　晴

擠　公　車

　　由於愈來愈接近年關，公共汽車在早晚的交通擁擠時間都擠得要命。每一輛公車都過度擁擠了，老人家、婦女和小孩子，都必須冒著生命危險搭上車子。

＊＊

rush hour （早晚之）交通擁擠時間

overcrowded〔͵ovɚ'kraʊdɪd〕 **adj.** 過度擁擠的

risk〔rɪsk〕 **n., v.** 冒險；賭注　　**at the risk of** 冒著……的危險

Sat., Dec. 3　Fine

English grammar

In the hour of English grammar, we were taught the usage of the articles. According to the explanation of the teacher there are many rules and exceptions in the usage of the articles. We think that we cannot make light of the articles.

十二月三日　星期六　晴

英文文法

　　英文文法課時，我們上冠詞的用法。根據老師的說明，冠詞的用法有許多的規則及例外的地方。我們認爲不可忽視了冠詞的重要性。

＊＊

article〔'ɑrtɪkl̩〕 **n.** 冠詞

explanation〔͵ɛksplə'neʃən〕 **n.** 說明；解釋

exception〔ɪk'sɛpʃən〕 **n.** 例外

make light of 低估；輕視

Sun., Dec. 4 Fine

Going out

There's nothing like going out with friends on a
Sunday. George, Chris and I went bowling today. It
was really a lot of fun. We started out in the morning by meeting each other in front of the Taipei Railroad Station. Chris was late again by thirty minutes,
but we had already come to expect this from him.
After he arrived we set out to look for the bus that
would take us to Shihlin. Once we arrived at our
destination we got off the bus. There weren't many
people yet when we got to the bowling alley. We then
paid for the three of us and borrowed some bowling
shoes.

Chris is very good at bowling. He always beats
George and me. No matter how hard we try somehow he
always wins. I am a bit better than George. We played
until noon. At noon, the three of us felt hungry so
we decided to grab something to eat nearby. We went
to Ting Gua Gua for some chicken. While in there, we
talked about some of our teachers and made fun of
them. It was really hilarious. We just couldn't stop
laughing. After that we walked around Shihlin for a
few minutes, half an hour to be exact. There wasn't
really anything that we wanted to buy, we just wanted
to take a look around. After that, we watched a movie,

the title of the movie was "I was a Teen-age Vampire."
I don't really care much for horror movies, but since the
other two guys wanted to watch it, there was nothing more
I could do. Majority wins. With that, we went home. I have
to study some more before I go to sleep. Next week, we
probably will do something different.

十二月四日　星期日　晴

外　出

　　沒有什麼比得上星期天和朋友出去。喬治、克里斯和我今天去打
保齡球，實在是很有趣。我們早晨出發，在台北火車站前集合。克里
斯又遲到了三十分鐘，但是我們早就料到他會如此。他到達後我們開
始找到士林的公車。我們一到目的地就下車。我們到達保齡球館時，
還沒有很多人。接著，我們付了三個人的錢，並借了保齡球鞋。

　　克里斯很擅於打保齡球，他總是打敗喬治跟我。不管我們多努力，
最後他總是贏。我比喬治好一點。我們一直打到中午。中午時，三個
人都覺得餓了，所以我們決定到附近找一些東西吃。我們到頂呱呱吃
炸雞。在那裏，我們談論一些老師並且嘲弄他們。那實在很有趣，我
們笑個不停。然後我們在士林逛了幾分鐘，實際上是半小時。事實上
沒有我們想買的東西，我們只是想四處看一看。然後我們看了一場電
影，片名是「少年吸血鬼」。我不是真的很喜歡恐怖片，但因為另外
兩個人想看，我也沒辦法。少數服從多數。看完後，我們回家。睡覺
前，我得多讀一些書。下星期，我們可能要做一些不同的事。

---

bowling alley 保齡球館　　　　grab〔græb〕*v.* 急抓
hilarious〔həˈlɛrɪəs〕*adj.* 有趣的；妙的
vampire〔ˈvæmpaɪr〕*n.* 吸血鬼

Sun., Dec. 4 Fine

House-cleaning

During the morning helped my family clean the house and in the afternoon repaired all the screen-doors with the help of my sister. It was pretty hard to wash the screens as the north wind was cold. At night was dog-tired so went to bed earlier than usual.

十二月四日　星期日　晴

大　掃　除

早上我幫忙家人清掃房子，下午妹妹幫我把紗門修好。在北風冷颼颼地吹著的時候清洗紗窗實在很艱苦。到了晚上我累得半死，所以就比平常早睡了。

＊＊
_____

screen〔skrin〕 *n.* 紗；帳；簾
dog-tired〔'dɔg'taɪrd〕 *adj.* 極疲的；甚倦的

Mon., Dec. 5 Windy

The north wind

It was extremely cold today with a cutting north wind and the cold of this morning penetrated to my very bones.　At school we listened to the teacher's lecture, shivering with cold in the classroom where we had no stove.

十二月五日　星期一　有風

北　風

今天天氣極度寒冷，刺骨的北風和早晨的寒氣都使我冷透骨髓。在學校時，我們一邊聽著老師講課，一邊在沒有暖爐的教室裏面冷得發顫。

＊＊

cutting〔'kʌtɪŋ〕 *adj.* 刺骨的　　penetrate〔'pɛnə‚tret〕 *v.* 透入
lecture〔'lɛktʃɚ〕 *n.* 演講；教訓　　shiver〔'ʃɪvɚ〕 *v., n.* 顫抖

Wed., Dec. 7　Fine

Assorted fire pot

It was a wonderful dinner tonight. We had a fire pot with beef, shrimp, squid and all kinds of vegetables. I didn't have any of the broth at the end though. I was afraid the broth had too many germs after everybody had stuck their chopsticks in it.

十二月七日　星期三　晴

吃　火　鍋

今晚的晚餐非常棒。我們吃的是放了牛肉、蝦子、魷魚和各種蔬菜的火鍋。但是最後我沒有喝湯。我擔心在每個人把筷子放進湯裡後，湯裡頭有太多的細菌。

**

assorted〔ə'sɔrtɪd〕*adj.* 什錦的　　shrimp〔ʃrɪmp〕*n.* 小蝦
squid〔skwɪd〕*n.* 烏賊；魷魚　　germ〔dʒɝm〕*n.* 細菌

Thurs., Dec. 8　Cloudy

My favorite singer

Michael Jackson is coming to town! I can't believe it! This is a dream come true! He is my favorite singer in the whole world. I stood in line for three hours to buy tickets for his concert. All my friends at school are going. Oh, I can't wait!

十二月八日　星期四　多雲

我最喜愛的歌星

麥克・傑克森就要來鎮上了！真不敢相信，我的夢想實現了！他是全世界我最喜愛的歌星。我排了三個小時的隊去買他演唱會的票。我在學校裡的所有朋友都要去。哦，我真等不及了！

**

favorite〔'fevərɪt〕*adj.* 最喜愛的　　*in line* 排成隊

Sat., Dec. 10　*Fine*

Reminding classmate
of her health

I went to cheer up Nancy this afternoon. She was so depressed about failing her English examination that I think she's gonna be sick. She told me she will pass the next one at any cost.

I reminded her that the most important thing is her health and told her to take care of it.

十二月十日　星期六　晴

提醒同學注意健康

今天下午我去安慰南西。她因為英文考試不及格而非常沮喪，我想她可能會生病。她告訴我下次不計任何犧牲都要通過考試。

我提醒她最重要的是她的健康，並且告訴她要注意自己的身體。

**　

cheer up 使高興；使快樂

depressed〔dɪˈprɛst〕*adj.* 沮喪的

examination〔ɪɡˌzæməˈneʃən〕*n.* 考試

take care of 照顧；看護

Mon., Dec. 12 *Cloudy*

My English class

Today, during my English period, I was told by my teacher to give a speech. I felt really terrible. I have been memorizing my speech for a week now but I felt I was still not yet prepared. My hands were cold and wet with perspiration. My teacher said not to worry and that I should just do my best. Then I started delivering my speech.

Oh, standing up there seeing all the faces staring at me I nearly froze to death. Then the first word came out and then the second, then the third. Finally I finished my speech. Then everybody clapped their hands. My teacher said that I talked too softly and too fast. I should've just relaxed. Then I remembered that I forgot to say a whole paragraph. It was really terrible.

Like they say, there's always a first time for everything. Hopefully next time I can do better. Actually I didn't do that bad. My other classmates did worse than me (if that's any consolation at all). But, I have to get used to it for this wasn't going to be my first and last time.

十二月十二日　星期一　多雲

我的英文課

今天，在英文課上，老師告訴我要演講。我覺得眞糟，我背了一個禮拜，但還是覺得沒有準備好。手發冷出汗。老師敎我別擔心，只要盡力就行了。然後，我開始演講了。

噢！站在那兒，看見所有的臉都盯著我看，我嚇得幾乎要癱在原地了。一個字，兩個字，三個字。終於講完了，然後大家都鼓起掌來。老師說我講得太輕太快，應該放輕鬆點。後來我才想起我漏了一大段。眞是糟透了。

正如人們所說，凡事都有第一次。希望下次我能做得更好。事實上，我也沒講得那麼糟。其他的同學比我還爛，（如果這是一種安慰的話）然而，我必須習慣，因爲這不會是我的第一次，也不會是最後一次。

**————————————————

deliver〔dɪˈlɪvə〕v. 發表　　clap〔klæp〕v. 拍手；鼓掌
consolation〔ˌkɑnsəˈleʃən〕n. 安慰　　*get used to* 習慣於

《表示緊張的常用語》

♤ I got nervous at the English examination.
在英文考試時我有些神經緊張。

♤ She is shy and nervous. 她膽小而羞怯。

♤ The audience was growing restless.
觀衆漸漸不安起來。

♤ When the news came that the ship had sunk, she was
deeply agitated.
消息傳來船已沈沒，她心裏卽焦慮不安。

Wed., Dec. 14　Fine

The punk hairdo

Day in and day out, there's nothing that I hear but my mother yelling at me. Sometimes I want to shout back but what's the use? I might just get slapped. When I really can't stand it anymore, I sometimes get out of the house in order to breathe some fresh air.

Take today for example. I was simply listening to some cassettes when my mother hollered at me to turn down the volume. I did just that but a minute later she banged again into my room and turned off the tape player herself. Ugh! I could have killed her for that. She just doesn't seem to understand what teenagers like me go through. I mean, I study hard, I help in the house chores but music is my only way of relaxation. I never say anything when she watches those Chinese operas on the TV and yet I can't say anything to her when she scolds me for listening to rock'n roll.

A friend of mine today was sporting a punk hairdo. She had all her hair cut short and it was standing up in the center. She says it's the latest fad in the United States. I wonder what my mother will say when she sees me in such a hairdo. Obviously she can't turn me off like she does with the radio. Hmm. The idea is really appealing to me.

十二月十四日　星期三　晴

龐 克 頭

日復一日，我只聽見媽媽對我大吼大叫。有時我真想對她吼回去，但有什麼用呢？我大概會挨一巴掌。我實在沒辦法再忍受下去了，有時我衝出屋外，爲了呼吸點新鮮空氣。

就拿今天來說好了，我只是在聽一些錄音帶，當時媽叫我把音量關小一點，當我剛剛照做之後，她却衝進我房裏，自己把按鍵給關掉。嘔！我真想殺了她。她似乎就是不了解像我這樣的青少年在搞什麼。我是指，我用功讀書，我幫忙做家事，而音樂，是我紓解的唯一方式。當她看電視上那些平劇時，我從不說什麼，然而當她爲了我聽搖滾樂而罵我時，我也不能說什麼。

今天我一個朋友炫耀著她的龐克頭，她把頭髮全部剪短，在中間還豎立起來。她說這是美國最新流行的髮型。我真想知道媽媽看到我留這種髮型時，會說什麼。很明顯地，她不能像關收音機那樣地把我關掉。嗯，這個主意真是讓人心動。

**────────────────────

day in and day out 每天；繼續不斷地　　yell〔jɛl〕*v.* 喊叫
slap〔slæp〕*v.* 掌擊；摑　　holler〔'hɑlə〕*v.* 叫喊
scold〔skold〕*v.* 責罵　　hairdo〔'hɛr‚du〕*n.* 女人的髮型
appealing〔ə'pilɪŋ〕*adj.* 令人心動的

《表示責罵的常用語》

♠ That woman is always scolding the children in our
neighborhood. 那婦人常責罵我們附近的孩子。

♢ He chided her for carelessness.
他爲她的粗心大意而責備她。

♢ She blamed him for being late. 她責備他遲到。

Thurs., *Dec.* *22*　　*Clear*

The winter solstice

According to the calendar, this is the winter solstice and the day is the shortest of the year. But from tomorrow the days will get longer day by day and we are somewhat delighted to think about it.

十二月二十二日　星期四　晴

冬　至

根據日曆，今天是冬至，也是一年裏頭最短的一天。但從明天開始，日子就會一天一天地變長起來，想到這裡，我們有些兒歡喜。

＊＊────────────────

calendar〔'kæləndɚ, 'kælɪn-〕 *n.* 日曆

solstice〔'sɑlstɪs〕 *n.* 至；至日　　delightful〔dɪ'laɪtfəl〕*adj.* 愉快的

Sat., *Dec.* *24*　　*Fine*

Christmas Eve

In the evening went with Mr. Ku to church to celebrate Christmas. There was a hymn, reading of the Bible, English speeches and prayers. After the ceremony there were many entertainments, such as a drama, a tableau vivant, etc.

十二月二十四日　星期六　晴

耶　誕　夜

傍晚和顧先生一起去教堂望彌撒。我們唱聖歌，唸聖經裏面英文的講道和禱告。儀式結束後，有許多餘興節目，如戲劇，活人畫等等。

＊＊────────────────

celebrate〔'sɛlə,bret〕 *v.* 慶祝；舉行宗教　　hymn〔hɪm〕*n.,v.* 聖歌

prayer〔prɛr, prær, 'preɚ〕 *n.* 祈禱　　ceremony〔'sɛrə,monɪ〕 *n.* 典禮

Wed., Dec. 28 *Fine*

No pains, no gains

I went through the day again like I have done so often so many times before. It was the same routine: school, home, study, sleep. I was kind of frustrated with my test results today. I got lower than what I had expected to get. I did pass though. At lunch when I was a bit down a friend of mine, Lisa, saw how depressed I was and she asked me if there was anything the matter with me. I said I was just a little disappointed about the test we had. She tried to cheer me up and said it didn't matter that much. I am glad to have such a friend like her. I felt better after a few laughs and jokes with her.

I knew for certain why I didn't do half as well as I should, I didn't study hard enough. I kept asking myself, why I couldn't be as good as my other classmates were. Then I found out that they took more time out to study than I did. I can't say that I'm dumber than they or anything, it's just they exerted more effort to do better in our exams. I read in a magazine an advertisement which said, " no pains, no gains ". Though the words may have been worn out already through repeated use, it still holds a lot of truths for us students. This is why the words, " no pains, no gains " will be my motto from now on.

十二月二十八日　星期三　晴

不勞則無穫

　　我又像以往一樣地度過了今天。一樣的例行公事，一樣的學校、家庭、讀書、睡覺。今天我對我的考試成績感到挫折，因為我考得比想像中還低，雖然我及格了。吃午餐時，我有點消沈，我的朋友莉莎看到了，問我是不是發生了什麼事。我說我只是對考試成績有些失望罷了。她企圖使我高興起來，並說它沒那麼嚴重。很高興我有像她那樣的朋友，在和她一陣嬉笑打趣之後，我覺得好多了。

　　我確實地明白為什麼我沒有做到我應該做到的一半好。我不夠努力用功。我不斷質問自己，為什麼我不能像其他同學一樣好？然後我發現他們都比我花更多的時間唸書。我不能說我比他們笨或諸如此類的，只是他們用較多的努力，以求取更好的考試成績。我在雜誌上讀到一則廣告，寫著：「不勞則無穫。」雖然這已是老生常談，對我們學生而言，仍然是真理。這就是為什麼這句「不勞則無穫。」從現在起就是我的座右銘了。

**─────────────────────────────

routine〔ruˊtin〕*n.* 例行公事　　exert〔ɪgˊzɝt〕*v.* 施行
motto〔ˊmɑto〕*n.* 座右銘

《表示挫折的常用語》

♠ My trouble is that I get frustrated much too easily.
　我的毛病就是我很容易感到挫敗。

♡ I admit my defeat. 我承認敗北。

♡ Gambling was his ruin. 他因賭博而落得身敗名裂。

♡ Our holidays were spoiled by bad weather.
　我們假期的樂趣被惡劣的天氣所破壞。

Fri., Dec. 30   *Fine later cloudy*

Traffic regulations

On my way home today, I witnessed a traffic accident. A fast moving car collided with a truck. Because it occured in the intersection, there was a traffic jam. There were a lot of people who gathered around the crashed car. Soon the police came and cleared everyone away.

Later in the evening, I saw the accident reported on the television news. It said that four passengers were injured and the drivers of both the car and the truck died.

I thought that the accident was really stupid. If the car had not speeded up in order to get through the yellow light the accident would never have happened. Even if the driver had gotten through he would probably have saved only a few minutes of his time. What's a few minutes to your life? The man should have thought ahead then nothing like this would have happened.

The state of traffic here in Taipei is really bad. People often disregard the traffic rules and regulations, pedestrians and drivers alike. Now if everyone just followed these rules and regulations then everyone would be safer and everything would be more orderly.

十二月三十日　星期五　晴時多雲

交通規則

今天回家途中，我目睹一場車禍，一輛開得很快的汽車撞上一部卡車。因為事故發生在十字路口上，所以發生交通堵塞。有許多人聚在撞壞的車周圍，警察很快就來把他們驅走。

傍晚時，我看到電視新聞報導了這場車禍，據說有四名乘客受傷，而汽車和卡車的司機都死了。

我認為這場車禍真是很愚蠢。如果汽車不為了闖黃燈而超速，這場車禍就不會發生，即使司機通過了，他也可能只省了幾分鐘。就生命而言，幾分鐘算什麼？這個人應該預先想到，那麼，像這樣的事就不會發生了。

台北的交通狀況實在很差，人們常常忽視交通規則；行人和駕駛都一樣。如果每個人都遵守這些規則，那麼每個人會更安全，一切會更有秩序。

---

intersection〔͵ɪntəˈsɛkʃən〕*n*. 交叉點　　*clear away* 清除
pedestrian〔pəˈdɛstrɪən〕*n*. 行人

《表示混亂的常用語》

♤ There was confusion in the street after the accident.
　　意外發生後街上很混亂。

♤ Much of the information he gives is muddled.
　　他所給的消息都亂七八糟。

♤ The teacher always mixed me up with another student with the same name.
　　老師老是把我和另一位同名的學生搞混。

MONTH

January

Fri., Jan. 1　Fine

The New Year

Today is the first day of 1994. People all over the world are celebrating the new year. Many people spend their New Year's vacation traveling, shopping and so on.

But we should remember that there are still a lot of people elsewhere such as in Africa who are suffering from hunger and illness. To them a New Year means nothing. I don't think that they even know that today is the beginning of a new year. Anyway we who are enjoying a good life should remember these people and try to help them.

Although I am not suffering right now, I should not spend my vacation playing. This is because I have to study hard during the vacation in order to prepare for the coming entrance examination. So I'll just dig into my books right now and I'll think of having fun during the summer vacation.

一月一日　星期五　星期五　晴

元　旦

　　今天是一九九四年的頭一天，全世界的人都在慶祝新年。許多人利用旅遊、購物等等度過新年假期。

　　但是我們應該記得，其他地方還有很多人，例如在非洲的人，正在受飢餓及疾病的煎熬。對他們來說，新年毫無意義，我想他們甚至不知道今天是新年。無論如何，我們這些過著好日子的人應該記得那些人，並且試著幫助他們。

　　雖然我現在並沒有受苦，我還是不該把假期浪費在玩樂上，因為我必須在假期中用功讀書準備即將來臨的大學聯考。所以我現在只要努力讀書，等暑假的時候再來想玩樂。

** ———————————————————————

　　dig into 努力於

Sun., Jan. 3　Fine

MTV Center

I spent all day with Cindy at MTV. We watched so many movies that I was falling asleep. Cindy wanted to watch more but I wanted to get out and breath some fresh air. After being cooped up in that little room for seven hours I was beginning to loose my mind.

一月三日　星期日　晴

去看MTV

　　我和辛蒂花了一天的時間待在MTV中心。我們看了太多的電影以致於我都睡著了。辛蒂還想再看，但我想出去呼吸些新鮮空氣。關在那種小房間中達七小時之後，我已開始迷迷糊糊了。

Mon., Jan. 4 *Fine later cloudy*

An English diary

My English diary has only ten pages left. In the afternoon went to the bookshop near the station to buy a new English diary for this year. There were still lots of beautiful Christmas and New Year's cards.

一月四日　星期一　晴時多雲

英文日記

我的英文日記本只剩十頁了。下午我便跑到火車站附近的書店去買今年要用的新日記本。那裏仍然還有許多美麗的耶誕卡片及賀年卡。

**————————————————————

left〔lɛft〕*v.* pt. & pp. of leave 剩餘；留下
bookshop〔'bʊkˌʃɑp〕*n.* 書店

Wed., Jan. 6 *Cloudy later rainy*

Desire for the first snow

I wonder what snow is like. I wish we could have a snowstorm in Taipei this winter. I want to go out and have snowball fights and build snowmen. But it will never snow in Taipei, it only rains.

一月六日　星期三　多雲轉雨

渴望初雪

我一直想知道雪是什麼樣子。我希望今年冬天台北會有一場大風雪。我想出去打雪仗和堆雪人。但是台北從不下雪，只會下雨。

**————————————————————

wonder〔'wʌndɚ〕*v.* 想知道　　snowstorm〔'snoˌstɔrm〕*n.* 大風雪
snowman〔'snomæn〕*n.* 雪人（用雪堆成的人形）

Thurs., Jan. 7　*Very fine*

A sunny day

I got up early today to watch the sunrise. While I waited for the sun to rise, I sat beside my window and thought of my future. Soon I will be a grown man and I won't be a baby anymore. Maybe I'll be going to college if I pass the college entrance examination. I didn't want to think of not passing this important examination for my parents are counting on me to do so.

Anyway, if I don't pass this one I should try again next year. I thought about my parents too. They have worked so hard to give us children a good life. Now, they are getting older little by little. There are more grey hairs now in mother's hair. As for my father, he's beginning to have a hard time to read the newspaper. He uses a pair of glasses now. All these thoughts touch me and tell me that time is indeed swiftly passing by.

The sun was coming out of the horizon. First it was just a ray of light. But little by little the whole circle started coming into view. The sky was a bright orange with a blue haze surrounding the emptiness. Soon I could feel the warmth of the sun as its rays passed through my window pane. The view was really beautiful, more beautiful than any picture I had ever seen. In a few minutes everyone was awake and everyone went on their own way with their lives. Another day had started and it was another beginning for all of us.

一月七日　星期四　大晴

陽光的日子

　　我今天早起想看日出。等太陽升起的時候，我坐在窗戶旁邊，思考著未來。不久我就是個大人了，不再是小嬰孩了。如果我通過聯考，也許我會上大學，我不願想像我沒有通過這重要的考試的情況，因爲爸媽指望我金榜題名。

　　無論如何，假如我沒考上，我明年會再重考。我也考慮到爸媽。他們辛苦工作，爲了要給我們過好的生活。現在，他們逐漸老了，媽媽的頭上出現了更多的白頭髮。至於爸爸，他看報紙變得很吃力，需要戴眼鏡。所有這些想法都感染了我，告訴我時光的確匆匆飛逝。

　　太陽已經升出水平面了，首先是一道光。但漸漸地整個圓形就出現在眼前。天空呈現明亮的橘色，空的部分則鑲著藍色。當太陽光穿過我的窗玻璃時，我很快地就感覺到陽光的溫暖。這眞是我曾經看過最美麗的景色了。過不久，每個人都醒來，繼續他們的生活方式。一天又開始了，對我們大家而言，又是一個起點。

**

count on 期望；信賴　　　view〔vju〕 *n.* 景色
circle〔'sɝkl〕 *n.* 圓　　　pane〔pen〕 *n.* 窗玻璃

《 表示日出的常用語 》

♠ The sunrise was a wonderful scene.
　日出是很美的景象。

♤ Don't stand in the sunshine. 不要站在陽光下。

♠ The sunrise is beautiful beyond description.
　這日出美得無法形容。

♤ I have never seen such a fine view as this.
　我從未見過如此美的景色。

Fri., Jan. 8 *Fine*

Byron's poetical works

On my way home from school, dropped in at a second-hand book-store, and bought Byron's poetical works with a lot of beautiful illustrations. The book was rather difficult for me, but it was a recent lucky find.

一月八日　星期五　晴

拜倫的詩

我放學回家的路上，跑到一家舊書店，買了拜倫的詩集，裏面還有許多美麗的插圖。這本書對我而言相當困難，但它是近來一個幸運的發現。

❋❋ ───────────────────────

drop in 不期而至；過訪　poetical〔po'ɛtɪk!〕*adj.* = poetic　詩人的
illustration〔ɪ,lʌs'treʃən〕*n.* 插圖；圖解；舉例

Sat., Jan. 9 *Fine*

Depression

Owing to the slowness of business, high-priced goods are not much in demad for year-end presents. Various stores in the city have made themselves attractive with the lottery sale, but they have few customers.

一月九日　星期六　晴

不　景　氣

由於商業的蕭條，顧客並不太需要高價位的商品作爲年終禮物。於是各個城市不同的商店都使出渾身解數，以中獎特賣來吸引顧客，但生意仍然清淡。

❋❋ ───────────────────────

dullness〔'dʌlnɪs〕*n.* 不景氣　　attractive〔ə'træktɪv〕*adj.* 動人的

Sun., Jan. 10　Fine

Climbing Mt. Hohuan

A letter came from my friend who climbed Mt. Hohuan. It ran as follows : — "We have just come to the 8th station. It is very cold here because of a severe snowstorm. It is rather foolish to complain of the heat, staying in Taipei. The whole place was mantled in a street of white snow. Dogs and children were playfully romping in the snow, but persons in high clogs were very much troubled as the snow got in between the supporters of their clogs."

一月十日　星期日　晴

銀色世界

我一個去爬合歡山的朋友來信了。內容如下:「我們才剛到達第八站,這裡由於暴風雪的緣故,所以非常寒冷。留在台北,抱怨著天氣熱真是很愚昧的事情。整塊地方都被一街的白雪所覆蓋,狗兒和小孩子在雪裏嬉鬧玩樂,但是穿著高木屐的人可麻煩了,因為雪總是掉進木屐的鞋跟之間。」

**

as follows 如下

station〔'steʃən〕 *n.* 車站;營所;根據地

severe〔sə'vɪr〕 *adj.* 劇烈的;酷烈的　clog〔klɑg, klɔg〕 *n.* 木屐

supporter〔sə'portə, -'pɔr-〕 *n.* 支柱;支持者

Mon., Jan. 11　*Fine*

A chance to meet a strange man

While I was waiting at the bus stop this morning, I saw a man in ragged clothes walking aimlessly in the streets. I thought to myself this man must be really sick. But I didn't give much thought about it after that.

While I was looking out to see if my bus had arrived, I sensed that there was someone looking at me. When I turned my head it was that strange man who wore ragged clothes. I tried to move away without causing any commotion but the man kept on following me and staring at me in a strange way.

Finally I decided to run. I caught the first bus I could reach and got inside. Before the man could get into the bus, luckily, the bus was already moving. On the bus I was catching my breath from the scare I had. At the next bus stop, I changed buses.

This evening, I told my mother about my peculiar experience. I told her how upset I was about the incident. What made it worse was that she did nothing but laugh at my story. She thought it was funny. After that I laughed, too. Boy, I hope I'll never have to meet another man like that again.

一月十一日　星期一　晴

碰見陌生人

今天早晨在車站等車時，我看到一個穿著破舊衣服的人漫無目的地在街上走著。我心裏想這個人一定是生病了，之後卻沒有再多想這件事。

當我向外看車子來了沒時，我察覺到有人在看我。我轉頭，發現是那位穿著破舊衣服的陌生人。我試著不引起騷動而移開，但是這個人一直跟著我，並用奇怪的眼光盯著我。

最後我決定跑掉，我搭上我能趕上的第一班公車，跑了進去。很幸運地，公車在這個人進來前起動了。在車上我鬆了一口氣，不再害怕。我在下一站換了公車。

傍晚，我告訴媽媽我的奇遇，我告訴她我為這件事有多麼困擾。更糟的是她只是笑，她認為那很有趣，之後我也跟著她一起笑。天啊！希望我永遠不要再遇到這樣的人。

**

sense〔sɛns〕 *v.* 覺得；感知　　commotion〔kə'moʃən〕 *n.* 騷動
catch one's breath 鬆了一口氣

《表示陌生的常用語》

♤ He heard a strange voice in the next room.
　　他聽到鄰室有一個陌生的講話聲音。

♠ The city was strange to me.
　　那都市對我來說是陌生的。

♠ That face is unfamiliar to me.
　　那個面孔我以前不常見過。

Wed., Jan. 13 Fine

The death of a president

Today, my uncle came back from the United States. In order to welcome him, my father and I took him to see a movie. The movie was about the assassination of President Kennedy. After we arrived home, my uncle told me what he was doing when he heard that President Kennedy had been killed. He was sitting in class when somebody came in to say that the president had been shot. At first, people didn't believe it, but then, when they realized it was true, many people were in shock ; some cried. The whole country came to a stop to watch the news.

For Americans over 40 years old, this was a day they can never forget. Ask anyone and they can tell you what they felt when they heard the news. People were especially sad because the President was so young with a young family that would not now have a father. He won the election because he seemed able to express people's feelings for the future. When he died, many people no longer felt confident about the future of the country. Even today, Americans cannot forget the president they lost.

一月十三日　星期三　晴

甘迺迪總統之死

今天，我叔叔從美國回來。為了歡迎他，爸爸和我帶他去看了一場電影。這部電影是有關甘迺迪總統被暗殺的事。回家後，叔叔告訴我當甘迺迪總統遇刺時，他正在做什麼。當時，他正坐在課堂上，而有人進來說總統被射殺了。起初，人們都無法相信，但後來大家了解這是真的以後，許多人都感到震驚，有些人哭了。全國人們都停下來看這條新聞。

對四十歲以上的美國人來說，這是永難忘懷的一天。隨便問一個人，他都會告訴你，當他聽到這項消息時的感覺。尤其令人傷心的，是這位總統那麼年輕，現在，他的幼小孩子將永遠失去父親，他贏得選舉，是因為他似乎能表達人們對未來的感受。他死了，人們不再對這個國家的未來抱著信心。甚至今天，美國人仍無法忘記他們失去的總統。

---

assassination〔əˈsæsn̩ˈeʃən〕 n. 暗殺

《 有關死亡的常用語 》

♤ It shocked me very much to learn of your father's death.
得知你父親去世，我很震驚。

♤ I'm speechless with shock and sorrow.
我震驚、難過得說不出話。

♤ I was deeply grieved to learn of the bad news.
聽到這個壞消息，我十分難過。

♤ My heart bled when I heard of the sudden passing of our English teacher.
得知我們的英文老師遽逝，我心裏很難過。

Fri ., ***Jan.*** *15* ***Cloudy***

Women's smoking

The smoking habit seems to be getting more popular among young women nowadays. According to a certain doctor, smoking has an injurious effect upon women from a physiological point of view.

一月十五日　星期五　多雲

女性吸煙問題

吸煙的習慣現在在女性之間似乎愈來愈普遍了。據某醫生說，以生理學的觀點來看，抽煙對女性有不良的後果。

＊＊────────────────

injurious〔ɪn'dʒʊrɪəs〕*adj.* 有害的；不公平的
effect〔ə'fɛkt〕*n.* 結果；影響
physiological〔ˌfɪzɪə'lɑdʒɪkl〕*adj.* 生理學的；生理的

Sun., ***Jan.*** *17* ***Fine***

Sleep

As it was Sunday and moreover rainy today, I overslept till 10 o'clock in the morning. It was very hard to get up in the cold morning. Someone said "Sleep is an important element of health." This is quite true.

一月十七日　星期日　晴

睡　眠

因爲今天是禮拜天，更因爲今天是雨天，所以早上我睡過頭了。一直到十點鐘才起牀。在寒冷的早晨起牀是件相當艱鉅的事情。有人說：「睡眠是健康的要素。」眞是沒錯。

＊＊────────────────

oversleep〔'ovɚ'slip〕*v.* 睡過（某一時刻）；睡眠過久

Mon., *Jan*. *18* *Rainy*

Trains

I went to bring my sister to the train station. I wish I could've joined her on the train. I prefer train travel over any other type. The best part is looking out the window in the middle of the night when everybody else is asleep. It's the best time to imagine that ghosts and spirits really do exist in the world.

一月十八日　星期一　雨

火　車

我去帶妹妹到火車站。我希望我能一起去，我喜歡火車旅行勝過任何其它型式的旅行。最棒的是當夜深人靜其他人都入睡時，從窗外望出去，這是想像鬼靈的確存在這個世界的最佳時刻。

＊＊────────────────

type〔taɪp〕 *n.* 型式　　spirit〔'spɪrɪt〕 *n.* 幽靈

Tues., *Jan*. *19* *Clear*

Skating

According to the letter from my friend in Keelung province, skating is now in full swing in skating rinks there. It must be awfully pleasant to slide on the ice frozen all over the lake to one's heart's content. But it's an impossible scene in Taiwan.

一月十九日　星期二　晴

溜　冰

我在基隆的朋友來信說，那兒的溜冰場正盛行溜冰這項活動。在整條結了冰的河上盡情滑行一定十分快樂。然而，在台灣，這是不可能見到的景象。

＊＊────────────────

province〔'prɑvɪns〕 *n.* 省　　slide〔slaɪd〕 *v.* 滑動；溜過

Fri., Jan. 22   Fine

The meaning of life

This morning I didn't feel like going to school. This is because I was already tired of my life at school. The days seemed to be dragging on longer and longer with each passing day. Therefore I tried to pretend that I was sick in order that I wouldn't have to go to school but I failed. The reason was because I am not a good liar. So, off I went to school.

On my way to school, I tried singing a song to make myself feel happier. To my surprise, I suddenly realized the joy of living doesn't come from what we search for in life but comes from what we put into life. The moment I realized this, the sky seemed to be brighter than ever. With this frame of mind, I was able to carry on my day.

一月二十二日　星期五　晴

生活的意義

今早我不想到學校去，因為我已經厭倦學校的生活了。一天天過去，日子似乎愈來愈長，因此，我試著去假裝我生病了，以便不用上學，然而我失敗了。因為我不是一個在行的說謊者，所以，我還是去了。

在上學途中，我試著唱歌來使自己快樂一點，令我吃驚的是，我突然領悟到生活的喜悅並不來自我們從生活中得到什麼，而是來自我們過著什麼樣的生活。我一了解了這些，天空似乎也比從前明亮多了。帶著這樣的心情，我能繼續過我的日子。

Wed., Jan. 27 *Fine later rainy*

Staying up

I stayed up again last night. Last night was different though from the other nights when I stayed up. Instead of studying the whole night through ,last night I had a slumber party with my friends,Michelle, Jennifer and Amy. We talked about a lot of things. We talked about our favorite movie idols and the boys we had a crush on. James Dean is our favorite movie idol. We collect everything which has his picture on it. I showed my collection of James Dean to the other girls and I could see they were very jealous of what I had. We also ate a lot of potato chips and drank a lot of Coke. All of us hardly got any sleep.

When we were able to sleep at last, it was already five in the morning. When we got up at seven, the radio was still on. After having some breakfast,the girls left. Now, I have a throbbing headache, though I slept the whole afternoon. It's time to hit the books. Tomorrow will be another school day again.

一月二十七日　星期三　晴後轉雨

熬　夜

我昨天晚上又熬夜了。然而昨晚的熬夜和以前的熬夜都不同。我不是整晚唸書,而是和朋友們,蜜筱、珍妮佛和艾咪膩了一晚上。我們聊了許多事情。談著心目中最喜愛的電影偶像以及我們所迷戀的男孩子們。詹姆斯狄恩是我們最崇拜的電影明星,我們收集一切上面有他照片的東西,我把我收集的拿給其他的女孩看,就能感到她們都非常嫉妒我有這些東西。我們也吃了不少洋芋片和喝了許多可樂。大家都幾乎沒有闔眼。

當我們終於可以上牀睡覺的時候,已經是凌晨五點鐘了。我們七點醒來時,收音機還在響著。吃了一些早餐,女孩們都走了。現在,我的頭痛得不得了,雖然我睡了一下午。現在是摸書的時候了。明天又要上學。

---

have a slumber party　小女生們的聚會,在其中一人的家中聊天、玩樂,然後睡覺。

idol〔'aɪdl̩〕*n.* 偶像　　have a crush on　迷戀

potato chip　馬鈴薯片　　throbbing〔'θrɑbɪŋ〕*adj.* 悸動的

hit〔hɪt〕*v.* 碰撞

《有關娛樂的常用語》

♤ I read novels for amusement. 我以看小說爲樂。

♤ Pingpong is a good recreation. 乒乓球是一種好的娛樂。

♤ I went to the movie theater. 我到電影院去。

♤ We sang the song in chorus.
　我們合唱這首歌。

Today is the only time we can possibly live. Let's not turn it into a physical and mental hell by aimless worry about the future. Let's also stop fretting over the blunders we made yesterday.

— *Carnegie*

今天是唯一我們能眞正生存的時刻。我們不要因爲對未來盲目的擔憂，而把今天變成是一種身體與精神上的煉獄。讓我們也停止爲昨天所犯的過失煩躁。

3

LIFE SERIES

生活環境

Unit 1

The Nature 大自然篇

Thurs., May 5　Very sunny

A strawberry

At the fruit shop, strawberries as red as rubies were on show and they attracted the attention of the passers-by, but the price was so exorbitant that nobody could buy them.

五月五日　星期四　陽光普照

草　莓

在水果商店裏，正展示著紅得如紅寶石般的草莓，吸引了行人的注意力，但是價錢太貴了，以致於沒有人會買。

＊＊

ruby 〔'rubɪ〕 *n.* 紅寶石
passer-by 〔'pæsɚ'baɪ, 'pɑs-〕 *n.* 行人
exorbitant 〔ɪg'zɔrbətənt, ɛg-〕 *adj.* 過分的；過度的

Mon., May 16　Cloudy

The wisteria flower

As our mathematics teacher was absent, we had no lesson in the afternoon. Went to the New Rark. The wisteria flowers were at their best and they were very beautiful. An old couple was taking their lunch under the wistaria-trellis.

五月十六日　星期一　陰

紫 藤 花

由於數學老師沒來，我們下午沒課。到新公園去，紫藤花正盛
開而且非常漂亮。一對老夫婦在紫藤棚下吃午餐。

**

wistaria〔wɪsˈtɛrɪə〕*n.* 紫藤　　trellis〔ˈtrɛlɪs〕*n.* 格子架；格子棚

Sun., Oct. 23　Fine

The chrysanthemum flowers

The chrysanthemums, yellow and white, out in the garden
have all blossomed beautifully. When I opened the screen door,
a good smell assailed my nostrils. There are various kinds
of chrysanthemums but the yellow and white chrysanthemums
are the best of all so far as nobleness is concerned.

十月廿三日　星期日　晴

菊　花

外面花園的菊花，黃色的和白色的，全都綻開了美麗的花朵。
一打開紗門，一股清香就撲鼻而來。菊花有千百種，但就高貴而言，
黃菊和白菊是其中的佼佼者。

**

chrysanthemum〔krɪsˈænθəməm〕*n.* 菊；菊花
blossom〔ˈblɑsəm〕*v.* 開花
assail〔əˈsel〕*v.* 攻擊；被（某種感情）所困擾
nostril〔ˈnɑstrəl〕*n.* 鼻孔
so far as … be concerned 至於…；就…而論

Tues., Jul. 26 *Rainy*

A rainy day

It was a rainy day. I like the smell of rain and the feeling it brings to me. I seem happiest when it rains. Rain is a refreshing thing. It clears away the dirt that is around us and makes everything seem like new. The leaves in the trees, the grass on the ground are greener too after a brief rainshower. The flowers seem brighter too after the rain. As today is a summer day, the rain is a real welcome sight. I hate it when it is hot, but when the rain comes as today, I feel cool and my mood is lighter.

What did I do the whole day? Naturally I just stayed at home. I was able to catch up with my reading today. In the afternoon, Joan came over and we had a chat. We also watched a movie on the video machine. The title of the movie was: "Sleepless Seattle". It was a touching and moving film about love. That reminds me, when will I ever fall in love? The scenes looked so romantic but who'd ever fall in love with me? Well, until I do, I'll just keep on dreaming.

七月二十六日　星期二　雨

雨　天

　　今天是雨天。我喜歡雨的氣息及它帶給我的感覺。我似乎在下雨時覺得特別快樂，雨能使人精神振奮。它清除了我們周遭的灰塵，使每樣東西看來像新的一般。一場短暫的陣雨過後，樹上的葉子和地上的青草也會變得較綠些。花兒似乎也明亮多了，因為在夏季的今天，雨是最受歡迎的了。我討厭熱，但像今天這樣地下雨時，我會覺得涼爽，而且心情會愉快些。

　　我這一整天做了什麼事？自然，我是待在家裏嘍。今天我可以跟得上我自己唸書的進度。下午，瓊來找我聊天。我們還看了一部錄影帶。片子名稱是：「西雅圖夜未眠」。這是一部關於愛情的感人影片。它使我想到，不曉得什麼時候我才會談戀愛？電影的情節如此地浪漫，可是，誰將與我談戀愛呢？唉，除非我真的戀愛了，不然我只有繼續夢想。

**———————————————————————

refreshing 〔rɪ'frɛʃɪŋ〕 *adj.* 令人精神爽快的；提神的　　*clear away* 清除；消散
rainshower 〔'ren,ʃauɚ〕 *n.* 陣雨　　*catch up with* 趕上；追及
chat 〔tʃæt〕 *n.* 閒談　*come over* 訪問　video 〔'vɪdɪ,o〕 *n.* 電視
romantic 〔ro'mæntɪk〕 *adj.* 浪漫的；有浪漫思想的

《表示雨天的常用語》

♤ It is threatening to rain. 很可能會下雨。

♤ It stopped raining. 雨停了。

♤ The rainy season has set in. 雨季開始了。

♤ I got wet in the rain. 我被雨淋濕了。

♤ It looks like rain. 好像要下雨的樣子

Mon., Jun. 20　Fine

The yellow rose

I gave Betty a basket of yellow roses. She wanted to know the meaning behind the color yellow. I told her there's no special meaning and that it's only because the florist had no red roses left. " In that case, " she asked " why couldn't you try another florist? " Some people are so hard to please.

六月二十日　星期一　晴

黃 玫 瑰

我送給貝蒂一籃黃玫瑰。她想要知道隱藏在黃顏色之後的意義。我告訴她沒有什麼特別的意義，而只是因為花店沒有紅玫瑰的緣故。「如果是這樣，」她問，「為什麼你不試試別家花店？」有的人就是如此難以取悅。

**───────────────

florist〔'florɪst,'flɔr-,'flɑr-〕*n.* 花店
in that case 假使那樣
hard to please 難以取悅

Fri., Sept. 9　Rainy

The begonia flower

It rained softly but incessantly from morning. The sound of the autumn rain falling through the rainpipes was heard constantly. The begonia flowers in the garden were beaten by the autumn rain and fell off.

九月九日　星期五　雨

秋 海 棠 花

從早晨開始天空就不斷地飄著細雨。一直聽著秋雨由排水管滑
落的聲音。園裏的秋海棠被雨淋打而墜落。

＊＊─────────────────

incessantly〔ɪnˈsɛsntlɪ〕*adv.* 不斷地
rainpipe〔ˈrenˌpaɪp〕*n.* 排水管　　begonia〔bɪˈgonjə〕*n.* 秋海棠

Sat., Sept. 10　Fine

The tone of insects

As it was pretty cool at night, read a book by the lamp
light. Outside, the sad tone of insects that gathered in the
bush made us feel the solitude of the autumn night.

九月十日　星期六　晴

蟲　　鳴

由於夜間天氣非常涼爽，我在燈下閱讀。而外面，聚在樹叢中
的蟲，鳴聲悲切，使我們感覺到秋夜的孤寂。

＊＊─────────────────

tone〔ton〕*n.* 聲音
solitude〔ˈsɑləˌtjud〕*n.* 孤獨；孤寂

Wed., Jul. 27　Fine later cloudy

Sea-gulls

The roar of waves dashing on the beach was heard distinctly.
The sea was blue and calm, and the mountains in all directions
were clearly seen. Two or three white sails like sea-gulls in
the offing made a picturesque view.

七月廿七日　星期三　晴後多雲

海　鷗

清楚地聽到海浪拍打在岸上的咆哮聲。海水藍而平靜，四面的山都看得很清楚。二三點白帆像在不遠處的海鷗一樣，構成一幅如畫的景觀。

**

sea-gull〔'si,gʌl〕*n.* 海鷗（= *sea gull*）　　roar〔ror〕*v.,n.* 怒號
dash〔dæʃ〕*v.* 濺；撞　　distinctly〔dɪ'stɪŋktlɪ〕*adv.* 清楚地
in the offing 在不遠處　　picturesque〔,pɪktʃə'rɛsk〕*adj.* 如畫的

Fri., Jun. 17 　Rainy

A snail

The rain has kept falling for a week. Everything has become damp and musty. Even our bodies feel damp. A snail was creeping on the wall of the gloomy kitchen.

六月十七日　星期五　雨

蝸　牛

雨持續下了一個星期，每樣東西都變得潮濕發霉。連我們的身體都覺得潮濕。我看見一隻蝸牛正在陰暗的厨房牆上爬著。

**

plenty〔'plɛntɪ〕*n.* 充分；多
musty〔'mʌstɪ〕*adj.* 發霉的　　gloomy〔'glumɪ〕*adj.* 幽暗的

Sun., Jun. 5　Rainy later cloudy

An eclipse of the moon

As I read in the morning paper that there would be an eclipse of the moon tonight, waited for night with delight. To my disappointment, it began to rain toward the evening. The astronomers will be exceedingly dejected.

六月五日　星期日　雨後陰

月　蝕

由於在早報上看到今晚會有月蝕，我欣喜地等待夜晚的來臨。令人失望的是，接近傍晚時，天開始下雨了。天文學家將大爲沮喪。

**

eclipse〔ɪˈklɪps〕*n.* 蝕　　astronomer〔əˈstrɑnəmɚ〕*n.* 天文家
exceedingly〔ɪkˈsidɪŋlɪ〕*adv.* 過度地；非常地
dejected〔dɪˈdʒɛktɪd〕*adj.* 失望的

Sat., Jun. 11　Rainy

A fire-fly

In the evening, when the rain cleared for a while, took a walk in Youth Park,　and caught a fire-fly, so wrapped it in a sheet of paper.　The green light could be seen through the paper.　It is a pity that there is no place noted for the fire-fly and other insects in Taipei

六月十一日　星期六　雨

螢　火　蟲

傍晚，雨已停了一會兒了，我在青年公園散步，捉到一隻螢火蟲，於是將它包在一張紙裏面。透過紙張，螢火蟲的綠光仍隱約可見，在台北，沒有地方以螢火蟲或者其它昆蟲而聞名眞是一大憾事。

**

wrap〔ræp〕*v.* 包；捲；纒
a sheet of paper 一張紙　　pity〔ˈpɪtɪ〕*n.* 憾事；可惜之事
noted〔ˈnotɪd〕*adj.* 著名的；顯著的　　*be noted for* 以⋯著名
insect〔ˈɪnsɛkt〕*n.* 昆蟲

Mon., Jul.4 *Rainy later fine*

Rainbow

There was a beautiful rainbow this morning. It appeared like a bridge to heaven. I wonder why God created rainbows. There always seems to be a rainbow after a violent thunderstorm.

Is the rainbow a message from God? Is He trying to tell us that if we persevere in the worst of times that a rainbow will await us? I wonder.

七月四日　星期一　雨後晴朗

彩　虹

今天早晨有一道美麗的彩虹。彩虹像通到天國的橋樑。我很好奇，上帝爲什麼創造彩虹。在强烈的雷雨後，似乎總會有彩虹出現。

彩虹是上帝給予的啓示嗎？祂是不是想告訴我們，如果我能在逆境中堅忍，彩虹將等待我們？我很想知道。

---

thunder storm 雷雨　　persevere〔͵pɝsə'vɪr〕*v*. 堅忍

Mon., *Feb.* *1* *Fair*

Morning Voices

Whenever I wake up in the fine, fresh morning, I like to lean my body out of the window, in order to breathe deeply the cool, fragrant air. I also like to lend my ears to the merry birds who sing ever so cheerfully.

There are many different kinds of morning voices. All are joyful. Now listen, the birds are jumping in the green pasture. And the dogs bark, the cats mew welcoming the rising sun.

All these early morning voices are pleasant to hear. I consider myself a lucky girl to live in the suburbs and am able to enjoy these lovely sounds.

二月一日　　星期一　　晴

早晨的聲音

每當我在美好、清新的晨間醒來，我就喜歡將身子靠向窗外，以深深呼進涼爽，芬芳的空氣。我也喜歡傾聽愉快的鳥兒，總是在歡樂地唱著。

早晨的聲音有很多種，全都是令人喜悅的，現在聽吧，鳥兒在青草地上跳躍。小狗汪汪叫，小貓咪咪叫，都在歡迎著上升的太陽。

所有這些早晨的聲音真悅耳，我想我是個頗為幸運的女孩子，住在郊區，能夠享受到這些可愛的聲音。

Sun., *Apr.* *24* *Fine*

The Pacific Ocean

Last week my father promised to take us to the beach one of these days. Today, he fulfilled his promise. We set out early in the morning. Our destination: Keelung. I've always been to the beach. My fondest childhood memories were those that were spent at the beach. Upon reaching Keelung, we saw many ships anchored at its harbor. When I gazed out to the open sea, I could see the edge of the sea meeting the edge of the sky. It was a fantastic feeling. The blue waters of the Pacific are really truly beautiful. I could sense serenity all around me. I'll never forget this day in my life.

四月二十四日　星期日　晴

太 平 洋

上星期爸爸答應我們這幾天找一天要帶我們到海邊玩，今天他履行了這個承諾。我們一大清早出發，目的地是基隆。我常常到海邊，童年的回憶中我最喜歡的就是那些在海邊渡過的日子。一到基隆，我們就看到許多船停泊在港口。向遼濶的大海望去時，我可以看到海之涯與天之際相會合，這是一種奇異的感覺。太平洋湛藍的海水眞是漂亮極了。我可以感覺到周遭的寧靜。我一輩子都不會忘記這一天。

** anchor 〔'æŋkɚ〕 *v*. 泊船；拋錨
　　serenity 〔sə'rɛnətɪ〕 *n*. 寧靜

Sun., May 15　Clear

The magic shell

　　I found a magic shell on the beach. Whenever I hold it to my ear I can hear the wind and waves of the seashore. I bet I have the only magic shell in the whole world.

　　My big brother says my shell is not magic. He says the sounds are caused by the conical structure of the shell and that every shell like it will produce the same effect. I hate my brother. He always tries to spoil everything.

五月十五日　星期日　晴

奇妙的貝殼

　　我在海邊發現一個奇妙的貝殼。每當我把它靠近耳畔，我就能聽到風嘯以及來自海邊的浪濤聲。我打賭我有全世界獨一無二的奇妙貝殼。

　　大哥說我的貝殼並不奇妙。他說聲音是由貝殼的圓錐形構造所形成的，每個像這樣的貝殼都會產生同樣的效果。我討厭哥哥，他總是企圖破壞一切。

---

conical〔'kɑnɪkl〕*adj.* 圓錐的
spoil〔spɔɪl〕*v.* 破壞

Sun., Sept. 25　　*Fine*

Nature

I went to the park today. It was a lovely day. I had a chance to be with " nature " once more. I stayed in the park for at least four hours today. I watched the carps in the pond and fed them some bread that I had brought with me. How I wish I could sometimes be a fish. In their underwater world, everything is peaceful. Away from all the noise and troubles of the world, they glide gracefully in the water at an unhurried pace. After I finished feeding the fish, I took a walk under the shade of the trees. I could hear birds chirping all around me. Occasionally, I'd see a butterfly flutter past me. Here with nature's creation, I could find rest.

Later in the day, I just sat on a bench to enjoy the scenery around me and think of some pleasant thoughts about the past week. I noticed that the flowers were all blooming. I watched the sky too, where the fluffy white clouds drifted by. There couldn't have been a better day to be out here in the park. Later on, I heard some children playing in the distance. Their laughter reminded me of my own days when I was younger. Back then, my parents would bring me and my brother to the park to take time out from our busy schedules. When I went back home, I was fully recharged and ready to face the task that lay before me. This was how the day went.

九月二十五日　星期日　晴

大自然

　　我今天到公園去。天氣很好。因此我又有機會與大自然再度共處。今天我至少在公園裏待了四個小時。我觀賞池裏的鯉魚並用我帶來的一些麵包餵牠們。眞希望我有時候可以變成一條魚，在牠們的水底世界裏，一切都很平靜。牠們遠離塵世的喧囂及紛擾，在水中悠游自如。餵完魚後，我在樹蔭下散步。我可以聽到小鳥兒在我四周啁啾。有時候，還可以見到蝴蝶翩翩飛過。在此與自然界的萬物共處，我可以找到寧靜。

　　稍晚，我就只是坐在長凳子上享受四周的景色並想想上星期發生的一些愉快的事。我注意到花兒都盛開了。我也觀看天空，柔軟的白雲從中飄過。這種日子到公園去再好不過了。後來，我聽到一些小孩在遠處玩耍，他們的笑聲使我回憶起自己年幼的日子。那時候，父母會帶我和哥哥到公園去忙裏偷閒一下。回家後，我覺得又徹底地充電了，於是準備去面對堆積在眼前的工作，今天就是這麼過的。

＊＊

carp〔kɑrp〕*n.* 鯉魚　　chirp〔tʃɝp〕*v.* 啁啾而鳴
flutter〔ˈflʌtɚ〕*v.* 鼓翼；拍翅　　fluffy〔ˈflʌfɪ〕*adj.* 鬆軟如絨毛的
schedule〔ˈskɛdʒul〕*n.* 時間表　　recharged〔riˈtʃɑrdʒd〕*adj.* 再充電

《表示寧靜的常用語》

♤ He lives a tranquil life. 他過著平靜的生活。

♤ May God rest his soul, give repose to his soul.
　　願上帝使其靈魂安息。

♤ Calm yourself. 請你安靜下來。

♤ I like the serenity of a country life. 我喜歡鄉間生活的寧靜。

Sun., Apr. 24　Fine

A spring picnic

The sun was out today. It being spring we decided to go out to have a picnic. After breakfast, we started off for the suburbs. About ten minutes later, we arrived. We spread the picnic cloth on the grass and all of us sat down and started talking.

Later on we brought out the picnic basket and began to lay out the food. There was ham, cheese, apples and bread. We also brought along some hot chocolate and some cans of soft drinks. After that we all fell asleep. At five o'clock we started to head back home. We enjoyed ourselves very much on this beautiful spring day.

四月二十四日　星期日　晴

春　郊

今天太陽出來了。因為是春天,所以我們決定出去野餐。早餐後我們向郊外出發,約十分鐘後,我們就到達了。我們把野餐布舖在草地上,全部坐下來開始談天。

稍後,我們拿出野餐盒,開始準備食物,有火腿、乳酪、蘋果及麵包。我們還帶了些熱巧克力及幾罐冷飲。然後我們都睡著了,五點時我們踏向歸途。在這個美好的春日裏,我們都玩得非常愉快。

---

lay out 打開備用

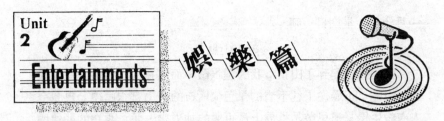

Sun., Jun. 19   Fine

A picnic

Our school went on a picnic today. I hate these social activities. I never know how to handle myself in them. All the other people were having fun but I was miserable. I don't know how to have fun, I'm too much of a book worm. I wonder if there are other people like me.

六月十九日　星期日　晴

野　餐

我們學校今天舉行野餐。我討厭這些社交活動。我從不知如何在其中自處。其他人都很高興，只有我可憐兮兮。我不知如何娛樂，我是不折不扣的書蟲。我懷疑是否有其他人像我一樣。

**

handle〔'hændḷ〕v. 對待　　miserable〔'mɪzərəbḷ〕adj. 可憐的

Sun., Jan. 10   Clear

Climbing Mt. Ali

We've finally made it to the top. My legs are sore and I almost stepped on a snake on the way up. But the view from up here makes all the effort worthwhile. It's an awesome sight, this must be one of the loveliest regions on earth. Now the problem is going down.

一月十日　星期日　晴

阿里山風光

　　我們終於爬到了山頂。我的腿很酸，而且在上山的路上差點踩到一條蛇。不過從上往下看的景色使所有的努力都很值得。風景令人凜然生畏，這兒該是世界上最可愛的地方之一了。現在的問題倒是該如何下去啦。

**——————————————————————————————

　　sore〔sor,sɔr〕*adj.* 酸痛　worthwhile〔'wɝθ'hwaɪl〕*adj.* 值得的
　　awesome〔'ɔsəm〕*adj.* 引起敬畏的

Mon., *Aug. 15*　*Fine*

David's magic

I don't know how David Copperfieid did it. He made an elephant disappear out of thin air. How did he hide an elephant? Amazing, absolutely amazing. I wonder how he got hold of an elephant in Taipei. The only elephants we have are at the zoo. He must have brought one with him.

八月十五日　星期一　晴

大衛魔術

　　我不知道大衛‧考柏菲爾德是如何做的。他使一隻大象從空中消失。他是如何藏起一隻大象的？驚奇，真是讓人驚奇。我想知道他在台北怎麼樣取得大象。我們擁有的大象都在動物園。他必定是自己帶了一隻來的。

**——————————————————————————————

　　amazing〔ə'mezɪŋ〕*adj.* 可驚異的
　　absolutely〔'æbsə,lutlɪ, ,æbsə'lutlɪ〕*adv.* 完全地；絕對地
　　get hold of 獲得；取得

Sun., Oct. 23　Fine

Camping

I love camping, but camping isn't for everyone.
Last Summer I convinced mom and dad to spend
their weeklong summer vacation camping up in the
mountains. We came home after one night. Father
said it was crazy to sleep outside on the ground and
cook dinner over an open fire. He complained there
weren't even any hot showers or flush toilets. He
couldn't understand why some people would go out
of their way to leave behind the conveniences of
modern life.

十月二十三日　星期日　晴

露 營

我喜愛露營，但是露營並不適合每一個人。去年夏天我說
服爸媽到山裏露營，渡過一星期的暑假。一個晚上後，我們就
回家了。爸爸說在外面地上睡覺和在野外的火堆中煮晚餐簡直
是瘋狂。他抱怨連熱水浴跟抽水馬桶都沒有。他無法了解爲什
麼有些人會失常到丟棄現代生活的便利設備。

---

flush toilet 抽水馬桶　　　　*go out of one's way* 逸出常規
leave behind 丟棄

Tues., Feb. 18 Fine

A hot disco

After school we had a class meeting. Mr. Chen danced a hot disco, by way of entertainment, which was highly welcomed by all. It put even a professional dancer to shame. I wonder when and where he learned such a dance.

二月十八日　星期四　晴

狄　斯　可

放學後我們舉行班會。陳先生跳了一支熱門的狄斯可舞，做爲餘興節目，很受我們大家歡迎。甚至勝過職業舞者。我很想知道他在何時何地學會這種舞蹈。

---

by way of　意在；當作

entertainment〔͵ɛntɚˊtenmənt〕*n.* 娛樂；表演

put to shame　勝過；使黯然失色

Mon., May 30　Fine

Going to the opera

I got up at six o'clock this morning. I ate a boiled egg and a piece of buttered bread for my breakfast. Then, I read the newspapers. After that I went to the bus stop to wait for buses at about seven. Because my house is not far from school, I got to the school pretty soon.After a day of studying, the classes were over. I left for the Opera Hall to see Verdi's Opera, Aida. It began at seven. There were many people at the Opera Hall.

"Aida" is a very famous opera. I thought it was very long. A lot of people clapped and cheered for the performers after the curtains were brought down. I must admit I didn't understand much of the opera but I thoroughly enjoyed myself watching the stage props and the elaborate costumes of the performers. The people who went to see the opera were also dressed very nicely. Pa and Ma talked about the opera on our way home. I could only listen. I hope to see something like this again, sometime in the future.

五月三十日　星期一　晴

去看歌劇

今天早晨六點起牀。早餐吃了一個煮蛋及一片奶油麵包。接著，看報紙。然後，大約七點時我到公車站等車。因爲家裏離學校不遠，我很快便到達學校。一日的學習之後，放學了。我前往歌劇院看韋瓦弟的歌劇「阿伊達」。歌劇七點開始。歌劇院門口有許多人。

阿伊達是一齣非常有名的歌劇，我認爲這齣劇很長。幕落下後很多人爲演出者鼓掌喝采。我必須承認我對這齣劇不是相當了解，但是我全然以觀賞舞台道具及精緻的服裝爲樂。去看歌劇的人也穿得很講究。回家路上爸媽談論這齣歌劇。我只能聽。我希望以後能再看一些像這樣的東西。

---

prop〔prɑp〕*n.* 道具

《有關音樂的常用語》

♤ I am crazy about rock music. 我熱愛搖滾樂。

♤ I went to see the Taipei Municipal Chinese Classical Orchestra. 我去看台北市立國樂團。

♤ I like classical music best. 我最喜歡古典音樂。

♤ I often go to concerts. 我經常參加音樂會。

♤ Whenever I am free, I like to listen to records.
　　只要有空，我就喜歡聽唱片。

♤ I am much interested in music. 我對音樂很有興趣。

♤ My favorite rock group is the Beatles.
　　我最喜歡的搖滾樂團是披頭四。

Sat., Jan. 2　Clear

The Taipei Art Museum

Recently, a so-called "Modern Sculpture Exhibition" was held in the Taipei Art Museum. Since art appeals to me very much, I invited one of my friends to visit the Museum this morning.

When we entered the art hall, I saw a notice that said: "Don't touch these works! Some of them are precious and dangerous." We didn't understand what the sign meant. Only after we had gone through the exhibition for five minutes did we understand what the sign meant. The exhibition was really what the title of the exhibition said. It was a collection of modern sculpture. They were almost entirely composed of wires, coloured lights, metals and many electrical contraptions. These works were not only art pieces but also scientific works. They were full of the creativity and imagination of their creators.

On the way home, we talked about this display and we both marvelled at the power of science and art.

一月二日　星期六　晴

台北市立美術館

　　最近，所謂的「現代雕刻展」在台北市立美術館舉行，因爲我對藝術非常有興趣，所以我今天早晨邀請一位朋友去參觀美術館。

　　　進入藝術廳時，我看到一個告示牌上寫著：「請勿觸摸！有些作品貴重而且危險。」我們不明白這個告示牌的意思。直到看完展覽五分鐘後，我們才了解告示牌的意思。這項展覽誠如展覽名稱所說的，是現代雕刻品的滙集。這些作品幾乎全是由電線、有色的燈泡、金屬和電子機件組成的。這些作品不僅是藝術成品，也是科學作品，他們充滿著創作者的創意和想像力。

　　在回家途中，我們談論這項展覽，我們兩人都對科學和藝術的力量感到驚奇。

** sculpture 〔'skʌlptʃɚ〕 *n.* 雕刻；雕塑　　notice 〔'notɪs〕 *n.* 告示
precious 〔'prɛʃəs〕 *adj.* 貴重的
contraption 〔kən'træpʃən〕 *n.* 機巧品；機械
display 〔dɪ'sple〕 *n.* 展覽

《有關藝術的常用語》

♤ Writing compositions is an art; grammar is a science.
　作文爲藝術，文法則是科學。

♤ He is a great artist. 他是一個大藝術家。

♤ I like to read the masterpieces in English literature.
　我喜歡讀英國文學名著。

♤ He played a piano sonata, that he himself had composed.
　他彈奏了一首自作的鋼琴奏鳴曲。

Sun., Mar. 20　Clear

Yangminshan Park

I had the chance to go to Yanmingshan Park today.
Today is the first day of Spring. Many people went
to the park to view the blossoms. This is the one
time of the year when the park is at its best. This
is so because all the flowers are in bloom. The whole
place was a carpet of red, white and green. The air
was also crisp and clean.

Most of the people who went there were old people.
Old people usually appreciate flowers more than young
people. I took a camera with me too and took some
photos of me with my family and friends. Then I spent
some time wandering along the pathways of the park.
I came across a natural waterfall. The water was very
cold but clean.

I noticed that there were some disposed food
wrappings floating on the water. This made me angry.
I was angry about the thoughtlessness of some people
here. Their careless acts only spoiled the beauty of
the park.

At midday we had gone through all of the park
already and were ready for the trek back home. We
went to a seafood restaurant to have lunch. We had
fish, squid and crabs. I spent the rest of the day
cleaning my room. I arranged my books in order,

> swept the floor and cleaned the window. I threw out a
> lot of things that I didn't need anymore too. I guess
> that's all for now.

三月二十日　　星期日　晴

陽明山公園

今天有機會到陽明山公園去。今天是春天的頭一天。許多人到公園賞花。這是公園一年當中的顛峯時期，因爲所有的花朵都盛開了。整個地方一片紅、白及綠，空氣新鮮清爽。

到那裏去的人大部分是老人，老年人大都比年青人更欣賞花。我還帶了照相機，和家人及朋友照了一些相。然後我花了一些時間在公園的小徑上漫步。我找到一處天然瀑布。水很冷但卻清澈。

我注意到有一些廢棄的食物包裝浮在水面上，這使我念怒。我對此地某些人的自私感到念怒，他們不負責任的行爲只破壞了公園的美觀。

中午時我們已逛完整個公園並且準備好緩慢而艱辛地踱回家。我們到一家海產店午餐，吃了魚、烏賊和螃蟹。我用其餘的時間來打掃房間，把書排好，地掃乾淨並且擦窗戶，我還丟了許多不再需要的東西。我想現在，這就是全部了。

---

at one's best　處於最佳時期　　　*a carpet of grass*　碧草如茵

crisp〔krɪsp〕*adj.* 新鮮的　　　*come across*　偶然遇到；找到

disposed〔dɪ'spozd〕*adj.* 放棄

thoughtlessness〔'θɔtlɪsnɪs〕*n.* 自私

trek〔trek〕*n.* 旅行　　　squid〔skwɪd〕*n.* 烏賊；魷魚

crab〔kræb〕*n.* 蟹

Sat., *Jul*. *30*　*Fine*

The zoo

　　The Mucha Zoo just recently opened. The other day I went to visit it for the first time. The zoo is one of the best and biggest in Asia. In it we saw all kinds of animals in dwellings that were as close as possible to their original habitats. We saw lions, tigers, elephants, beautiful birds, monkeys and so on. Besides these, we were able to see an interesting monkey show. It was all fun. At four p.m. we were already on our way home. We were very pleased with the trip and we wished to visit it again on another day.

七月三十日　　星期六　　晴

動　物　園

　　木柵動物園最近剛開放，前天我第一次去那裏。這座動物園是亞洲最好最大的動物園之一。在裏面我們看見各種的動物，牠們的住處都建造得儘可能接近牠們的原產地。我們看見獅子，老虎，大象，美麗的鳥類，以及猴子等等。除此之外，我們能夠欣賞有趣的猴子秀。眞好玩。下午四點的時候，我們已經在回家的路上了。我們對於這次的旅遊覺得很開心，而且希望改天再去一次。

---

dwelling〔'dwɛlɪŋ〕 *n*. 住處
original〔ə'rɪdʒənl〕 *adj*. 最初；最早的；原來的
habitat〔'hæbə,tæt〕 *n*.（動植物的）產地；棲息地
on one's way home 某人回家途中

Sat., Aug. 27　Fine

A birthday party

The highlight of the day was John's birthday party. All of John's friends were there including his family and relatives. We had a marvelous time. There were balloons, lots of food, games, dancing and singing. I arrived at John's place at around seven. There were already a lot of people when I got there. I gave John a record of the latest album of Madonna. I hope he will like it.

We had our dinner at around an hour later. After that we turned off the lights and lighted the birthday cake. When all the candles were lit, we began to sing " Happy Birthday " in Chinese and in English. He made a wish, blew out the candles and then everybody clapped and wished Johnny a happy birthday. The cake was delicious. At around ten, I told John goodbye. I took a taxi back home. Tomorrow I have to start exercising in order to take off the extra pounds I've added on tonight.

八月二十七日　星期六　晴

慶 生 會

　　今天的高潮是約翰的慶生會。所有約翰的親友家人都來了。我們玩得很愉快。有汽球、許多食物、遊戲、舞蹈和歌唱。我在七點左右抵達約翰家的。我到的時候，那兒已經有許多人了。我送他一張瑪丹娜最新專集的唱片，希望他會喜歡。

　　我們大約一個小時後吃晚餐，吃完之後把燈都熄掉，點亮了生日蛋糕。當所有的蠟燭都點好之後，我們開始唱中文和英文的生日快樂歌。約翰許了願，把蠟燭吹熄，然後大家鼓掌，祝福約翰生日快樂。蛋糕很好吃。大概十點時，我向約翰說再見，然後搭計程車回家。明天我必須要開始作運動了，以減掉今晚增加的體重。

---

highlight 〔'haɪˌlaɪt〕 *n.* 最精彩、重要的部分或場面
balloon 〔bə'lun〕 *n.* 汽球　　**album** 〔'ælbəm〕 *n.* 唱片集

《有關生日的祝福語》

♤ Happy birthday greetings！賀生日快樂！

♤ Happy birthday to you！祝你生日快樂！

♤ My best wishes for your happy birthday！
　恭賀你生日快樂！

♤ Many many happy returns on this memorable day！
　祝你擁有無數個快樂生日！

♤ I congratulate you on your birthday.
　祝你生日快樂。

♤ I wish you a very happy birthday. 祝你生日快樂。

Sun., Sept. 18   Fine

Youth park

I went to the Youth Park today. My father was doing something important for business, so he didn't go with us. I went with mom, and my two younger brothers. My Aunt Susan also came along with us. Ted and Roy brought their kites with them while I just brought some books with me. When we got there, the park was already teeming with people. A lot of people come here during Sundays. It is really a huge park and there are a lot facilities to do your favorite recreation. For example, there are tennis courts, a golf practicing range, a place to ride horses, skating and others. There were also a lot of vendors selling all kinds of food and toys.

I like the quiet part of the park, where there are few people. After finding a more secluded place, Mom, Aunt Susan and I sat down on the chairs, while the other two boys flew their kites. I had to help them fly their kites at the start. But once they were up in the air I left them alone. While Mom and Aunt Susan talked I read my book silently. In the afternoon we decided to go home. Today was a fine day.

九月十八日　星期日　晴

青年公園

今天到青年公園去。爸爸因為生意上的關係，沒跟我們一起去。我們有媽媽、兩個弟弟，還有蘇珊姑媽。泰德和洛依都帶了風箏，而我則帶了一些書。當我們到那兒的時候，公園裏正是人山人海。許多人都喜歡在星期假日來這裏玩。這真是一個大公園，有許多遊樂設施，讓你做你最喜歡的遊戲。有網球場、高爾夫球場、騎馬場、溜冰場等等。還有販賣各種食物和玩具的小販。

我喜歡公園裏寂靜的地方，人比較少。發現了一個比較隱密的地方之後，媽媽、姑媽和我就坐在椅子上，另外兩個男生則在玩他們的風箏。剛開始的時候，我必須幫他們飛，但一旦風箏都飛上天空之後，我就離開了。媽媽和姑媽在談話，我靜靜地在讀書。下午我們決定回家，今天真是美好的一天。

**————————————————

　　teem〔tim〕*v.* 充滿；多　　facility〔fə'sɪlətɪ〕*n.* 設備（常用複數）
　　vendor〔'vɛndə〕*n.* 自動販賣機；小販
　　seclude〔sɪ'klud〕*v.* 隔離；隱居

≪有關假日的常用語≫

♤ New Year's Day is a national holiday. 元旦是國定假日。

♤ Mr. Wu is away on holiday at present. 吳先生目前正在度假。

♤ There is a vacation from schoolwork every year in summer.
　每年夏季學校放假。

♤ He asked for leave. 他請假。

♤ The soldier has two weeks' furlough.
　那士兵有兩週的休假。

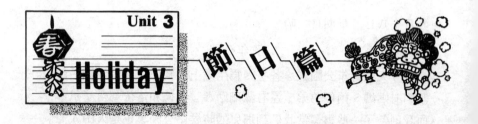

Unit 3

Holiday

節日篇

Sat., March 12   Fine

Arbor Day

Today is Arbor Day. This day was observed throughout the country by planting hundreds or thousands of saplings. Owing to this day mountains in Taiwan become greener every year. Considering the recent situation of nation-wide fuel shortage, we should plant more trees in the mountains. In the afternoon, planted two lilac trees in our garden. They will surely bloom next year.

三月十二日　星期六　晴

植　樹　節

今天是植樹節，全國各地藉種植成千上百的樹苗來慶祝這個日子。因為這一天，台灣的山變得一年比一年綠。鑒於最近全國性能源短缺的情勢，我們應該在山區種植更多的樹才是。下午在園裏種了兩棵紫丁香。明年它們一定會開花。

Arbor Day 植樹節　　observe〔əb'zɝv〕 *v.* 慶祝；紀念
sapling〔'sæplɪŋ〕 *n.* 樹苗　　***fuel shortage*** 能源缺乏
lilac〔'laɪlək〕 *n.* 紫丁香

Mon., April 4　Fine

Children's Day

Today is Children's Day. At Sports Field in Taipei the ceremony was attended by some 3,000 children and citizens, and Children's Park gave free admission to children.

So we took two small children of my aunt's with us to go there. There were so many people there that we were very careful not to let the children get lost.

There were free balloons given to small kids, but at all rides there were long lines of people. By the time we got home, we were a little tired, but we felt like happy small children again.

四月四日　星期一　晴

兒　童　節

今天是兒童節。台北的體育場約有三千名兒童及市民參加典禮，而且兒童樂園免費招待兒童入場。

於是我們帶著阿姨的兩個小鬼去兒童樂園玩。那兒人真多，因此我們必須很小心，以免小鬼走丟了。

那兒有免費贈送給小朋友的汽球，但每個項目後面都大排長龍。當我們回到家時，都有點疲倦，但彷彿又回到了童年一般，快樂無比。

Sun., Jun. 5 Fine

Sports day

Our school had a sports day. The 400-meter relay was especially exciting. I was the anchor for our team. It was a close race. I fell down at the corner. I was encouraged by the crowd. Although I ran as fast as I could, our team came in last.

After the race, the coach said to us, "To be a good loser is more important than to win the race." I knew his words were wise, but really I wanted to cry.

六月五日　星期日　晴

運　動　會

學校舉辦運動會。四百公尺接力特別刺激。我是我們隊的最後一棒。這是閉幕賽。我在轉彎處跌倒了。觀衆一直鼓勵我，但是儘管我盡力跑快，我們隊還是最後一名。

比賽結束後，教練告訴我們，「做一個有風度的失敗者，比贏得比賽更爲重要。」我知道他的話很有道理,但是我眞想哭。

sports〔spɔrts〕*n.pl.* 運動會　　relay〔rɪ'le〕*n.* 接力賽跑
anchor〔'æŋkɚ〕*n.* 最後一棒　　*come in* 得
coach〔kotʃ〕*n.* 教練；老師

Thur., Jun. 30　Fine.

My plans for Summer vacation

The summer vacation will start tomorrow.We all have many plans. After dinner, we talked about our plans for the vacation. Harry, Emi and I will visit our uncle in Tainan and will go to Kaoshiung. Watching high school baseball games will be great fun.

Grandma and Dad will visit the family grave in Yunlin. Mother said, "I'd like to take a rest at home."

六月三十日　星期四　晴

暑假計畫

暑假明天開始，我們都有許多計畫。晚餐後我們討論暑假的計畫。哈利、愛美和我要去拜訪住在台南的叔叔並且要到高雄去。看高中棒球賽一定很有趣。

祖母和爸爸要祭掃在雲林的祖墳。媽媽說：「我想在家裏休息。」

---

grave〔grev〕*n.* 墳墓　　*the family grave* 祖墳
take a rest 休息

Sat., Dec. 24 *Fine and windy*

Christmas Eve

There's nothing like Christmas Eve. It's cold outside but warm in here. We've just exchanged gifts with each other. I bought Mom a sweater and Dad a tie. For my younger sister, I bought her a doll. I also got a lot of presents from my family, but I won't know what they are until tomorrow. After we went to church, Dad took all of us to the Hilton to have dinner. The Christmas tree in the hotel was very tall and beautiful. While we were having dinner I could hear a lot of music. I love the chocolate mousse cake that I had. When we finished our dinner we went outside to listen to a choir sing Christmas songs. It was really lovely.

When we came home it was almost eleven. Mother was very happy with the gift I gave her. The gifts were placed around the foot of our own Christmas tree. Father said, we will all be surprised tomorrow morning with the gift he had for us. After this, Father and Mother tucked me and my sister in bed. Though I am tired, I can't sleep. I am just too excited about tomorrow.

十二月二十四日　星期六　晴朗有風

聖誕夜

沒有什麼比得上聖誕夜。外面很冷，但這兒卻很溫暖。我們剛剛互相交換了禮物。我爲媽媽買了一件毛衣，爲爸爸買了一條領帶。至於妹妹，我給她買了一個洋娃娃。我也從家人那兒得到許多禮物，不過要到明天才知道是些什麼東西。上教堂做完禮拜後，爸爸帶我們去希爾頓大飯店吃晚餐。飯店裡的聖誕樹高大又漂亮。用餐時，我聽到許多音樂。我很喜愛我的巧克力慕思蛋糕。吃完晚餐我們走到外面去聽唱詩班唱聖誕歌曲。眞是美妙極了。

回到家已是近十一點了。母親對我送她的禮物感到很高興。所有的禮物都放在我們自己的聖誕樹下。父親說明天我們都會對他所準備的禮物感到驚訝。之後，爸和媽替我跟妹妹把被子蓋好睡覺。雖然我很累，卻睡不著。想到明天的一切，我就覺得很興奮。

**────────────────────────

mousse〔mus〕*n.*（以乳酪、蛋白、膠、糖及香料等混合製成之一種）泡沫冰淇淋

choir〔kwaɪr〕*n.*（教堂中的）唱詩班

tuck〔tʌk〕*v.* 很暖適地圍裹或覆蓋

≪表示溫暖的常用語≫

♤ She sat in the warm sunshine. 她坐在暖和的陽光中。

♤ The fire soon warmed the room. 爐火很快地使室內溫暖起來。

♤ I had a tepid bath. 我洗了個溫水澡。

♤ The weather has been very hot. 這些天來天氣都很熱。

Sun., *Dec.* 25　*Clear*

Christmas Day

　　We have Christmas on Taiwan just like in America. We celebrate Christmas even though we're not Christians, but that's all right. I hear many Americans aren't Christians either but they still celebrate Christmas. Every year we get a Christmas tree and go to Midnight Mass just like the Americans. The only problem with Christmas on Taiwan is that there's never any snow.

十二月二十五日　星期日　晴

耶　誕　節

　　我們在台灣和在美國一樣地有耶誕節。僅管我們不是基督徒，我們却照樣慶祝耶誕，但那無所謂。我聽說許多美國人也不是基督徒，但他們也仍然慶祝耶誕。每年我們都準備一棵耶誕樹並且像美國人一樣去參加午夜彌撒。在台灣，耶誕節的唯一問題就是從不下雪。

＊＊ Christian〔'krɪstʃən〕*n*. 基督教徒
　　celebrate〔'sɛlə,bret〕*v*. 慶祝
　　Midnight Mass 午夜彌撒

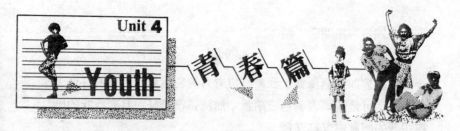

Unit 4 Youth　青春篇

Tues., Jul. 26　Fine

Hair-styles

Some of the girls at school are appearing with all kinds of strange hair-styles. One of them even had her hair dyed purple. I think girls look prettiest with their hair clean and natural. Why do they go through all that trouble to change their hair? I don't understand girls.

七月二十六日　星期二　晴

髮　型

學校的某些女孩以各種奇怪的髮型出現在校園裏。其中一位甚至把頭髮染成紫色。我認爲女孩子頭髮乾淨自然看起來最漂亮。爲什麼她們要透過那種麻煩來改變自己的頭髮？我不了解女孩子。

***

dye〔daɪ〕 *v.* 染色

Wed., Sep. 14　Clear

Dance party

I went to a dance party tonight. I was afraid that nobody would ask to dance with me, but someone did. I wish he hadn't asked though, he was a lousy dancer and kept stepping on my feet. My toes are all red and sore.

九月十四日　星期三　晴

舞　會

今晚我去參加一個舞會。我擔心沒有人請我跳舞，不過有一個人來
請我跳。可是我真希望他沒請我，他跳得很不好而且老踩我的腳。
害得我的腳趾頭又紅又痛。

Mon., Nov. 14　Fine

The generation gap

Today's grown-ups are less mature and responsible than
grown-ups of previous generations. They're off in their own
little worlds and don't make any time to be with us.

Why won't they take the time to talk with us？ Why
won't they take the time to listen to us？ They're always rushing off to work in the morning and when they come
home they read the newspapers or watch TV. I don't understand today's grown-ups. Maybe this feeling is called the generation gap or the communication gap. Maybe they don't understand
today's teenagers, either.

十一月十四日　星期一　晴

代　溝

今日的成人比前一代的成人較不成熟且不負責。他們總是遠在
自己的小世界中而不爭取任何時間來與我們相處。

他們為什麼不花時間和我們談話？他們為什麼不花時間傾聽我
們？他們總是在早晨衝出去工作，回家後他們就看報紙或看電視。
我不了解今天的成人們。也許這種感覺就是「代溝」或者「溝通差距」
吧。也許他們也不了解今天的青少年呢。

**

generation gap 代溝　　　　*make time* 爭取時間

Thur., Dec. 15　*Fine later rainy*

A disturbing age

These are disturbing times. But then, when was there a time not disturbing? Sure, the older people talk about the good old days, but these days will be my good old days.

It's funny how we like to look for bad things in current times while our memories recall only the good portions of our past. In truth, our pasts were not as pleasant as we remember and the current times are not as bad as we say.

十二月十五日　星期四　晴後雨

動盪不安的時代

這是一個動盪不安的時代，但是，又有哪個時代不動亂呢？當然，老一輩的人談論過去美好的時光，但現在這些日子將成爲我的昔日好景。

很可笑的是，我們很喜歡在現在尋找不好的事物，而我們的記憶卻只回想過去美好的部分。實際上，我們的過去不像我們回憶中那麼愉快，現在也不像我們所說的一樣糟糕。

---

portion〔ˈpɔrʃən〕*n.* 部分

Sun., Sep. 18　*Overcast*

Fast food shop

I went to try McDonalds today for the first time. I don't see what the big deal is. The hamburger and fries were nothing special. However, I liked the music they played there. Next time I go I'll just order a cup of coffee and listen to the music.

九月十八日　星期日　多雲

速　食　店

　　今天我第一次去試試麥當勞。我不明白它有多稀奇。漢堡和薯條沒什麼特別的地方。可是，我很喜歡他們放的音樂。我下回去只要點一杯咖啡並聽音樂就好了。

**

　　hamburger〔'hæmbɚgɚ〕*n.* 漢堡
　　fry〔fraɪ〕*n.* 油炸食物　　order〔'ɔrdɚ〕*v.* 點（食物）

Tues., *Aug.* 16　*Fine*

The types of teenagers

There are many types of teenagers at my school, but I divide them into two groups: the popular and not so popular. Everybody wants to be with the popular people. I don't know what makes them so popular, they're not always the best look-ing. I belong in the not so popular group. I can't seem to attract people to be with me. Do they have something that I don't have ? I wonder.

八月十六日　星期二　晴

青少年的類型

　　在我的學校有許多類型的青少年，但我把他們分為兩類：受歡迎和不很受歡迎的。每個人都想跟受歡迎的人在一起。我不知道是什麼使他們這麼受歡迎，他們並不一定是最好看的人。我屬於不受歡迎的一群，我似乎不能吸引別人和我在一起，他們是不是有什麼我所沒有的東西呢？我真想知道。

**

　　teenager〔'tin,edʒɚ〕*n.* 十幾歲的少年
　　popular〔'pɑpjəlɚ〕*adj.* 受歡迎的

Sat., Jan. 9　Fine

What do you want to be
when you grow up?

　I hated when my parents badgered me with that question. "What do you want to be?" It was hard enough to be a youngster without having to worry about my future. When I'm a parent with little ones of my own I won't pester my children with that question. Being wiser than my parents I will tell my children they can pursue any field they want so long as they enjoy it and strive to be the best in it. And, most important of all, get a Ph. D. in it.

一月九日　星期六　晴

你長大後想做什麼？

　我討厭父母用那個問題:「你長大後想做什麼?」來困擾我的時候。做一個年青人而無須煩惱未來實在很困難。當我有自己的小孩而為人父母時，我不會用那個問題來困擾我的孩子。我會比我的父母明智，告訴孩子們只要喜歡，並且努力在這領域中出人頭地，他們可以追求任何一個他們想追求的領域。而且，最重要的是，取得那個領域的博士學位。

---

badger〔'bædʒɚ〕*v.* 困擾　　　　pester〔'pɛstɚ〕*v.* 使困擾
field〔fild〕*n.* 界；領域
Ph. D. = Doctor of Philosophy　博士學位

Thur., *Sep. 8*   *Clear*

We are young but once

Oh no, I'm getting older and older. Soon I'll have to be a grown-up. I don't want to be a grown-up. I like being a teenager. I want to be a teenager forever. How can I slow down time? Time always goes by fast when I'm having fun. Wait! I know how I can slow down time. I'll bore myself. Time always slows down when I'm bored. I think I'll go sit in the closet and bore myself. Maybe I can live longer this way.

九月八日　星期四　晴

我們只年輕一次

噢，不！我變得越來越老了。很快地我就得成為大人了。我不要變成大人，我喜歡當一個青少年，我要永遠當青少年。我怎樣才能使時間慢下來？時間總是在我高興的時候很快地消逝。慢著！我知道怎樣使時間慢下來了。我要讓自己厭煩。當我煩的時候，時間總是慢下來。我想我要去坐在廁所裏，讓自己厭煩。這樣或許我可以活得久一點。

** go by 過去；逝
　closet〔ˈklɑzɪt〕*n.* 小房間；廁所（＝water closet）

Unit 5

Emotion 心情篇

Sun., Nov. 6　Cloudy

My pain

My dog got hit by a car. She is in a lot of pain and can't walk anymore. What should I do? I can't afford to take her to see a doctor but I can't bear to see her in pain. I will have to put her to sleep.

十一月六日　星期日　多雲

痛　苦

我的狗被車撞了。牠很痛而且再也不能走路了。我該怎麼辦？我沒有錢帶牠去看醫生，但我也不能忍受看著牠痛苦。我必須使牠長眠。

afford〔ə'ford, ə'fɔrd〕v. 力足以；能堪　　　bear〔bɛr〕v. 忍受

Wed., Nov. 30　Cloudy later fine

Anger

I was so angry at myself for making a stupid mistake on today's test. I knew the answer but wrote down the wrong thing. How could I have been so stupid? I should have had a one-hundred, oh well, it's too late to do anything about it now.

十一月三十日　星期三　多雲時晴

憤　怒

我眞氣我自己在今天的測驗裏犯了一個愚蠢的錯誤。我知道答案却寫錯答案。我怎麼會這麼笨？我本可以拿一百分的，哦但是，現在做什麼都太遲了。

Wed., Oct. 5   Fine

Hatred

I hate that jerk Fred. He thinks he's so great, but what does he have to be proud of? He thinks he's God just because he went to National Taiwan University. I bet his rich father bribed NTU officials to let him in.

十月五日　星期三　晴

憎　恨

我恨那個未經世事的佛瑞德。他以爲他很偉大，但他有什麼好驕傲的？只因爲他唸台大他就以爲他是神。我敢打賭是他那有錢的老爸賄賂台大的職員才讓他進去的。

✷✷

jerk 〔dʒɝk〕*n.* 〔俚〕未經事故的人；愚笨的人　　bet 〔bɛt〕*v.* 打賭
bribe 〔braɪb〕*v.* 賄賂　　official 〔ə'fɪʃəl〕*n.* 官吏；職員

Mon., Jun. 27   Fine

Love

Martha still hasn't replied to the love letters I send her every day. I don't think she likes me. I don't understand it. I'm tall, handsome, charming, intelligent, and rich. I'm the perfect gentleman. How could she not like me?

六月二十七日　星期一　晴

愛　情

瑪莎仍然沒有回我每天寄給她的情書。我認爲她不喜歡我。我眞不懂。我長得高、英俊、迷人、聰明又有錢。我是個完美的紳士。她怎麼會不喜歡我呢？

Wed., Apr. 20　Clear

Pursuing happiness

Ever since the word "happiness" was invented people have been pursuing it as if it really exists. Some people try to buy happiness with money, but the wisemen tell us that happiness can't be bought. The wisemen are right; how can you buy something that doesn't exist? The really smart people know happiness is an illusive goal and have learned to live with the fact. It's only the dumb people who don't know any better that are happy, such as children.

四月二十日　星期三　晴

追求快樂

自從「快樂」這個字發明以來，人們就一直在追求快樂，好像快樂眞的存在似的。有人試著用金錢購買快樂，但是智者告訴我們，快樂是買不到的。那些智者是對的；人如何買不存在的東西呢？眞正聰明的人知道快樂是個虛幻的目標，並且學會接受事實。只有那些什麼都不懂的笨瓜才會快樂，例如小孩。

---

illusive〔ɪˈlusɪv〕*adj.* 虛幻的

live with　接受；忍受　　***know better***　了解事情的錯誤

Fri., Aug. 26   *Cloudy*

Happy birthday

I'm in a good mood today. Why? Because it's my birthday. When I woke up this morning I found a card on my table. It was from Helen. It was a birthday card. Then when I went to have breakfast Mother greeted me happy birthday too. She said to come early for she will prepare some food for us to eat. Then she gave me some money to treat my friends at school.

At school, my class sang the Birthday Song for me. The class wrote on the blackboard in big words, "Happy Birthday, Yuh-Jen, From your friends and classmates". Then I wrote "thank you" in one corner. The words stayed there the whole day as is the practice of the class. My teachers were extra nice to me today. I felt uneasy about it though. Why? I don't know why. During lunch I bought some ice cream and treated everyone in my class and my teachers to some ice cream. When I went home, my family was already waiting for me. My mother gave me some books and my father gave me five thousand dollars. We ate the food mother cooked and then I blew out the candles on the birthday cake. Then the day was over and I was also a year older.

八月二十六日　星期五　多雲

快樂的生日

今天我心情很好。為什麼呢？因為今天是我的生日。我早上起來的時候，在桌上發現一張卡片，是海倫寄來的生日卡。後來我在吃早餐的時候，媽媽也對我說生日快樂。她教我們早點去，因為她要準備一些食物給我們。然後她給了我錢去請學校的朋友。

在學校，班上為我唱生日快樂歌。黑板上寫著大字：「玉眞，生日快樂。妳的朋友和同學敬上。」於是我在角落寫上「謝謝」。那些字整天留在黑板上面，就像本班的慣例一樣。老師們今天也對我特別好。但是我覺得有點不安，不知道為什麼。吃午餐時，我買了些冰淇淋請老師和同學吃。回家的時候，家人已經在等著我了。媽媽送我一些書，爸爸給我五千塊。我們吃了媽媽羹的東西，然後我吹熄了生日蛋糕上的蠟燭。一天便結束了，我也老了一歲。

**

practice〔'præktɪs〕n. 習慣；慣例
treat〔trit〕v. 請客

≪表示快樂的常用語≫

♤ The children seem to be very happy. 孩子們似乎很快樂。

♤ I enjoy it very much. 我高興極了。

♤ He cheered up at once when I promised to help him.
　　我答應幫忙他時，他立刻高興起來。

♤ They lived happily ever after.
　　他們以後就一直過著快樂的生活。

♤ I am happy that you are here.
　　你的光臨使我快樂。

Sat., Mar. 19　*Drizzling*

Departing

Next to death, the most depressing thing in life is a farewell between those beloved — even though it is but for a short time.

Yesterday my father left for Singapore. It was a quiet morning; no one spoke much, and the air was filled with the sound of packing. Not a morsel of food passed my mouth, nor did I taste a drop of liquid the whole morning. The thought that my beloved father would be leaving us in the afternoon was too much for me to bear. He has never been so far away from us before since he last went to Hong Kong.

三月十九日　星期六　細雨

次於死亡，生命中最悲傷的事情就是和所愛的人分離了，即使時間很短。

昨天爸爸去了新加坡，那是個寂靜的早晨，沒人說話，只聽見整理行李的聲音。整個早上我吃不下東西，也沒喝水。想到親愛的爸爸下午就要離開，真教我受不了。自從上回他去香港以來，就沒再離開過我們。

---

morsel〔ˈmɔrsl〕*n.*（食物的）一口

Sat., Mar. 5　Rainy

Missing

Today was a very lonely day for me. Michael was on my mind all day. I read his letters over and over again. In the afternoon after reading his letters I cried myself to sleep. I miss him so much. My heart aches for him. If I could I would like to fly to him but there's no way I can. I wish he was back with me right now. I have just written a letter to him and all that I can do is wait for his reply. Waiting for his letter seems to take forever. Oh why does life have to be this way?

三月五日　星期六　雨

思　念

今天對我而言是個十分寂寞的日子。我整天都把麥可放在心上。我一遍又一遍地讀著他的來信。下午讀了信之後，我哭著睡著了。我好想他。爲他心痛。如果能夠，我要飛到他身邊，但我一籌莫展。希望他現在就回到我身邊，跟我在一起。我剛寫了一封信給他，所有我能做的事就是等候他的回信。等這封信的時間彷彿永恆。噢，爲什麼人生必須是這樣的呢？

＊＊

reply〔rɪˈplaɪ〕*n.* 回信；答覆

Fri., Apr. 15 Fine

Something about me

It just dawned on me that I don't know myself very well. I give more thought to understanding other people than myself. I know a few of my simple likes and dislikes, for example I like oranges over apples. But I don't know how I would act in crisis situations. Would I give up my life to save another? I know a few people who would, but am I as un-selfish?

四月十五日　星期五　晴

有關我的一些事

我剛剛才明白，我並不十分了解自己。我比了解自己花更多心思去了解別人。我知道自己一些簡單的好惡，例如我喜歡橘子勝於蘋果。但是我不知道自己在危急的情況下會如何反應，我會放棄生命去拯救另一個人嗎？我認識一些會這麼做的人，但是我是不是和他們一樣無私？

---

dawn〔dɔn〕v. 覺醒；了解
crisis〔'kraɪsɪs〕n. 危機

Thurs., *Aug*. *18*　　*Fine*

My happiness and fears

It was sunny today. While I was studying I put on my favorite cassette tape to listen to some music. I like music very much. Wherever I go, I always have a walkman with me so that I can listen to my favorite songs. I think I would die if I didn't have music even for a day. Music expresses my feelings so rightly. When I listen to a song, I feel as if the music was meant for me. I can identify my fears and happiness with the music I hear. With music I can go into a world of my own where no one can disturb me. Music means so much to me.

八月十八日　　星期四　　晴

我的快樂與恐懼

今天陽光普照。當我讀書時我打開我最喜愛的卡式錄音帶，放一些音樂來聽。我非常喜歡音樂。不管去哪裏，我總是隨身攜帶隨身聽，以便能夠聽我喜愛的歌曲。我想我如果一天沒有音樂，我就會死。音樂十分精確地表達了我的情感。當我聽一首歌時，我就覺得那音樂是爲我做的。我能夠藉著我所聽的音樂來辨別我的恐懼與快樂。我能隨著音樂一直走到一個自我的境界，沒有人能來打擾我。音樂對我意義良多。

---

cassette〔kæ'sɛt〕*n.* 裝卡式錄音帶的長方形扁盒
identify〔aɪ'dɛntə,faɪ〕*v.* 認明；識別

Fri., Jul. 1   Fine

The first day of the Entrance Examination

I was exhausted today. Today was the first day of the Entrance Examination. I was grilled in four subjects. After finishing them I was already feeling burned out. I didn't do as well I would have liked to because I was feeling tense throughout the tests. In order to relax, I decided to take a walk home after the tests. I passed by the Chiang Kai-shek Memorial Hall. I saw many people playing games and doing exercises. All of them looked so happy. I envied them. When I got home I decided to have a good night's sleep so that I'd do better on tomorrow's exam. That's all.

七月一日　星期五　晴

大學聯考的第一天

我今天累死了。今天是大學聯考的第一天,我考了四科,考完後,我已精疲力竭。我沒有表現得如預期中好,因爲整個考試中,我都感到緊張。爲了放輕鬆,我決定考完試後走路回家。經過中正紀念堂。看到許多人在玩遊戲做運動。每個人看起來都很愉快。我好羨慕他們。回家後我決定晚上好好睡,明天才能表現得好一點,就是這些了。

** ───────────

exhausted 〔ɪgˊzɔstɪd〕*adj.* 疲憊的　　grill 〔grɪl〕*v.* 燒;烤
burn out 燒壞
envy 〔ˊɛnvɪ〕*v.* 嫉妬;羨慕

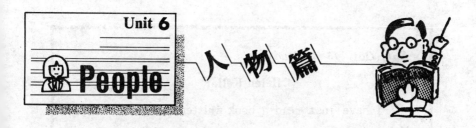

People

Sat., Apr. 9　Fine

The story of Li Po

In class today the teacher told us the story of Li Po, one of China's greatest poets. Our teacher said the key to Li Po's success was determination. With determination, she told us, we can do anything.

I don't agree with her. I don't think determination is enough. Also necessary is brains. Anybody can be determined, but not everyone can be smart.

四月九日　星期六　晴

李白的故事

今天課堂上老師告訴我們中國最偉大的詩人之一——李白的故事。老師說李白成功的關鍵是決心，她告訴我們，憑藉決心，我們可以做任何事。

我不同意老師的看法，我不以爲有決心就足夠了，聰明才智也是必要的。任何人都可以下決心，但並不是每一個人都聰明。

---

determination〔dɪ,tɝməˈneʃən〕*n.* 決心;毅力　brains〔brenz〕*n.*智慧

Sat.,Oct. 15　Cloudy.

Helen Keller

I have just read a book written by Helen Keller. Helen could not see, hear, or speak. She lived in darkness. She was just like an animal. How surprised she was when she first learned that everything had a name! How glad Miss Sullivan, her teacher, was too!

Helen Keller was a great woman because she gave light to many of the handicapped people of the world. I hope the world will have more people like Helen Keller.

十月十五日　星期六　多雲

海倫凱勒

我剛讀完一本海倫凱勒寫的書。海倫不能看、不能聽、也不能說話。她活在黑暗中，就像動物似的。當她第一次明白每件事物都有個名稱時有多驚訝呀！而她的老師，蘇利文小姐也非常高興。

海倫凱勒是位偉大的女性，因為她給世界上許多殘障的人們帶來光明。希望世界上會有更多像海倫凱勒一樣的人。

---

handicapped〔'hændɪ,kæpt〕*adj.* 殘廢的；身體有缺陷的

Thur., July 14　Fine

My uncle

My uncle who had finished his study abroad in America after three years arrived at Chung Jenq Airport in Taoyuan this afternoon. He is planning to teach Physics at a college in Hsinchu.

According to him, what he felt keenly in foreign countries is that people living there are surprisingly ignorant of our country. On the other hand, when we are asked in foreign countries about things in Taiwan, we are often surprised to find how ignorant we are about our country.

七月十四日　星期四　晴

我的叔叔

在美國深造三年，學成歸國的叔叔，今天下午抵達桃園的中正國際機場。他計畫到新竹的一所大學教物理。據他說，他在國外感覺最深刻的是，住在那裏的人很令人驚訝地，竟不知道我們的國家。另一方面，當我們在國外被問及臺灣的事情時，我們常常驚奇地發現，我們對自己的國家多麼缺乏認知。

Physics〔'fɪzɪks〕*n.* 物理學

keenly〔'kinlɪ〕*adv.* 深刻感覺地

ignorant〔'ɪgnərənt〕*adj.* 顯示無知的；不明白的

Sun., Nov. 27　Fine

My best friend came back

Last Sunday I had a surprise visit. My friend came to visit me. She was my best friend during junior high school. She went abroad with her family when we graduated.

I couldn't believe that she was standing in front of me. I hugged her for a long time. Then I saw how much she had changed. She had grown more beautiful and she dressed just like an American. We had been in touch with each other all throughout the years. I really missed her so much.

We talked about her new school in America. She told how different things were in America. She also talked about her many interesting experiences.

She told me the most difficult thing for an immigrant was the language. She made a lot of effort to study English. Now, she can speak English very well. I was really proud of her. I was happy she could visit me. We both had a very good time on this unforgettable Sunday.

十一月二十七日　星期日　晴

<h3 style="text-align:center">好友歸來</h3>

　　上星期天我有一個意外的驚喜。我的朋友前來拜訪我。她是我國中時最好的朋友，我們畢業後，她和家人一起到國外去。

　　我無法相信她就站在我面前，我緊擁住她好長一段時間。然後我看到她改變了好多，她變得漂亮多了，而且穿得像個美國人。這些年來，我們一直互相聯絡，我實在非常想念她。

　　我們談論她在美國的新學校，她告訴我在美國事物有多麼不一樣，她談了許多有趣的經驗。

　　她還告訴我，對一個移民來說，最困難的事情是語言，她花了很多功夫學英文，現在，她英文說得相當好。我真以她為榮。我很高興她能來拜訪我，在這令人難忘的週日，我們兩人都非常愉快。

＊＊─────────────────────

　　junior high school 國中　　hug〔hʌg〕*v.* 緊抱；摟抱
　　immigrant〔ˈɪməgrənt〕*n.* 移民　　*be proud of* 以…為榮

<h3 style="text-align:center">≪有關語言的常用語≫</h3>

♤ How many languages do you speak? 你能說多少種語言？

♤ The Negro dialect is hard to understand.

　　黑人的方言難以了解。

♤ He spoke in the idiom of the New England countryside.

　　他講新英格蘭鄉下的方言。

♤ He speaks several dialects. 他會說好幾種方言。

♤ He just doesn't speak my language.

　　他和我所持立場不同。

Sun., Sept. 4   Wind and rain

My boy friend

My boy friend came here today. He brought some roses for me. After I placed the roses in a vase of water, we had a talk in the living room. He asked me how I was doing with my homework and he offered to help me. It was really sweet of him. But I said I would be alright. We talked until the sun went down. In the evening we ate in a restaurant and watched a movie after that. At around nine, my boy friend took me home. Before he said goodbye, he looked into my eyes. I could have melted right there and then. He had the most beautiful pair of eyes that I have seen. He kissed me lightly, then he was gone.

I sighed a deep breath as I closed the door and I slowly went back to my room. How long has it been since we've been together? It's been only six months. I wonder how he felt about me. He's always in my mind. Even when I'm asleep, I dream of him. I wish I could see him everyday but we both still have to go to school so we can only see each other during the the weekends or any time when we can steal away.

九月四日　星期日　風雨

我的男朋友

　　我的男朋友今天來這裡。他為我帶來一些玫瑰。我把花放在花瓶裡之後，我們便在客廳談起天來。他問我作業寫得如何，並且提議幫我做。他真是好。不過我說功課沒問題。我們一直聊到太陽下山。晚上我們去一家餐廳吃飯，而且看了一場電影。大約九點鐘左右，我男朋友送我回家。在他說再見之前，他注視著我的眼睛；那時我幾乎被他的目光溶化在那裏。他有一雙我見過最漂亮的眼睛。他輕柔地吻我，然後離去。

　　關門時我深深地嘆了一口氣，然後慢吞吞地回到房間。我們在一起已經有多久了？只有六個月。不知道他對我的感覺如何。他時常縈繞在我心中。甚至睡著了也會夢到他。我真希望能每天看到他，但是我們兩個都還得上學，所以我們只能在週末，或是偷找時間見面而已。

** ――――――――――――――――――――

　　vase〔ves〕*n.* 花瓶；瓶　　　　***steal away*** 悄悄走掉；偷偷走掉

≪有關戀愛的常用語≫

♤ They are in love. 他們在戀愛中。

♤ He fell in love with her at first sight. 他對她一見鍾情。

♤ He was crossed in his first love. 他的初戀不得意。

♤ I like my teacher, but feel no affection for her.
　　我喜歡我的老師，但並不愛她。

♤ He wrote her a letter with great adoration.
　　他給她寫了一封信，備致愛慕之意。

♤ She was an old love（flame）of mine years ago.
　　她是我多年前的舊情人。

True learning is not a matter of the formal organization of knowledge of books. It is a series of personal experiences.

— *Harold Taylor*

眞正的學習不是書本中的知識形式上的組合。它是個人經驗的累積。

...... I was rich, if not in money, in sunny hours and summer days.

— *Thoreau*

縱然我不富裕，但却擁有無數個陽光的日子和夏季。

APPENDIX

附　錄

中外節日一覽表

●中國節日●

≪一般節日≫

- 一百年紀念
  centennial〔sɛn'tɛnɪəl〕

- 二百年紀念
  bicentennial〔,baɪsɛn'tɛnɪəl〕

- 三百年紀念
  tercentennial〔,tɝsɛn'tɛnɪəl〕

- 五十週年紀念
  jubilee〔'dʒublˌi〕

- 公衆假日　*public holiday*

- 年節　festival〔'fɛstəvl̩〕

- 花季　*flower season*

- 紀念日　*memorial day*

- 除夕　*new year's eve*

- 假日
  holiday〔'hɑləˌde〕, day off

- 國定假日
  statutory（legal）holiday

- 勝利紀念日　*Victory Day*

- 節日
  holiday〔'hɑləˌde〕, feast day

- 節慶　a festival〔'fɛstəvl̩〕

- 新年　*the new year*

≪國曆節日≫

【1月1日】
中華民國開國紀念日　Founding Anniversary of the Republic of China

【1月1日】
陽曆年　Solar（western）New Year

【1月23日】
自由日　Liberty Day

【3月12日】
植樹節　Arbor Day

【3月12日】
國父逝世紀念日　Memorial Day of Dr. Sun Yat-sen's Death

【3月29日】
青年節　Youth Day

【4月4日】
兒童節　Children's Day

【4月5日】
蔣公逝世紀念日　Memorial Day of President Chiang Kai-shek's Death

【4月5日】
清明節　Tomb Sweeping Day

【5月1日】
勞動節　Labor Day

【5月4日】
文藝節　Literary Day

【6月3日】
禁煙節　Opium Suppression Movement Day

【8月8日】
父親節　Father's Day

【9月1日】
記者節　Reporters' Day

【9月3日】
軍人節　Armed Forces Day

【9月28日】
教師節　Teacher's Day（Confucius Birthday）

【10月10日】
雙十節　Double-Tenth Day

【10月25日】
光復節　Taiwan Restoration Day

【10月31日】
蔣公誕辰紀念日　The Late President Chiang Kai-shek's Birthday

【11月12日】
國父誕辰紀念日　Dr. Sun Yat-sen's Birthday

【12月25日】
行憲紀念日　Constitution Day

≪陰曆（農曆）節日≫

【陰曆正月初一】
春節　Spring Festival

【農曆1月1日】
陰曆年　Lunar New Year

【陰曆1月8日】
農民節　Farmer's Day

【陰曆1月15日】
元宵節　Lantern Festival

【陰曆5月5日】
端午節　Dragon Boat Festival

【陰曆7月15日】
中元節　Ghost Festival

【陰曆8月15日】
中秋節　Mid-Autumn（moon）festival

【陰曆9月9日】
重陽節　Double Ninth Festival

● 西洋節日 ●

【1月6日】
主顯節　Epiphany〔ɪˈpɪfənɪ〕

【2月2日】
聖燈節　Candlemas〔ˈkændl̩məs〕

【2月12日】
林肯誕辰　Lincoln's Birthday

【2月14日】
情人（范倫泰）節　（St.）Valentine's Day

【3月8日】
婦女節 Women's Day

【3月21日】
復活節 Easter Sunday

【4月1日】
愚人節 April Fool's Day

【4月5月的某一天】
植樹節 Arbor Day

【5月第2個禮拜天】
母親節 Mother's Day

【5月30日】
美紀念陣亡將士日 Memorial Day

【6月15日】
美國父親節 Father's Day

【7月4日】
美獨立紀念日 Independence Day

【美：9月之第一個星期一】
勞工節 Labor Day

【10月12日】
美國哥倫布紀念日 Columbus Day

【10月31日】
美國萬聖節前夕 Halloween

【11月1日】
萬聖節 All Saints' Day；All Hallows Day

【11月第4個星期四】
感恩節 Thanksgiving（Day）

【12月25日】
聖誕節 Christmas

節氣時令用語

【 2 月 5 日 】
立 春　spring begins

【 2 月 19 日 】
雨 水　the rains

【 3 月 5 日 】
驚 蟄　insects awaken

【 4 月 5 日 】
清 明　clear and bright

【 5 月 5 日 】
立 夏　summer begins

【 6 月 21 日 】
夏 至　summer solstice

【 7 月 23 日 】
大 暑　great heat

【 8 月 7 日 】
立 秋　autumn begins

【 9 月 23 日 】
秋 分　autumnal equinox

【 11 月 7 日 】
立 冬　winter begins

【 12 月 21 日 】
冬 至　winter solstice

【 1 月 21 日 】
大 寒　great cold

• 上午
morning〔'mɔrnɪŋ〕; a.m.

• 下午
afternoon〔,æftɚ'nun〕; p.m.

• 中午　noon〔nun〕

• 正午　mid-day〔'mɪd,de〕

• 世代　generation〔,dʒɛnə'reʃən〕

• 世紀　century〔'sɛntʃərɪ〕

• 陰曆　*lunar calendar*

• 週一至週五
weekdays〔'wik,dez〕

• 週末　weekend〔'wik'ɛnd〕

• 閏月（日）
intercalary month（day）

• 閏年　*leap year*

• 陽曆　*solar calendar*

• 微明　twilight〔'twaɪ,laɪt〕

• 黎明　dawn〔dɔn〕

• 薄暮　dusk〔dʌsk〕

氣 象 用 語

≪氣象一般用語≫

- 小雨　*light rain*
- 大雨　*heavy rain*
- 毛毛雨
  drizzle〔'drɪzl̩〕; *fine rain*
- 反常的天氣　*freakish weather*
- 天氣預報　*weather forecast*
- 北風　*north wind*
- 甘霖　*welcome rain*
- 冰　ice〔aɪs〕
- 西北風
  northwester〔,nɔrθ'wɛstɚ〕
- 西風　*west wind*
- 西南風
  southwester〔,saʊθ'wɛstɚ〕
- 冷鋒　*cold front*
- 低氣壓
  low-pressure〔'lo'prɛʃɚ〕
- 雨天(季)　*rainy day (season)*
- 雨量
  precipitation〔prɪ,sɪpə'teʃən〕;
  rainfall〔'ren,fɔl〕
- 雨點
  raindrop〔'ren,drɑp〕
- 東北風
  northeaster〔,nɔrθ'istɚ〕

- 東風　*east wind*
- 東南風
  southeaster〔,saʊθ'istɚ〕
- 炎熱　*scorching heat*
- 虹　rainbow〔'ren,bo〕
- 南風　*south wind*
- 陣雨　shower〔'ʃaʊɚ〕
- 高氣壓
  high-pressure〔'haɪ'prɛʃɚ〕
- 氣溫　*air temperature*
- 氣象報告　*weather report*
- 氣團　*air mass*
- 閃電
  lightning〔'laɪtnɪŋ〕(flash
  〔flæʃ〕)
- 陰
  be overcast〔'ovɚ,kæst ; ,ovɚ-
  'kæst〕
- 陰天　*cloudy day*
- 涼　be cool〔kul〕
- 雪　snow〔sno〕
- 乾燥
  dryness〔'draɪnɪs〕; aridity〔ə-
  'rɪdətɪ〕
- 晴　be clear〔klɪr〕

戀愛婚姻用語

≪戀愛≫

- 一見鍾情　*love at first sight*
- 女（男）朋友
  girl（boy）friend
- 山盟海誓　*lovers' vows*
- 互相吸引　*mutual attraction*
- 失戀
  to lose one's love；be jilted
- 自由戀愛　*free love*
- 成雙成對
  be a couple（man and woman,
  married or unmarried）
- 男女的三角關係　*love triangle*
- 男女間之約會　date〔det〕
- 求愛
  court〔kɔrt〕；woo〔wu〕
- 初（私）戀　*first（secret）love*
- 相思病
  lovesickness〔'lʌv,sɪknɪs〕
- 情人
  lover〔'lʌvɚ〕；sweetheart
  〔'swit,hɑrt〕
- 情人眼裡出西施　"*Love is blind*"
- 情不自禁　*no self-control*
- 理想對象　*ideal catch（mate）*
- 單戀
  unrequited（one-sided）love

- 愛的故事；浪漫史
  love story；romance〔ro'mæns〕
- 畸戀　*perverted love*
- 精神戀愛　*Platonic love*
- 墜入情網　*fall in love*
- 獨身生活
  celibacy〔sɪ'lɪbəsɪ〕
- 戀情　*love affair*
- 心心相印
  to know each other's mind
- 求婚　propose〔prə'poz〕
- 含情脈脈　*look of love*
- 柔情似水
  softness & sentiment

≪西洋婚姻紀念名稱≫

【一週年】
　紙婚　paper（wedding）anniversary
【二週年】
　棉布婚　cotton（wedding）anniver-
sary
【三週年】
　皮婚　leather（wedding）anniver-
sary
【四週年】
　絲婚　silk（wedding）anniversary

【五週年】

　木婚　wooden（wedding）anniversary

【六週年】

　鐵婚　iron（wedding）anniversary

【七週年】

　毛（銅）婚　woolen（copper）（wedding）anniversary

【八週年】

　電器婚　electrical applicance（wedding）anniversary

【九週年】

　陶器婚　pottery（wedding）anniversary

【十週年】

　錫婚　tin（wedding）anniversary

【十一週年】

　鋼婚　steel（wedding）anniversary

【十二週年】

　蔴婚　linen（wedding）anniversary

【十三週年】

　花邊婚　lace（wedding）anniversary

【十四週年】

　象牙婚　ivory（wedding）anniversary

【十五週年】

　水晶婚　crystal（wedding）anniversary

【二十週年】

　瓷婚　china（wedding）anniversary

【廿五週年】

　銀婚　silver（wedding）anniverary（jubilee）

【卅週年】

　珍珠婚　pearl（wedding）anniversary

【卅五週年】

　珊瑚婚　coral（wedding）anniversary

【卅五週年】

　碧玉婚　jade（wedding）anniversary

【四十週年】

　紅寶石婚　ruby（wedding）anniversary

【四十五週年】

　藍寶石婚　sapphire（wedding）anniversary

【五十週年】

　金婚　golden jubilee, golden（wedding）anniversary（jubilee）

【五十五週年】

　翠玉婚　emerald（wedding）anniversary

【六十週年或七十五週年】

　鑽石婚　diamond（wedding）anniversary（jubilee）

人 間 百 態

- 一本正經者；自命不凡者
  prig〔prɪg〕
- 人妖（男扮女者）
  transvestite〔træns'vɛstaɪt〕
- 大人物　*big shot（wig）；V IP*
- 大亨　tycoon〔taɪ'kun〕
- 小氣鬼
  scrooge；miser；（colloq）
  skin-flint〔'skɪn,flɪnt〕
- 小偷
  burglar〔'bɝglɚ〕；thief〔θif〕；
  prowler〔'praʊlɚ〕
- 文抄公
  plagiarist〔'pledʒərɪst〕
- 不良少年；阿飛
  hoodlum〔'hudləm〕
- 反常的人　freak〔frik〕
- 中國事務（問題）專家
  China watcher；Pekingologist
  〔,pɛkɪŋ'alədʒɪst〕
- 中國通　*old China hand*
- 扒手　pickpocket〔'pɪk,pakɪt〕
- 生在美國的中國人
  America-born Chinese（ABC）
- 老油條
  *an old fox；a nonchalant sophis-
  ticate*

- 衣冠楚楚的人
  fashionplate〔'fæʃən,plet〕
- 守財奴　*slave of wealth*
- 劣等學生
  dunce〔dʌns〕；booby〔'bubɪ〕
- 百萬富翁
  millionaire〔,mɪljən'ɛr〕
- 交際花
  socialite〔'soʃə,laɪt〕；*society
  belle（beauty）*
- 忘恩負義者
  betrayer〔bɪ'treɚ〕
- 吹牛大王
  boaster〔'bostɚ〕；bragger
  〔'brægɚ〕
- 投機主義者
  opportunist〔,apɚ'tjunɪst〕
- 青年才俊
  a young talent
- 和事佬
  peace-maker〔'pis,mekɚ〕
- 知識份子
  intellectual〔,ɪntḷ'ɛktʃʊəl〕
- 看手相者　palmist〔'pamɪst〕
- 政客
  politician〔,palə'tɪʃən〕

- 香客；朝山進香者
  pilgrim 〔'pɪlgrɪm〕
- 恩人
  benefactor 〔ˌbɛnə'fæktə〕
- 捉刀人（私下代人寫作者）
  ghost-writer 〔'gost,raɪtə〕
- 烈士　martyr 〔'mɑrtə〕
- 酒肉朋友　*fair-weather friend*
- 書呆子　bookworm 〔'buk,wɝm〕
- 馬屁精
  flatterer 〔'flætərə〕; *book lickcr*;
  (*vulg*) *brown nose*; (*vulg*) ass-
  kisser 〔'æs,kɪsə〕
- 流浪漢
  wanderer 〔'wɑndərə〕; rover
  〔'rovə〕
- 缺德鬼　*public nuisance*
- 破產者　bankrupt 〔'bæŋkrʌpt〕
- 神童
  prodigy 〔'prɑdədʒɪ〕; *wonder child*
- 假才子；自作聰明的人
  witling 〔'wɪtlɪŋ〕
- 混血兒
  mixed-blood 〔'mɪkst,blʌd〕;
  halfbreed 〔'hæf,brid〕(*often
  used as term of abuse*)
- 推卸責任者
  goof-off 〔'guf,ɔf〕
- 淘氣鬼　urchin 〔'ɝtʃɪn〕
- 寄膳不寄宿的人；通學生
  day-boarder 〔'de,bordə〕
- 問題兒童　*problem child*

- 媒人
  matchmaker 〔'mætʃ,mekə〕;
  gobetween 〔'gobə,twin〕
- 新手；見習者
  novice 〔'nɑvɪs〕; greenhorn
  〔'grin,hɔrn〕
- 愛出風頭的人
  showboar 〔'ʃo,boə〕
- 節食者　dieter 〔'daɪətə〕
- 搞亂份子　saboteur 〔ˌsæbə'tɝ〕
- 慈善家
  philanthropist 〔fə'lænθrəpɪst〕
- 厭世（悲觀）者
  pessimist 〔'pɛsəmɪst〕
- 偽君子
  hypocrite 〔'hɪpə,krɪt〕;
  dissembler 〔dɪ'sɛmblə〕
- 瘋狂的影迷　*movie fanatic*
- 撞人而逃的司機
  hit-and-run driver
- 熱心於防止環境污染的人士
  ecology-activist
- 線民；告密人　*stool pigeon*
- 調情聖手
  a great lover; a Romeo
- 應聲蟲　*a yes-man*
- 戴綠帽子的人　cuckold 〔'kʌkld〕
- 總統夫人　*the first lady*
- 職業婦女　*career woman*
- 藍領階級的人　*blue collar worker*
- 難民　refugee 〔ˌrɛfju'dʒi〕

學 生 用 語

≪教育活動≫

- 戶外活動　outdoor activity
- 升旗典禮　flag raising ceremony
- 軍訓　military training
- 級會　class meeting
- 校友返校聚會
  homecoming 〔'hom,kʌmɪŋ〕
- 校慶　Founder's Day celebration
- 家庭訪問　home visit
- 惜別會　send-off (farewell) party
- 畢業典禮
  graduation (commencement)
  exercises
- 畢業旅行　graduation travel
- 朝會　morning meeting
- 開學典禮
  inauguration (opening) ceremony
- 新生訓練
  orientation 〔,orɪɛn'teʃən〕

≪學生用語≫

- 女大學生
  (Am slang) co-eds 〔'ko'ɛdz〕
- 下課時間　(slang) play time
- 工讀生
  co-op (part-time) student

- 方帽子
  (slang) square cap; mortarboard
  〔'mɔrtɚ,bord〕
- 分數蟲（只注意分數的大學生）
  (slang) grade grabber
- 用功的學生；書呆子
  (slang) grind 〔graɪnd〕;
  bookworm 〔'bʊk,wɝm〕
- 母校
  (Am slang) alma mammy;
  (L) alma mater
- 死用功（勞而無功）
  to study diligently without
- 同窗好友
  chum 〔tʃʌm〕; buddy 〔'bʌdɪ〕
- 活字典
  walking (living) dictionary
- 校花　school beauty
- 留級生　（Am）repeater 〔rɪ'pitɚ〕
- 逃學
  to play hooky (truant);
  truancy 〔'truənsɪ〕
- 通宵讀書
  (slang) pull an all-nighter
- 開夜車
  (colloq) to burn the midnight
  oil

- 獎學金生
  prize-fellow; scholarship student

- 隨便翻閱　to browse〔braʊz〕

- 臨時抱佛腳
  （Eng slang) to swot〔swat〕;
  to cram〔kræm〕

- 醫科學生　medico〔'mɛdɪˌko〕

- 翹（曠）課
  to skip school (class)

≪教育用語≫

- 人才外流　*brain drain*

- 入學資格　*admission qualifications*

- 小過　*small offence (demerit)*

- 下課
  to get out of (dismiss) class

- 上課　*to attend (go to) class*

- 三學期制　*trimester system*

- 天才兒童
  gifted child; baby genius

- 日間部學生　*day student*

- 用功讀書　*diligence in study*

- 代課　*teach as a substitute*

- 全日制
  full-time (schooling) system

- 因材施教
  differentiation & adaptation to suit the teaching to the ability of pupils

- 自修　*be self-taught*（cultured）

- 同校同學　schoolmate〔'skʊlˌmet〕

- 同班同學　classmate〔'klæsˌmet〕

- 考倒數第一　*get the lowest score*

- 休學　*to stop attending school*

- 有教無類
  to teach everyone without prejudice

- 男女同校制
  coeducation〔ˌkoɛdʒə'keʃən〕

- 抄筆記　note-taking〔'notˌtekɪŋ〕

- 招生廣告
  advertisement for pupils

- 性向分組制　streaming〔'strimɪŋ〕

- 夜間部學生
  night school student

- 兩學期制　*two-term system*

- 例題（文法）
  praxis〔'præksɪs〕

- 重修　*to repeat a course*

- 品學兼優
  be excellent in character & learning

- 校友　alumnus〔ə'lʌmnəs〕

≪考試用語≫

- 入學考試　*entrance examination*

- 小考　quiz〔kwɪz〕

- 口試　*oral exam*

- 大學入學考試
  college board (entrance)
  examination
- 不及格；未錄取
  to flunk 〔flʌŋk〕, fail 〔fel〕
- 不對題
  impertinence 〔ɪm'pɚtṇəns〕;
  irrelevance 〔ɪ'rɛləvəns〕
- 月考　monthly examination
- 及格　to pass 〔pæs, pɑs〕
- 心理測驗　psychological test
- 升等及檢定考試
  Examination for Promotion and
  Qualification
- 分數　mark 〔mɑrk〕; grades 〔gredz〕
- 平均分數　average mark
- 可看書的考試
  open-book examination
- 出題　to compose an examination
- 扣分　deduction 〔dɪ'dʌkʃən〕
- 考試失敗　to fail an examination
- 托福考試
  Test of English as a Foreign
  Language (TOEFL)
- 改卷子　to correct papers
- 抽考
  poptest (quiz); a test given to
  a group of randomly chosen
  students
- 放榜
  to post the result of an
  examination (test)

- 是非題　true-false question
- 准考證
  admission card for entrance
  exam
- 密封　seal 〔sil〕
- 畢業考　graduation examination
- 智力測驗　intelligence test
- 智商　intelligence quotient (IQ)
- 期中考試　mid-term exam
- 期末考試　final exam
- 補考
  (Am) make-up (test) 〔'mek, ʌp〕
- 報名表
  entry (registration) form
- 報名費　registration fee
- 筆試　written examination
- 測驗題　test materials
- 零分　zero 〔'zɪro〕
- 試卷　examination paper
- 試題
  examination subject 〔question(s)〕
- 滿分 full marks
- 監考
  to proctor (an examination)
- 類比式；配合題　matching test
- 繳白卷
  to turn in a blank essay (paper)
- 繳卷　to hand in the test paper
- 難題
  puzzle 〔'pʌzḷ〕; difficult question

外國文學家及其代表作

姓　　　名	年　代	代　表　作
大仲馬（法） Alexandre Dumas(*father*)	1802-1870	基督山恩仇記 The Count of Monte- Cristo 三劍客 The Three Musketeers
小仲馬（法） Alexandre Dumas（*son*）	1824-1895	茶花女 Camille 豐富之海 The Sea of Fertility
三島由紀夫（日） Yukio-Mishima（Jap）	1925-1970	金閣寺 The Golden Temple
川端康成（日） Yasunari-Kawabata	1899-1972	雪鄉 The Snow Country 千鶴 Thousand Cranes
毛姆（英） Somerset Maugham(Eng)	1874-1965	人性枷鎖 Of Human Bondage
王爾德（英） Oscar Wilde	1856-1900	陶林·葛雷的畫像 The Picture of Dorian Gray 快樂的王子 The Happy Prince
卡夫卡（德） Franz Kafka（G）	1883-1906	城堡 The Castle 審判 The Trial
卡繆（法） Albert Camus（F）	1913-1960	叛徒 The Renegade 黑死病 The Plague
艾略特（英） T S Eliot（Eng）	1888-1965	荒原 The Waste Land 普魯佛克的愛歌 The Love Song of J Alfred Prufrock
托爾斯泰（俄） Leo Tolstoy（R）	1828-1910	戰爭與和平 War and Peace 安娜·卡列尼娜 Anna Karenina
但丁（義） Dante Alighieri（It）	1265-1321	神曲 Divine Comedy 新生活 La Vita Nuova（*The New Life*）
狄更斯（英） Charles Dickens (Eng)	1812-1870	雙城記 A Tale of Two Cities 大期望 Great Expections

沙特（法）	1905-1980	嘔吐 Nausea
Jean-Paul Sartre（F）		牆 The Wall
杜斯妥也夫斯基（俄）	1821-1881	罪與罰 Crime and Punishment
Fёdor Mikhailovich		卡拉瑪佐夫的兄弟們 The Brothers
Dostoevski（R）		Karamazov
易卜生（挪）	1828-1906	玩偶家庭 A Doll's House
Henrik Ibsen（Nor）		赫達・賈柏萊 Hedda Gabler
		彼爾・金特 Peer・Gynt
芥川龍之介（日）	1892-1927	羅生門 Rashomon
Ryunosuke-Akutagawa（Jap）		
雨果（法）	1802-1885	悲慘世界 Les Miserables
Victor Hugo（F）		巴黎的聖母院 Notre-Dame de Paris
波特萊爾（法）	1821-1867	交響 Correspondences
Charles Baudelaire（F）		翻華樂 La Fanfarlo
吳爾夫（英）	1882-1941	燈塔 To the Light House
Virginia Woolf（Eng）		浪 The Waves
哈代（英）	1840-1928	還鄉記 The Return of the Native
Thomas Hardy（Eng）		隱居 Far from the Madding Crowd
拜倫（英）	1788-1824	唐璜 Don Juan
George Noel Gordon, Lord		拜倫詩集 The Selected Poetry of
Byron（Eng）		Lord Byron
契訶夫（俄）	1860-1904	櫻桃園 The Cherry Orchard
Anton Chekov（R）		
紀德（法）	1869-1951	德語斯 Theseus
André Gide（F）		
泰戈爾（印）	1861-1941	金船 Sonār Tari（*The Golden Boat*）
Sir Rabindranath Tagore		夢 Kalpanā（*Dreams*）
（Ind）		
馬克・吐溫（美）	1835-1910	湯姆・索耶 Tom Sawyer
Mark Twain（*Samuel*		密西西比河上的生活 Life on the
Langhorne Clemens）（Am）		Mississippi

海明威（美） Ernest Hemingway（Am）	1898-1961	日出 The Sun Also Rises 老人與海 The Old Man and the Sea 喪鐘 For Whom the Bell Tolls
朗費羅（美） Henry Wadsworth 　Longfellow（Am）	1807-1882	史丹狄希之求婚 The Courtship of Miles 　Standish 海野瓦達之歌 The Song of Hiawatha
夏綠蒂・勃朗黛（英） Charlotte Bronte（Eng）	1816-1855	簡愛 Jane Eyre
莎士比亞（英） William Shakespeare（Eng）	1564-1616	哈姆雷特 Hamlet 馬克白 Macbeth
莫里哀（法） Molière（*Jean Baptiste* 　*Poquelin*）（F）	1622-1673	塔杜菲 Tartuffe 唐璜 Don Juan
莫泊桑（法） Guy de Maupassant（F）	1850-1893	脂肪球 Boule de suif（*Ball of Fat*） 好友 Bel Ami
荷馬（希） Homer（Gk）	8th century BC	依利亞得 Iliad 奧德塞 Odyssey
密爾頓（英） John Milton（Eng）	1608-1674	失樂園 Paradise Lost
斯坦貝克（美） John Steinbeck（Am）	1902-1968	人與鼠 Of Mice and Men 憤怒的葡萄 The Grapes of Wrath
喬依斯（愛） James Joyce（Ire）	1882-1941	尤里西斯 Ulysses 年輕藝術家的畫像 A Portrait of the 　Artist as a Young Man
勞倫斯（英） D H Lawrence（Eng）	1885-1930	兒子與情人 Sons and Lovers 查泰萊夫人的情人 Lady Chatterley's 　Lover
屠格涅夫（俄） Ivan Turgenev（R）	1818-1883	父與子 Fathers and Sons 貴族的窩 A Nobleman's Nest
奧尼爾（美） Eugene O'Neill（Am）	1888-1953	榆蔭情慾 Desire Under the Elms 荒野 Ah, Wilderness！

奧斯丁（英） Jane Austen（*Eng*）	1775-1817	傲慢與偏見 Pride and Prejudice
愛米麗・勃朗黛（英） Emily Brontë（Eng）	1818-1848	咆哮山莊 Wuthering Heights
愛倫坡（美） Edgar Allan Poe（Am）	1809-1849	莫格街之謀殺案 Murders in the Rue Morgue 亞西家族之衰弱 Fall of the House of Usher
傑克・倫敦（美） Jack London（Am）	1876-1916	野性的呼喚 The Call of the Wild 海狼 The Sea Wolf
福克納（美） William Faulkner（Am）	1897-1962	喧聲與狂怒 The Sound and the Fury 入定 Sartoris
福樓拜爾（法） Gustave Flaubert（F）	1821-1880	包法利夫人 Madame Bovary 情書 Correspondence
歌德（德） Johann Wolfgang von 　Goethe（G）	1749-1832	浮士德 Faust 少年維特之煩惱 The Sorrows of Young Werther
賽珍珠（美） **Pearl Buck（Am）**	1892-1973	大地 The Good Earth 活草 The Living Reed

各月幸運花卉、寶石、星座

≪代表生日月份之鮮花≫

- 一月──荷蘭石竹；雪花；野玫瑰
  Jan — carnation 〔kɑr'neʃən〕; snowdrop 〔'sno,drɑp〕; wild rose

- 二月──櫻草花
  Feb — primrose 〔'prɪm,roz〕

- 三月──紫羅蘭；（黃）水仙
  Mar — violet 〔'vaɪəlɪt〕; jonquil 〔'dʒɑŋkwɪ〕; daffodil 〔'dæfədɪl〕

- 四月──延命（雛）菊
  Apr — daisy 〔'dezɪ〕

- 五月──鈴蘭
  May — lily of the valley

- 六月──玫瑰花；忍冬
  June — rose 〔roz〕; honeysuckle 〔'hʌnɪ,sʌkl〕

- 七月──香豌豆花；燕草
  July — sweet pea; larkspur 〔'lɑrk,spɝ〕

- 八月──水仙菖；睡蓮；罌粟
  Aug — gladiolus 〔,glædɪ'oləs〕; water lily; poppy 〔'pɑpɪ〕

- 九月──紫菀；秋麒麟草；牽牛花
  Sept — aster 〔'æstɚ〕; goldenrod 〔'goldn,rɑd〕; morning-glory
  〔'mɔrnɪŋ,glorɪ〕

- 十月──天竺牡丹；大波斯菊；金盞草
  Oct — dahlia 〔'dæljə〕; cosmos 〔'kɑzməs〕; calendula 〔kə'lɛndʒələ〕

- 十一月──菊花
  Nov — chrysanthemum 〔krɪs'ænθəməm〕

- 十二月──聖誕紅（俗）；冬青木；檞寄生；水仙
  Dec — poinsettia 〔pɔɪn'sɛtɪə〕; holly 〔'hɑlɪ〕; mistletoe 〔'mɪsḷ,to〕;
  narcissus 〔nɑr'sɪsəs〕

≪誕生石≫

- 一月——柘榴石；風信子石（忠實）
  Jan—garnet〔'gɑrnɪt〕；hyacinth〔'haɪə‚sɪnθ〕（ *Fidelity* ）
- 二月—— 紫水晶（眞摯）　　Feb—amethyst〔'æməθɪst〕（ *Sincerity* ）
- 三月—— 血石；碧玉；綠玉石（果敢）
  Mar—bloodstone〔'blʌd‚ston〕；jasper(ite)（'dʒæspɚ）；aquamarine
  〔‚ækwəmə'rin〕（ *Courage* ）
- 四月—— 鑽石（純潔）　Apr—diamond〔'daɪəmənd〕（ *Innocence* ）
- 五月—— 翡翠（幸福）　May—emerald〔'ɛmərəld〕（ *Happiness* ）
- 六月—— 珍珠；月長石；瑪瑙（健康）
  June—pearl〔pɝl〕；moonstone〔'mun‚ston〕；agate〔'ægət〕（ *Health* ）
- 七月—— 紅寶石；條紋瑪瑙（愛情）
  July—ruby〔'rubɪ〕；onyx〔'ɑnɪks〕（ *Love* ）
- 八月—— 紅條紋瑪瑙；橄欖石；紅玉髓（美滿良緣）
  Aug—sardonyx〔'sɑrdənɪks〕；peridot〔'pɛrɪ‚dɑt〕；carnelian
  〔kɑr'niljən〕（ *Conjugal bliss* ）
- 九月—— 藍寶石（智慧）　Sept—sapphire〔'sæfaɪr〕（ *Wisdom* ）
- 十月—— 玫瑰鋯石；蛋白石；電氣石（希望）
  Oet—rose zircon; opal〔'opl〕；tourmaline〔'tʊrməlɪn〕（ *Hope* ）
- 十一月—— 黃玉（友誼）　Nov—topaz〔'topæz〕（ *Friendship* ）
- 十二月—— 土耳其玉；琉璃（繁榮）
  Dec—turquoise（'tɝkwɔɪz）；lapis lazuli〔'læpɪs'læzjəlaɪ〕（ *Prosperity* ）

≪星座名稱≫

【 12 月 22 日～ 1 月 19 日 】	魔羯座		Capricorn〔'kæprɪ‚kɔrn〕
【 1 月 20 日～ 2 月 18 日 】	寶瓶座		Aquarius〔ə'kwɛrɪəs〕
【 2 月 19 日～ 3 月 20 日 】	雙魚座		Pisces〔'pisɪz〕
【 3 月 21 日～ 4 月 19 日 】	白羊座		Aries〔'ɛriz;'ɛrɪ‚iz〕
【 4 月 20 日～ 5 月 20 日 】	金牛座		Taurus〔'tɔrəs〕
【 5 月 21 日～ 6 月 21 日 】	雙子座		Gemini〔'dʒɛmə‚naɪ〕
【 6 月 22 日～ 7 月 22 日 】	巨蟹座		Cancer〔'kænsɚ〕
【 7 月 23 日～ 8 月 22 日 】	獅子座		Leo〔'lio〕
【 8 月 23 日～ 9 月 22 日 】	處女座		Virgo〔'vɝgo〕
【 9 月 23 日～ 10 月 22 日 】	天秤座		Libra〔'laɪbrə〕
【 10 月 23 日～ 11 月 22 日 】	天蠍座		Scorpio〔'skɔrpɪ‚o〕
【 11 月 23 日～ 12 月 21 日 】	射手座		Sagittarius（‚sædʒɪ'tɛrɪəs ）

心得筆記欄

Editorial Staff

● 修編 / 劉復苓

● 編著 / 武藍蕙

● 校訂 / 劉　毅・謝静芳・蔡琇瑩・陳子璇
　　　　高雅姿・劉宜芳

● 校閱 / David Brotman・Edward C. Yulo
　　　　John H. Voelker・Kenyon T. Cotton

● 封面設計 / 白雪嬌

● 版面設計 / 張鳳儀・林燕茹・黄新家

● 打字 / 黄淑貞・倪秀梅・蘇淑玲・吳秋香

如何寫好英文日記

修　　編 / 劉復苓

發 行 所 / 學習出版有限公司　　　　☎ (02) 2704-5525

郵 撥 帳 號 / 05127272 學習出版社帳戶

登 記 證 / 局版台業 2179 號

印 刷 所 / 裕強彩色印刷有限公司

台 北 門 市 / 台北市許昌街 10 號 2 F　　☎ (02) 2331-4060

台灣總經銷 / 紅螞蟻圖書有限公司　　　☎ (02) 2795-3656

本公司網址　www.learnbook.com.tw

電 子 郵 件　learnbook@learnbook.com.tw

售價：新台幣一百八十元正

2016 年 7 月 1 日二版三刷

ISBN 978-957-519-910-4